THE GREATEST CAKE
OF THE GLOBES

Ciara Jackson

*Special thanks to my love, Morgan Boone,
for supporting me throughout the entire process of
creating this story and much, much more.*

*Dedicated to my family, friends and my animals: I love
you all so dearly.*

Text copyright © 2014 by Ciara Jackson

Illustrations copyright © 2014 by Ciara Jackson

GATHER THE PIECES of your life & make your story

Ciara Jackson

The Greatest Cake Of the Globes

Written and Illustrated by Ciara Jackson

Doublemaximus Books

*In memory of Trent, my wonderful dog.
The entirety of this story was written with you on my lap.*

★ Chapters ★

Prologue...7

1. A Little World in the Clouds................8
2. An Announcement................................19
3. The Sweetest Thing..............................28
4. The Journey of Super Cirrus................37
5. Out Upon the Shelf..............................48
6. A Silly Boy in the Snow.......................53
7. Entering a Dreary Place.......................62
8. For Lorne...71
9. No Time to be Snoozing......................81
10. A Nightmare While Awake.................90
11. A New Keen Cat in Town....................99
12. The Clock is Ticking.........................109
13. Ticks, Tocks, and Applesauce............116
14. A Face Without Time........................127
15. The Withered Flower.........................136
16. To Others, a Weed; To us, the Queen......146
17. The Royal Faerie Proposition.............156
18. A Broken Unbroken Promise..............164
19. The Heart's Storm..............................172
20. There Will Always be Time................181
21. Let the Music Play.............................190
22. Home in the Clouds...........................204
23. Bake It or Break It.............................213
24. The Last Level...................................222

The Greatest Cake of the Globes

We all live in a globe. Everything, living or not, exists inside a globe called Earth. It is our world, our home—where we learn to love and grow. However, little do we know, there are thousands of globes within ours that exist as well. Perhaps you have seen them before—in a souvenir shop, a gift store, or have even received one as a present. These globes which I speak of are none other than snow globes. As they sit on our shelves not making a sound, another world flourishes within. The creatures that live in these tiny worlds are called "Globelings". Now, globelings look similar to humans, only smaller…a lot smaller.

As of now, a woman named Destiny sits at her desk in her study room. She likes to think of herself as an aspiring author who just finished writing her first story. As she reads through her freshly printed book, she looks up at her collection of snow globes and smiles to herself. Destiny had nearly lost all hope for her book, however. Months would go by and not a single creative idea would come to mind. There was even a time where she had almost given up her dream of writing, but something inspired her to continue. What could have possibly changed her mind?

☆Chapter One☆

A Little World in the Clouds

A few months ago, a bit of a mess occurred on a shelf. No, not a dust bunny invasion, but a problem with one of the creatures that lived inside one the snow globes. His name was Cirrus—Cirrus O'Zone, and what a shy fellow he was. He lived in the first globe that Destiny had sitting on her shelf, although she had no idea that he was even there—let alone an entire civilization. Inside the globe existed a world called Cloudscape Town and it was such a delightful place to live. The buildings in town were made up of pleasing puffs of clouds and the streets were paved with shimmering stars. Every day the streets would bustle with colorful characters that carried on each day with charm. On the main street, right down the road from the Cloud Courthouse of Mayor Sphere, was a bakery owned by Cirrus's parents called The O'Zone Bakery. Cleverly enough, the "O" in O'Zone was made to look like a donut, sprinkled in all of its glazed glory—dripping with plastic, lilac frosting.

One day, a green haired woman entered the bakery with her son. She seemed rather angry by the way she had dragged him into the bakery. He was young, cheeks bursting with freckles, and had a grim pout glued to his face. The woman, despite several customers peacefully observing the baked displays, did not seem to mind causing a scene. Cirrus peeked through the kitchen window looking quite worried. His chef hat sagged over his face like a deflated balloon.

"Hello! May I help yo—," said Cirrus's mother, Stara, who was suddenly interrupted by the customer.

"I bought a birthday cake for my son yesterday and it was as hard as a rock!" the woman said in a strict voice. "Just look at what it did to my son's tooth!" She pointed to his mouth. The freckled boy opened wide and there, plain as day, was a chipped front tooth. He looked like a little vampire who needed fang braces. Cirrus's father, Atmo, stood up from behind the counter and scratched the patch of purple hair on his chin.

"Well, Happy Halloween!" he mumbled with a mouthful of powdered donuts. He wiped the white powder off on his polka dotted apron. "You make a pretty scary vampire, kid! Although, I think you have a few more months until Halloween. No candy here. Well, I guess we do have some lollipops over there and some—"

"His tooth chipped because of *your* son's horrible cake!!" the mother bellowed.

"Oh, poppycloud! He is bound to lose that tooth any given day now." Atmo said as he wiped his hands on his apron and knelt back down. "Baby teeth come and go."

"How dare you!" she snarled. "He is thirteen years old! His baby teeth are long gone!" The son continued to pout as he crossed his arms.

"Thir-thirteen?!" Atmo peered back up from the counter and gawkily eyeballed the boy. He couldn't believe that the kid was thirteen. He really didn't know how to respond, so he continued to do whatever he was doing behind the counter that involved donuts. Stara punishingly glared at him.

"Whoever lets your son bake cakes around here is making a horrible mistake. He should be locked away from this place, never to touch a single measuring cup again!" the angry mother sneered and again snatched her son's hand aggressively.

"Owwuh!" the boy whined. Stara was flustered with the woman's remark on the baker of the cake, which was Cirrus after all. Her cerulean hair almost appeared purple when contrasted with her flushed, red face. No one mocks her son.

"Well, I should dare say," Stara said as she pushed up her large, round glasses with her middle finger. "I am always open to criticism, but if you don't like our cakes and can't give feedback politely, you can just leave!"

"That is precisely what I'm going to do, hmph!" The woman shook her grassy hair and nearly tore her son's arm off when they exited the bakery. The door jingled as it slammed and rattled the windows.

A few silent moments passed as the other customers slowly resumed their movements, while most quietly left the shop. Stara sighed and apologized to the customers while Atmo grumbled behind the counter. At that moment, Cirrus sluggishly walked out of the kitchen and his hat sank over his face more than ever. He took a seat by the counter and his head dropped on the glass. That woman marked the sixth customer that week to come into the bakery and complain about Cirrus's cakes. His first cake was too dry and nearly made people choke. His second cake had a puddle of uncooked batter than poured out when cut. The third was a batch cupcakes that were for a retirement party, and let's just say that the cupcakes weighed nearly fifteen pounds each despite their small stature—those poor old folks could barely lift them at all. Cirrus thought about his other cake failures, but refused to acknowledge them at the moment. All he wanted in life was to make great tasting cakes and other sweets for his family business, but nothing seemed to be going right for him. His father stood up, yet again dusting the powdered sugar off of his face, and patted Cirrus on the back while his mother started to rub his head. Cirrus shamefully sighed. Atmo slowly started to eat another powdered donut.

"For raincloud's sake, honey! Stop eating our entire inventory." Stara's voice clapped. "Rather than chow down on our donuts, why don't you go clean up the apartment next door that we've been trying to rent out, hm? Make yourself useful. We need some extra money to get the oven fixed before it goes kaput." She startled Atmo, causing him to drop the donut in which he then pretended to examine the bakery like he did nothing wrong, but needless to say his face showed true horror with the loss of the donut and the threat of having to clean. He cleared his throat and took a deep breath.

"Son," Atmo said sternly and struck fear in his son's heart. "Maybe it is time that *you* ran the cash register and take orders while your mother and I make the cakes—" Cirrus looked up at his father with a pale face and his fingers shook.

"B-but…Dad," his deep voice cracked but tried not to stutter. "You know I'm not good with…being social. Besides, I want to bake."

"I know you want to bake, son, but...." Atmo was about to admit that his son's baking was horrendous, but he refrained and changed the subject. "What's there to be social about anyway?" Atmo chuckled as he glanced over to Stara. "Really now, you don't have to strike up a speech. You're not gonna try and pitch an idea for company or anything. You can just say things like 'hi' or 'how are you', 'can I help you', 'have a good day' and so on. 'How's the weather' is a good topic. Little things, son. That is all."

"I know, I know..," Cirrus continued to look high-strung. "I just always get this feeling of panic in my stomach and I forget what to say and then I end up freezing up. I'm a failed raindrop since I always turn into a snowflake." His head fell and hit the counter again—several pastries and candies behind the counter glass shook from the impact.

"Stop doing that, sweetie! You are going to form a bump on your head." Stara said as she tugged on his short, purple ponytail. Just then a young woman who had been browsing the cakes near the bakery window started to approach the counter. She made eye contact with Cirrus and his parents.

"Oh, just in time. I think we've got ourselves a customer!" Stara whispered in Cirrus's ear. She glanced at her husband and flicked her head back toward the kitchen as if she were hinting toward something sneaky. Atmo subtly nodded and they both quickly took off to the kitchen and shut the door behind them.

"Now's your chance, big boy!" Atmo said through the kitchen panel.

"W-W-WHAT?" Cirrus shot up from the counter and tried to push his way back into the kitchen, but his parents held the door on him. "Mom! Dad! I don't know what to do!" Cirrus's heart stopped as he watched the young woman approach the counter. She examined all of the baked goods in the display shelves and smiled.

"Hmhm! These look delicious!" she giggled as she looked at Cirrus. He turned around from the kitchen door and tried to act professional as he clumsily paced behind the cash register and hoped she could not hear the pounding of his heart.

"Hi how are you can I help you have a good day how's the weather?" Cirrus jumbled his words in a fast mess—his stomach an ocean of tenseness. The woman looked confused, but she laughed.

"Haha, what?" she asked as she flung her sky-blue, marshmallow ponytail behind her.

"I meant to say…I mean..." Cirrus stumbled with words. He blushed and fiddled with his white gloves until he felt like he was about to faint. He couldn't take the pressure anymore and he scurried up the spiral staircase next to him, completely abandoning his post at the register. His parents came tumbling out the door in disbelief and called his name while the girl stood silently.

"Cirrus!" Atmo called. "Cirrus, you get back down here!"

"I can't believe he did that." Stara sighed and apologized to the girl. "I'm so sorry. He's...not good around others. I don't quite understand."

"He's too absorbed in those video game fantasy worlds, hun. I've told you. Besides, if he wants to become a baker so badly he's gonna have to get out of this phase." Atmo said disappointingly, but Stara shushed him for talking about it in front of a customer. For some reason, the young woman's eyes lit up at the mention of video games and she softly spoke.

"Is there a way I could speak to him?" she asked. "It's kind of important to me." She handed his parents a piece of paper and they clonked heads in order to read it together. They both went wide eyed and glanced back at the girl.

"Ahhh, I hardly recognized you." Stara laughed. "Certainly you may speak with him about this, but I doubt I can get him to come down here. Why don't you come along back here and head up to his room yourself? We give you permission." The woman thanked them and skipped up the stairs behind the register, leaving Cirrus's parents in thought.

"You think he will go through with it?" Atmo asked.

"When stars fall, perhaps." Stara sighed.

The marshmallow haired woman made her way upstairs and tip toed through the hallway. The second story of the bakery was actually a small housing area for the O'Zone family. It was very convenient for them to live above their own business. After a few moments of observing their cozy living area, she heard several beeps and boops coming from a door at the very end of the hallway. She carefully placed her ear against the door and could hear the sounds more clearly. They were sounds she was very familiar with, as a matter of fact. It was of a video game that she frequently played a few years back and she smiled from the fond memories she had with it. However, instead of prying any longer, she went ahead and tapped on the door. The sounds abruptly came to a stop and she knocked once more.

"Mom, I don't want to talk about it right now." Cirrus sighed, but then a few seconds later he got up and guiltily opened the door.

"Hello!" the woman gave a chipper wave as the door opened, but was startled by the instant slamming of it. Cirrus gasped and his heart resumed to drum through his chest. *What is she doing up here?* He thought. *This is so embarrassing!*

"Is that The Journey of Super LoLo?" she asked abruptly. Cirrus paused his breathing and blinked frantically in awe. Before he knew it, he had opened the door and stood face to face with the mysterious woman.

"Y-yes." he swallowed hard. "I'm playing it right now."

"It's a wonderful game isn't it?" she smiled and bounced in her shoes. "It's my favorite childhood game! The tale of the heroic baker, LoLo—the puzzles, the quests, the collectable items—I love it all." Cirrus could feel his body calming down the more she talked about the game. He had never met anyone who has played it before.

"Oh! But I don't want to bore you. I actually would like you to help me out with something." Her bulbous yellow shoes squeaked as she wiggled in her stance. Cirrus swallowed his fear and agreed. Before he closed his bedroom door, the girl noticed that his television displayed a PAUSE screen of the video game he was playing and, since she was so familiar with the game, she knew exactly how far along he was—near the very end of the game, as a matter of fact. "I would like you to see the cakes that you make." She spoke quickly. "Would you mind showing me?" *Oh, what could be worse? Now she wants to see the cakes I made.* He hesitated a bit, but he guided her down the stairs and led her to the cake display. She pointed to a frosted, purple cake covered in rainbow star sprinkles. "May I sample a piece of this cake?"

"Y-you wanna try a piece of this cake?" Cirrus said with a jittery voice. "You don't wanna to try a piece of this cake…eh…heh."

"Why not?" she shrugged.

The Greatest Cake of the Globes

"Well, because…I made that one." Cirrus looked ashamed.

"Oh, puddlepuff!" she said with a stern tone. "I would still be very happy to try it."

Cirrus became worried. He turned and saw his parents eavesdropping through the kitchen door's window yet again. They nodded vigorously and, since he was still feeling guilty about what happened earlier, he walked over to the counter and removed the cake from the shelf. The woman just smiled and watched as happily as she could. Cirrus gave in and began to cut out a slice of cake. His gut nearly dropped when he couldn't get the knife to cut through it because it was so hard.

"The weather is nice." she said softly.

"Huh?" Cirrus fumbled.

"You asked me how the weather was a few minutes ago, so I'm answering." she replied cheerfully.

"O-oh!" He continued to try and cut the cake.

"You look really cute in that chef outfit, you know?" she said bashfully. "You remind me of Super LoLo dressed like that." Cirrus blushed and stopped paying attention to what he was doing. Then, at that very moment, the knife unexpectedly became loose and cut quickly through the icing. The cake became unbalanced and began to topple over once Cirrus lost his grip on it. As it tumbled off of the plate the girl did not hesitate to lean over and help catch it.

"That was close!" She said as she helped Cirrus re-balance the cake.

"Yeah, heh, Thanks…" Cirrus felt humiliated as he finished cutting the cake. He noticed that she had gotten the purple frosting all over her hand so he fumbled quickly beneath the counter, retrieved a couple of napkins and gently wiped her fingers clean.

"A-ah! Thank you very much." The young woman's bubblegum cheeks were tickled pink. Cirrus couldn't believe that he actually touched her without hesitation. His face felt like it was pre-heated to 350 degrees. *What has become of me?* He wondered. He knelt down again and pulled out a plastic fork and handed her the slice.

"Thank you again!" she said in a chipper voice. She stuck the fork into the slice and took a bite. Cirrus didn't even want to watch, but he couldn't help it. His cake was being tasted by a kind, cute woman who has played Super LoLo. He didn't know what else to do. She made a slightly disgruntled face after a few seconds, as if she was eating a lemon and fought the urge to crinkle her nose from disgust. Her expressions made Cirrus become feeble. He knew the cake tasted horrible and he hated being reminded of it.

"It's bad, I know!" he said as he tried to not make eye contact with her. She finished chewing and swallowed.

"Hm, it *may* be a bit hard and bitter..." she said. "...and have bland flavor...and kind of smells just a bit odd..." Cirrus faced his head to the ground and slumped his shoulders passed his chest, but she placed her hand on his hand. "...but that doesn't mean you have to give up your dream of being a great baker. Gather the pieces of your life and make your story." she said peacefully. Cirrus looked back up at her and his cheeks became more of a rosy color rather than the intense redness he wore before.

"Inside the star beats the heart." she told him in a gentle voice and winked.

Cirrus felt a bit stunned. What she said sounded familiar to him—as if he had read it in a book somewhere—but he could not pinpoint it out. He thought she was going to rant about how awful his baking skills were and did not expect her to lend him kind words of wisdom. She nodded and showed him a pleasing smile, but then turned around to leave the bakery.

"My name is Luname," her voice sparkled. "Nice to finally meet you, Cirrus."

"Wait, how did you know my name?" Cirrus asked in surprise.

"Oh, I'm actually a frequent visitor!" she laughed. Cirrus looked down and felt embarrassed that he didn't recognize her. That just showed how much he tried to avoid customers—and, *wait, did she say it was nice to 'finally' meet me?* He blushed heavily, but then managed to laugh a bit too. Luname walked over and handed him a little card she pulled out from her pocket.

"I expect a great cake from you." She winked yet again.

Cirrus took a look at the card. It was a birthday invitation for Luname. He felt bubbles in his stomach, but couldn't tell if they were boiling with anxiousness or bouncing with joy. He went to say thank you, but she had already left. He looked at what was written on the back of the invitation. It read:

Congratulations! You are invited to participate in a joyous event for my daughter, Luname. Her 22nd birthday is just around the corner and I want a spectacular birthday cake that she and the whole town can enjoy. You were selected to be one of our contestants in the competition of cake baking. The grand prize winner will receive ☆1000 twinkles and will be given a wonderful trophy. Hope to see you there! Happy Baking!

~Mayor Sphere

"WHAT?!" Cirrus shouted and rattled the free lollipops on the counter. "This can't be! She is the mayor's daughter and she wants *ME* to participate in this competition? This has to be a cruel joke…"

★ CHAPTER TWO ★

AN ANNOUNCEMENT

Cirrus continued to stare at the invitation with disbelief as his parents secretly stood behind him reading the card.

"Look at you go!" his mother boasted. She nearly broke Cirrus's ear drum. "Your first customer ends up being your girlfriend." she chuckled.

"Mom! Don't…" he whined. His father placed his hand on Cirrus's head.

"So…" he began. "Are you going to do it?" Atmo looked a bit uneasy.

"I-I can't. I already know that I'll fail at it." Cirrus didn't hesitate to demote himself.

"You don't know that, Cirrus." Stara replied. She went to embrace him, but he quickly jerked away from her.

"Yes I do!" Cirrus responded angrily. "How can you say I don't know that? Because of me, we've lost several customers. I put the bakery to shame and you both know it. I can't do it. I don't even deserve to wear the O'Zone apron!"

His parents looked at each other in dissatisfaction as Cirrus tore the apron off of himself. They turned and took seats at the counter and said nothing. Then, they started to clean the counters and dust the shelves, pretending to disregard Cirrus's hurtful words about himself.

"I can remember little Cirrus, nearly four years old, wanting nothing more than to be a great cake baker." Stara sighed.

"Ya think it's those video games that made him this way? Made him afraid of the real world?" Atmo quietly asked her, although his son had heard. A hard lump formed in Cirrus's throat, so he stormed up the spiral staircase behind the shop's counter once again. As soon as he got upstairs, he overheard a few words his mother spoke.

"If only he could see what he is capable of…" her voice cracked. "That would mean everything."

Cirrus couldn't take it anymore. He clutched his wrinkled apron, ran into his bedroom, threw himself on his bed and began to softly weep. The sound of his sorrow became muffled underneath his celestial-patterned blanket.

☆*☆*☆

At that very moment, outside of the snow globe, in our world, the human woman sat at her desk. Destiny had been sitting there for hours as she stared at a blank sheet of paper. Day after day, she waited for an idea for a story to emerge from her head. Ever since she was little, she had dreamed of writing creative, imaginative stories for those who seek the enlightenment of fantasy. However, as she aged, she began to feel as if her creativity was losing its luster. She feared the thought of her imagination fading as she grew. As much as she worried about her thoughts vanishing, she was only twenty-four years of age. She was virtually a flower that had just blossomed.

"Gotten anything written yet, love?" her husband, Zachery, asked as he walked in the room with a steaming cup of tea. Her dog, Brent, was scratching himself while he sat on her lap. She nudged him gently so he would stop, but then turned to her love and shamefully shook her head.

"You know you will get an idea soon," he said in a positive voice as he handed Destiny the cup of tea. "and it will be the most unique story ever told!"

Destiny took the cup of tea and could smell the chamomile steam as it passed through her nose. It felt pleasing for a short moment, but then she quickly felt the guilt rise again.

"I don't think I can do it." she muttered. Her motivation had dropped to an all-time low.

"Why not?" he asked. He put his arms around her shoulders and his cheek squished against her strawberry, blonde hair.

"I just can't seem to think of anything original." she complained. "I feel like everything I think of is either too cliché or it has been done already. I'm no good at writing like I thought I was…and I never will be."

"You are stressing yourself to death, Destiny. Why not take a break and come out and watch a movie with me, huh?" Zachery asked as he kissed her head and began sniffing and snorting in her ear like a dog. It made the hair on the back of her neck rise and she twitched. She couldn't help but laugh.

"Alright, alright, give me a few minutes and I'll be out." she snickered. Zachery leaned over and kissed her before he left the room. Destiny sighed and lifted Brent off of her lap. He grumbled and shook his little, hairless body when she sat him on the ground—such a cute old pup. She stood, stretched, and took one last look at that blank sheet of paper that haunted her. A little groan managed to slip out, but she shook off the disappointment for now. The first snow globe on the shelf caught her eye as she began to leave the room. She turned and walked back to the globe and examined it. Inside the globe danced clouds, stars, and moons all in a colorful composition and it brought delight to Destiny—reminded her of her childhood. She then carefully picked up the globe and flipped it upside down. There was a wind up key that sat at the bottom of the globe. A clicking sound played as she twisted it, but when she stopped it began to play a soft, music box melody. She repositioned the globe on the shelf and gazed at the glittery stars floating about. After a moment or two, Destiny walked out of the room, along with Brent, as the music continued to play.

♩ ♪ ♫ ♪ ♫ ♩

Cirrus slowly lifted his eyes open from his nap. He could hear the chiming of the music box at a distance. He began to sense something strange— a nostalgic feeling as he heard the music play. His eyes, however, became heavier than they were before. In a matter of seconds, after he closed his eyes, he began to dream of a place from his childhood.

"I'm sitting on a large spiral staircase. No, that can't be the staircase in my house. Where am I? I feel like I've been here before. Where is this place? I feel so relaxed. That music…"
ZzZzZzzzz

A few hours had passed. The stars glittered and the moon lit the sky like a diamond. Cirrus was wrapped up in his blanket and was barely awake. He heard his bedroom door creak open and heard his parents whispering. As a crack of light from the door hit his face, he faintly opened his eyes.

"You feeling any better?" his mother asked Cirrus in a whisper.

"Honey," his father began. "He's not playing those bleep bleep video games. He must be sick."

"Oh, Dad. C'mon…" Cirrus groaned. "I'm fine. I'm just wallowing in self-pity. Every young man does this once in a while." He turned over in his cocoon of a blanket. His mother and father both stepped into his room.

"You *are* going to make yourself sick if you keep that up." Stara explained. Cirrus looked over at her with a pitiable face, eyes glossy and innocent.

The Greatest Cake of the Globes

"I'm a childish twenty-two year old who can't seem to do anything right for himself." Cirrus mumbled. "I'm just so sorry that you have to put up with a lousy son like me."

Stara was a bit bewildered to have heard Cirrus say such a thing. She turned over to Atmo expecting to have him help her say something that would cheer their son up. Atmo leaned against the bed post while Stara sat down at the end of Cirrus's bed.

"Cirrus…" she spoke gently. "…you never let us down. There are some times when we become a bit disappointed with you, but that doesn't change the fact that we love you. I know one day, perhaps even sooner than we all expect, you will make everything right for yourself."

"And you will make us all proud." Atmo interrupted as he untied his polka dotted bandana from his head. He gave Cirrus a smile and winked. Their kind words made Cirrus feel a bit more relieved, but he still felt at fault on the inside. He grinned at his parents as his eyes blinked slowly.

"Get some rest, son." Atmo held the door open for Stara.

"We love you." she said as her round glasses reflected the hallway light. "See you in the morning."

"Love you too…" Cirrus replied and rolled over in his puffy, padded bed. His parents both smiled, walked out, and closed the door behind them. Cirrus's grin gradually turned into a frown. He thought deeply for a few moments.

"I have to change somehow…" he said quietly to himself. Before he closed his eyes felt something hard rub up against his cheek from beneath his pillow. It was his video game controller. His father's words echoed in his mind.

'Ya think it's those video games that made him this way'

'He's not playing those bleep bleep video games. He must be sick.'

That must be the only thing my dad thinks I do, Cirrus thought to himself. To answer his father's question, no. No, video games did not make him shy and unsociable. It was just his hobby, at least that's what he wanted to think, but he suddenly began to question it himself. *I can easily talk to the characters in my video games*, he thought, *but why? Is it because they aren't real? Is it because I'm not afraid of them judging me? Why is it easier for me to talk to them, but not real globelings? Have video games taken the real out of my reality?* Cirrus had always admired the main character of his favorite video game, Super LoLo, who was a heroic baker with magical powers that was sent on a quest to rescue Princess LuLu and save everyone from the evil Poison Prince, the main villain who wanted nothing more than to take over the sugary-sweet kingdom and turn everything sour and bitter. Sadly, even Cirrus was unable to beat the video game and see how the story ended. Hours upon hours were spent trying to find the legendary Baker's Brooch—a golden, star shaped breastpin—that revealed the Poison Prince's hiding place, but he never found it. *I can't even complete my favorite game.*

Cirrus woke up early the next morning in a good mood. He decided that he would open the shop early before his parents woke up and that he would also get an early start on making some buttery, dinner rolls. Fortunately, rolls just so happened to be Cirrus's only specialty. *Who can mess up dinner rolls*, he thought. He turned on all of the lights in the shop, switched the CLOSED sign to OPEN, and then quickly scurried back into the kitchen to get started on the rolls.

After several moments had passed, Cirrus was already covered in flour and was kneading the dough. He could already feel his EXP increasing...or, his *experience points*. He separated the dough into miniature balls and placed them in an alignment on a greased baking pan. He felt his excitement rise like the dough he was kneading when he thought of his parents praising him for preparing the bakery all on his own as a surprise for them.

The Greatest Cake of the Globes

Seconds after he finished setting all of the pans in the oven, the sound of loud chattering came from outside the bakery. Cirrus peeked through the kitchen window and saw many citizens scattering down the road. Out of curiosity, he ran to the shop door. When he opened it and stepped out of the shop, he saw everyone heading down to the Cloud Courthouse. Cirrus wondered what could have caused the dispersion of the townspeople, so he decided to go investigate. He hastily switched the OPEN sign back to CLOSED and trotted down the street.

The closer he got to the Cloud Court house, he noticed that it was entirely engulfed in pastel, rainbow balloons. Marshmallow colors twisted around the pillars and made the courthouse almost seem edible. Cirrus squeezed through several crowd members to get a better look, but he could not see who was on the main porch. He then noticed that he was standing beside a street light. Thus, he was able to climb up just a smidgen to get a better view.

He saw a plump globeling in a baby blue suit approach the podium. Cirrus was certain that it was Mayor Sphere, though he has rarely seen the mayor let alone many of the other townspeople. Following behind him was a woman in a rosy pink dress decorated in yellow stars. It was Luname! Cirrus's heart began to flutter at the sight of her. He watched as she smiled and waved gracefully at the audience. Without a delay, the mayor began to speak into a microphone.

"Hello, everyone! Greetings to you all and thank you all for coming. I have a special announcement to make. My wonderful daughter, Luname, is going to be celebrating her twenty-second birthday in a just matter of two days. Kids grow up so fast, don't they? With that said, I am proud to announce the contestants that have been chosen to participate in the cake competition to bake the best birthday cake of all!"

The crowd cheered, but Cirrus was stricken with terror. He had a sick feeling that he was going to have his name called in front of all of the globelings in town since Luname had personally given him that invitation. Miss Eva Poration, the first contestant—who looked as if she just strutted out of a fashion magazine—was called to the veranda of the courthouse; Stratus the II, the second contestant, dressed in a golden tuxedo, swaggered up the steps; Crystal Droplett, the third, who was a very young girl, trotted up; and Nimbus, the forth, proudly marched to the top in his fancy, skin tight clothing.

"And the fifth and final contestant is…" the mayor began. A dab of sweat dropped from Cirrus's temple. His heart fell like rain and he wanted nothing more than to head back home to the bakery, but it was too late.

"Cirrus of the O'Zone Bakery!"

The mayor called his name just as he feared. The world stopped in Cirrus's mind. Despite hearing several crowd members mumble about what a horrible baker he was, he completely froze and could not think a single thought. He continued to tightly grasp the street light pole and tried to breathe. The mayor searched the audience to find him, but Luname spotted him first. She frantically waved to get Cirrus's attention and it surprisingly ended up being a success.

He kept a strong gaze on Luname and he unexpectedly jumped down from the pole and trekked through the crowd. In just a matter of seconds, Cirrus was unintentionally standing next to her in front of the whole town. His face persisted to look petrified. Luname, on the other hand, proudly smiled at the audience and at Cirrus. Though, she could tell that he was extremely nervous.

"These fine globelings are going to bake their best of cakes. I'm serious, folks. You all are going to be the judges of these cakes and you can vote for the best tasting ones as well. These bakers are going to make a cake that is big enough to feed the entire town! The grand prize of the competition is ☆1000 twinkles! The competition begins at six o'clock in two days! Gather your best recipe and let the preparations commence!!" Confetti surrounded the town and balloons were released. The crowd roared yet again and Cirrus remained in his uneasy daze.

☆*☆*☆

There was another problem that was about to occur outside of the snow globe. A massive hand began to enclose itself over the glass orb and it was lifted from the shelf. To us, the hand is not massive at all. It is just the hand of a mere, seven year old boy named Richard, who was partaking in something that he should not be doing. He watched the glittery stars intently as he started to shake the globe.

"Richard, no!" Destiny shrieked as she hurried to grab the globe from him. "You know not to touch those. If they broke, you could cut yourself very badly from the sharp glass." Destiny lifted Richard off of the chair that he was standing on and placed the globe back to where it belonged.

"But it was so sparkly!" Richard whined. Then he started to fiddle with his loose tooth. He made Destiny cringe every time he would wiggle his loose teeth.

"I know, but it's still something you shouldn't touch." She said as she glanced at the time. "Oh, better go hurry and get ready. Your mom will be here soon to pick you up." Richard scampered out of the room making airplane noises.

"Such a troublesome cousin…" Destiny muttered to herself. She looked back at the snow globe and let out a sigh of relief that it was not broken.

☆Chapter Three☆

The Sweetest Thing

The announcement was finally over and the mass group of globelings had gone back to their daily lives with the excitement of the cake competition stirring in their minds. However, it took Cirrus a few moments to realize that he wasn't outside of the Cloudscape Courthouse anymore.

"Ya know what I mean, son?" The mayor laughed and patted his shoulder.

Cirrus had snapped out of his daze. He hadn't a clue if the mayor was talking to him or not and he started to feel tongue-tied. Mayor Sphere, Luname and Cirrus were the only ones in the room, so he could only assume that the mayor was talking to him.

"Uh, yeah, of course!" Cirrus abruptly answered without thinking. Luname looked shocked and began to blush. The mayor patted her on the shoulder and cackled some more.

"See, honey?" he said to Luname. "This young fella agrees that you are the prettiest garsh darn girlie in this here entire town! No need to be worried about your age, darling."

"Oh, papa..." Luname rolled her eyes jokingly. "It's not my looks that I'm worried about. I just can't believe that I'm going to be twenty-two, is all. What I look like is no big deal."

Mayor Sphere laughed a bit more and then took the empty glass from Cirrus's hand where he had apparently been drinking water.

"Make sure he feels better, Luni." Mayor Sphere said to his daughter as he walked out of the room. After he had shut the door, Luname let out a prolonged sigh and sat next to Cirrus on the see-through, gel couch.

"Being the mayor's daughter can be quite embarrassing sometimes." she snickered. "But, um…are you feeling any better?"

"Ah…yes, I guess." he replied timidly. Cirrus didn't even realize that he was supposed to be feeling sick. All he could remember was that he was incredibly tense. He then realized that he must have had a severe nervous meltdown of some sort.

"Good! That's good. You were extremely flush-face out there. I was a bit concerned." she informed him. "I am so glad that you showed up for the recognition of the contestants, though!"

"T-thanks!" he softly smiled. He felt a peculiar vibe from Luname that struck his interest. She was one of the first globelings to ever start a conversation with him and not make him feel uncomfortable. To him, she was a very cute and outgoing young woman. It was nice to see her bubbly blue hair and puffy cheeks again. Her pastel colored appearance tickled him with delight. When she would smile, her large front teeth would poke out and set above her bottom lip. They reminded him of bunny teeth, which added a few more points to her adorable aspect. After how nice she had been to Cirrus, the thought had actually crossed his mind that they could end up being good friends, or so he had hoped.

"You will make a great cake, Cirrus." she said in a soft tone.

"What makes you think that?" he asked bashfully. Luname looked up at him and began to nudge herself closer to him on the couch, which made his heart gallop. She placed her hand on his once again.

"I see hidden potential within you." she replied. "You don't think it's there, but it is. I promise you that it is."

"How can you say that," Cirrus spoke. "…when you already know that my cakes taste like unhappy dirt clumps mixed together with powdered sadness?"

Luname was taken off guard from Cirrus's random words. She paused for a short moment, but then suddenly burst with laughter. Cirrus felt embarrassed and thought that she was laughing at his awkwardness.

"Oh, Cirrus!" she chuckled. "You are hilarious! Powdered sadness? Classic!" She took a couple of deep breaths between her little giggles that escaped. Cirrus blushed after hearing how cute her laugh was. It sounded like a mouse bouncing on a mushroom. "Powdered Sadness is a pretty rare item in Super LoLo, isn't it?" Luname asked as she held her chin. "I always have trouble finding where they are located."

"Yeah. I know you can find some hidden in the walls of the sugar caves in the third world." Cirrus replied. Both Luname and Cirrus became wide eyed and they stared at each other. Their faces looked like they were ready to go on a geek spiel.

"EEEeeek! You are so interesting! It makes me so happy to find someone else in this town that has played that game!" Luname started to bounce in her seat.

"M-me too!" Cirrus said gleefully, but before he could say anything else, he noticed that Luname paused for a moment as her eyes searched the room.

"Did you hear something?" she asked. They both sat silently and waited to hear a noise, but he couldn't hear anything.

"Aw, I think I heard my father call for me. I'm sorry. I'll be right back, okay?" Luname said as she scurried out of the room. He nodded as she stepped out.

As soon as he was left alone, he had to take a few moments to absorb all of the amazement that had just happened to him. After finding out that she had played one of his favorite video games in the whole globe, now she thinks he is interesting. *Is this what having a crush feels like?* What a thrilling event that was to him! He felt splendid. Maybe his video game hobby did change his life for the better after all.

However, the butterflies in his stomach turned into bats as something strange suddenly caught his attention and disrupted him from his daydreaming. A dark aura of purple smoke began to seep through the cracks of the door that Luname had closed moments before.

"What the…?" Cirrus mumbled.

SLAM!

The door slammed open and caused the dark purple smoke to spread like wildfire all throughout the room, morphing the room into a dark, pixelated nightmare. Cirrus yelped and curled into a ball on the couch, or, where the couch used to be that is. The smoke started to shape itself together with several cloud formations. He peeked through his fingers and saw a shadowy figure amidst the dark smoke. It was a very thin looking creature that was covered in a murky, oily cloak. He could barely get a look at whom or what it was.

"**HMM HMM HMM!**" Laughter encircled Cirrus and the toxic clouds absorbed all of the light in the room. The laugher was shriller than a cactus grazing glass. Cirrus lifted his head and tried to stop trembling, but the figure's voice pierced his soul. "**ARE YOU THE ONE CALLED…*CIRRUS*?**"

"M-m-my name is…Cirrus, yes." he stuttered fearfully. "H-how may I help you…?" That had always been the way he was taught to greet others so he hoped it did him some good.

"**DON'T SPEAK TO ME AS IF I WERE ONE OF YOUR CUSTOMERS, FOOL!**" the voice spattered, but then a suave laugh softly hummed through. "**DON'T YOU RECOGNIZE ME?**"

"What…?" Cirrus remained in fetal position over the abyss that was once the floor. He wondered if Luname or the mayor could hear the demonic noises that played around the walls. *Run away! Run away now!* That's all he wanted, but was too afraid to even lift his head to look at the mysterious figure that appeared before him in the newly distorted room. The hooded figure hovered on the dark cloud closer to Cirrus, causing him to sink further to the ground.

"Take a good look at me. I know you know who I am." the voice beckoned as its cloak vanished into a vortex of oily slime.

"Huh, w-what?" Cirrus questioned in fright, but then let his sight slip through his fingers. What he saw was impossible. What he saw was unimaginable. The lanky legs that draped over an acidic, violet cloud, the bulbous clothing that shifted from green to yellow and from blue to purple, the swampy purple hair that believed it was underwater—and the crown that drew in all things bitter. *There is no way!* "T-the Poison Prince?!" Cirrus caught his breath and flung his body to the seemingly bottomless pit of a ground. The atmosphere around him swirled like rainbow oil as the man's laughter rattled the stars.

"Ahh~ So nice to hear my name said with such detest." boasted the Poison Prince as he ran his long fingers through his grassy hair. *No. What is happening? This can't be actually happening, can it? Maybe my dad was right—I really do need to take it easy with the video games.* The amount of questions that raced through Cirrus's mind couldn't even fill a math book. The main villain from a video game stood right in front of him. What in the world was he supposed to do?

The Greatest Cake of the Globes

"**YOUR TOWN SEEMS VERY FUN, LOVING AND...*SWEET.*"** the prince sighed romantically. "**WHAT A SHAME IT WOULD BE FOR EVERYONE TO SUDDENLY, HM, WHAT'S THE WORD...EXPIRE? GO BAD? RUN OUT? SPOIL? ROT?**"

"W-what do you mean?" Cirrus asked, but then a gasp escaped through a shiver in his throat. The Poison Prince clapped his hands together and gleefully hovered around on his dark cloud.

"**IT'S EXACTLY WHAT YOU THINK.**" the prince widely grinned. "**THIS PLACE IS ENTIRELY TOO SWEET FOR ITS OWN GOOD. SURELY, A CAKE COMPETITION IS OUT OF THE QUESTION— UNLESS I HAD A BIT OF FUN WITH IT.**" Cirrus knew exactly what he meant. In the game, the Poison Prince despised everything sweet and did everything he could to keep the world bitter and rotten. Having the whole town gather for the baking competition was the perfect opportunity for him to strike.

"You can't!" Cirrus pleaded.

"**OH, I CAN~**" the prince sang while he whipped his way over toward Cirrus and stood inches away from his face. "**BUT, I CAN SPARE THE TOWN A SOUR DEMISE ON ONE CONDITION.**" The prince's nose glided its way up Cirrus's cheek, freezing him in place, as he sniffed around his head. Cirrus was sickeningly familiar with that action. In the game, the Poison Prince had a very keen sense of smell and could tell how sweet something was just by their scent, and would usually use that for piercing enemy defenses. "**HM, VERY SWEET, YOU ARE.**" the prince sniffed around more. "**BUT NOT SWEET ENOUGH. I GUESS THE GIRL WILL HAVE TO DO.**"

"Huh?!" A gust of wind blasted from the hands of the prince and knocked Cirrus to the ground once more. A strobe of venomous light encircled the prince and formed a magical orb that collapsed and expanded with each breath of laughter. A woman could be heard shouting from the orb.

"*Cirrus! Help me!*" her voice echoed as a blurry image appeared within the sorcerous orb. *Luname, no!* Cirrus felt the world stop around him once more as soon as he saw her in captivity.

"**THIS GIRL IS BY FAR THE SWEETEST THING I'VE EVER SMELLED—AND IT JUST SICKENS ME.**" the prince's face went sour. "**LET ME TURN THIS TOWN INTO A WONDROUS, TOXIC WASTELAND, OR I'LL TAKE THIS GIRL AND TURN HER SUGAR-COATED HEART INTO MOLDED BREAD.**"

"N-no..." he said as he leaned back on the corner of the wall and slid down to the floor. The amount of disarray that flooded Cirrus's mind caused him to feel light headed. He held his head and groaned. "There has to be a way out of this." But suddenly, the orb of light burst out of the Poison Prince's grasp and lit the room with an array of cotton candy clouds.

"*There is a way, Cirrus!*" Luname spoke and desperately reached her hand out of the aura of the orb. She was struggling to hold on to something. "*Here!*" She tossed a small item in to Cirrus's hands—which he was surprised to have caught so easily—and was sucked back into the orb. Without hesitation, he quickly examined what she had thrown.

It was a small, silver necklace that held a glass vial. It was about four inches long and it was attached to a thin chain. The top of the vial was sealed with a cork that had a blue gemstone and silver wings sculpted on the side. Cirrus was almost too distracted from its beauty to have realized that there was a piece of paper rolled up inside. He took out the paper and began to read it.

The Greatest Cake of the Globes

"This..this is a cake recipe?!" Cirrus stuttered out of puzzlement. All that was written on the paper was a list of ingredients. Luname tried as best as she could to keep the power of the orb under her control. The Poison Prince struggled to keep his eyes open from the immense light she was creating.

"Yes! This is the recipe for **The Greatest Cake of the Globes**! Only you can save me and the town from the prince's poisonous trickery!" Luname shouted. Her words were beginning to fade.

"What?!" Cirrus asked with worry. "What must I do?" His heart was racing faster than hail falling during a storm.

"You must gather those special ingredients from the seven globes!" Luname explained.

"That's impossible!" Cirrus cried. "No one ever leaves the globe. I rarely leave my room let alone the entire globe! I'm too weak-minded. I can't do this!"

"You can, Cirrus! You can!" cheered Luname. "This is the only way. The Poison Prince is cursed to where everything that is sweet is painful to him. The Greatest Cake of the Globes is the only thing in this world that is so sweet, he can't be anywhere near it!" Luname struggled to stay visible. "If you can bake The Greatest Cake of the Globes, we will all be saved! Do not tell anyone about this! Not my father, not your parents. You are the only one who can do this. Be my Super LoLo. Be my Super Cirrus!!!"

The Poison Prince suddenly clapped his hands together causing Luname and the orb to completely vanish. He gripped his hands together and panted heavily. The prince took one final look at Cirrus and hissed loudly, calling back his dark magic, which made the room feel uneasily calm again. The sounds of roaring winds had ceased and the walls were no longer painted in toxins. The same sunlight as before had shown through the window, but it seemed so much brighter to him. Everything was suddenly back to normal, though he remained in the corner of the room huddled in a ball. He could feel a knot in his throat and his eyes begin to weld up with tears—he had no idea what he was going to do. The only thing he could do was to go back home and recollect everything that had just happened—and he needed to make a decision fast! While trying to ignore his trifling thoughts, he left the Cloudscape Courthouse as fast as he could without being spotted by the mayor. However, once he stepped on to the terrace of the courthouse, there was another sight he wished he had not seen.

"Oh no..." he gasped and was stricken with terror. He saw a crowd of globelings gathered around his home where dark, black smoke was seeping from the bakery's windows. The bakery was on fire.

```
*Quest Unlocked:Find legendary
ingredients

HP: 10/10  *HP= Heart Points
BP: 10/50  *BP= Baker Points
MP: o o o o o o o   *MP= Magic Points
```

☆Chapter Four☆

The Journey of Super Cirrus

Cirrus scrambled his way through the nosy, gawking crowd and shouted for his parents. Before he reached the front door, his mother opened the window and let a gust of smoke pour outside. She was coughing uncontrollably. Cirrus stopped dead in his tracks.

"Cirrus!" Stara coughed. "There you are! You are alright!"

"Mom! What happened-" Cirrus was interrupted by his mother grabbing his arm and pulling him into the bakery.

"Quick!" she shouted. "Help your father fan out the smoke. Open some windows!" Stara turned back around and noticed the prying pack of globelings peeping into the bakery. "Haven't you ever heard of a fire drill? This is a phony flame rehearsal. Fake smoke and all! Off with ya!" Stara shooed off the snoopers and then quickly ran back inside. Lo and behold, his father had already doused the flames in the kitchen.

Roughly ten minutes later after frantically clearing the thick smoke out of the building, Atmo walked out of the kitchen with a pan full of burnt dust bits—the tray scalded and all. He sighed and turned to his son. Cirrus was sitting on a stool in fetal position by the counter. The way he was sitting looked rather difficult to maintain balance, but somehow he pulled it off. Stara was fanning out the last bit of smoke through a window on the other side of the room. She looked back at Atmo, who seemed upset.

"What is that?" Stara asked. Cirrus slightly lifted his head to get a glance of his father. As soon as he saw the scorched rolls, his head plopped right back down into his folded arms.

"I'm afraid to say," Atmo spoke with a gloomy tone. "...that the oven is broken."

"No, don't even say that!" Stara held her hand to her mouth. "It just overheated right? It will be back to normal when we clean it...right? It can't break now!"

"The top and bottom burners have completely overheated and they will not light anymore. I've tried several times. Burnt to a crisp." Atmo stated.

"W-well..." Cirrus began. "Let's give it a few hours and see how it goes, ah?" He tried to smile, but it ended up being way too obvious that he was near tears. Atmo sat the pan down on the counter and began to scratch his head.

"It won't be that easy, son. We are going to have to close down the shop for the day and even possibly tomorrow. What good is a bakery without an oven?" Atmo sighed and went to switch the OPEN sign to CLOSED, but then realized that it was already set to CLOSED. He turned back and looked at Cirrus with disappointment.

"Did you put rolls in the oven and just leave them unattended to?" Atmo asked. Cirrus was stricken with tremendous guilt.

"There was a crowd and...globelings everywhere..." Cirrus took a deep breath and sighed. "Yes... yes I did." He sat up from the stool and headed for the spiral staircase.

The Greatest Cake of the Globes

"Wait, wait, wait." Stara said. "Cirrus, why would you do that? You never prep the bakery."

"I wanted to do something good for you and Dad for a change. I wanted to surprise you by getting a head start on baking the rolls." he said accepting the blame. "Then, I got distracted by things outside and lost track of time. I'm really sorry…" Cirrus rapidly thudded up the steps and had sprung up to his room. His parents did not say a word.

As the door slammed behind him, he stopped. Something had struck his mind. He was tired of cowering to his room. Running to his room shouldn't be his first alternative for dealing with his problems. *No more acting like a child*, he thought. He re-opened his bedroom door, but then shut it back the right way; quiet and subtle, like a well behaved young man. He sat on his bed softly, rather than jumping on the bed pouting, and took a deep breath. At that moment, he remembered the vial necklace and pulled the chain up from beneath his blue shirt, which could not even remember when he placed it around his neck. He began to read the recipe, and what a large recipe it was!

Ingredients:

- 30 cups cake mix………………*~Cloudscape~*
- 8 cups water…………………*~Cloudscape~*
- 14 tbsp. of ground cinnamon …..*~ JingleJangle~*
- 12 cups milk…………………*~ O'Cottage~*
- 8 eggs…………………… *~O'Cottage~*
- 10 cups of butter………………*~O'Cottage~*
- 4 cups blueberries for frosting….*~DrearyDrough~*
- 100 malt balls………………*~Jukebopper~*
- 1 golden apple………………*~TockTick~*
- 11 tbsp. honeysuckle nectar………*~FaeAway~*

He felt a bit overwhelmed to see such a large recipe with an out of the ordinary cluster of ingredients. *Cloudscape* was written after two of the listed ingredients, which made him wonder if the other names listed were from other globes. There were six different locations following Cloudscape town, so they had to be the six other globes that Luname spoke of. Cirrus rolled up the recipe and placed it back into the vial. He swallowed the hardest he ever could.

Nearly twenty minutes had passed, and he came walking down the stairs dressed in virtually the same adventurous clothing that Super LoLo wore in the game: sturdy brown boots, loose blue pants, and a purple cape that his mother had made him when he was younger. He was carrying a large, velvet satchel around his shoulder. His parents both stopped what they were doing and looked at him in confusion.

"Are you going somewhere?" his mother asked concernedly. "My, I haven't seen you wear that cape ever since you were little."

Cirrus paused for a short moment and took the time to examine his parents. He could see that they were hiding the dissatisfaction with him underneath calm faces and recollected all of the times he had disappointed them. Hesitantly, he took the curled paper out if the vial, unfurled it, and handed it to his father.

"Ah, a shopping list." his father said with relief. "He's just going to do some shopping, Honey." Atmo took a second glance at the list and looked back up at his son. "Hold on, now. This is a pretty big order for a shopping list. How in the moon's craters are you going to buy all of this stuff?" Cirrus realized what his father said was true; there was no way he could purchase any of these items even if they were from different globes, but tried to ignore his doubt while his parents began to ramble on about money.

"How much money do you think one hundred malt balls would cost?" Atmo asked Stara jeeringly.

"Nearly fifty twinkles, I would say. More than what we are charging for rent next door, that's for sure." she replied. Cirrus finally spoke and interrupted them.

"I'm not going to buy them." Cirrus stated.

"Don't you start thinking of thievery!" Atmo objected. Cirrus was taken aback by such an accusation.

"No, never!" Cirrus defended himself. "I-I'm… going to travel to the other globes in search of these ingredients."

There it was. Cirrus had finally admitted what he was doing, though he still could not tell them about Luname being captured by the Poison Prince. They would think the video games took over his mind for sure. He felt a bit of relief that he had finally admitted it, but the look on his parents' faces still troubled him.

"Oh, don't say such a thing, sweetie." Stara awkwardly laughed.

"He's just playing around." Atmo hiccupped.

Cirrus wasn't laughing. There was a long, uncomfortable pause between all three of them as their eyes played an uneasy game of badminton.

"You're not playing around, are you?" Atmo embarrassingly asked. Cirrus faintly shook his head.

"B-but…uh…" Stara stuttered and quickly snatched the recipe from Atmo. "We should have some of these ingredients, right? You don't have to leave, Cirrus."

"No, mom." Cirrus said. "It says that I can only use the cake mix and water that we have here. See?" Cirrus pointed to where it said Cloudscape next to cake mix and water. "There are different globes listed by the other ingredients; that's why I must go."

"Where did you even find such a recipe?" Stara asked.

"I-I found it in an old cookbook under my bed." he lied. "I thought it would make a great and unique recipe for my cake in the competition. You know...something that stands out?" Atmo and Stara looked at each other and with mystified faces.

"But, son, I bet you-" Atmo was suddenly interrupted by Cirrus.

"Dad, no!" Cirrus raised his voice. "I know what you are going to say. Don't try and talk me out of this. I'm gathering these ingredients for the mayor's daughter's baking competition. I want to do something I've never done before and make you both proud of me. Besides, if I win the competition, I can buy us a new oven; an even better one than before. Let me do this as an apology for ruining the bakery and the fact that I always mess up everything."

Cirrus's throat swelled like a sponge and he could feel himself trembling a little. Never has he had such a serious discussion with his parents. It strangely gave him a good feeling, knowing that he was about to attempt something he would never have thought about doing in a million years. Atmo put his hand on Stara's shoulder and then stepped forward.

"If you would have let me finish," Atmo said as he cleared his throat. "I was going to say... I bet you don't remember how to exit the Cloudscape globe like you did when you were little."

"Like I used to?" Cirrus asked to his surprise.

☆*☆*☆

Nearly thirty minutes later, Atmo and Cirrus arrived at the supposed exit of the globe. Although Cirrus didn't quite see where the exit was, he was still soaking up the nostalgia from the flowery field that surrounded him.

"You've been here before, ya know?" Atmo said.

"I..." Cirrus murmured. He couldn't recall the area entirely, but he was certain that he had been around this flower field before.

"Ahhh, yep." Atmo sighed. "You always wanted to come here when you were a youngster; always wanting to ride the *swirly-swirl*." Atmo tugged on his small beard and winked at Cirrus.

"Swirly-swirl? Hey, that does sound kind of familiar now that you mention it." Cirrus faintly smiled.

"Well, I'm sure it does." Atmo chuckled. "It was the highlight of your life back then, you used to sneak out here all of the time. You were quite adventurous before you got sucked into those video games, that is." Cirrus's mouth went crooked and he scratched his head, embarrassingly. "Oh, I'm just kiddn' ya, son!" his father laughed while he forcefully patted Cirrus on the back. "But, really, you should take a break from those games."

"Dad," Cirrus groaned and rolled his eyes. "I'd appreciate it if you stop bringing up my gaming hobby. I'm not playing them now, am I?" He and his father shared a serious glare at one another. However, once several seconds of silence went by, they both smiled and playfully laughed with each other.

"You're a funny boy, Cirrus. A funny boy, but you are my funny boy and that's all that matters." Atmo squeezed his son tightly and let go. He walked over to a little mound of flowers and knelt down. Cirrus followed close behind him. He peeked over his father's spotted bandana and saw a large, bubble stuck inside of a hole in the ground.

"What's that? That looks familiar too!" Cirrus said in awe. Without hesitation, he crouched beside his father and went to touch it.

"WHAT IN RAINCLOUD'S SAKE ARE YOU DOING?" Atmo yelled furiously. Cirrus gasped and fell over, throwing his hands in the air as if he was surrendering.

"What, what?!" Cirrus asked gasping for breath.

"Nothin." Atmo smiled. "I'm just messing with ya again. Go ahead and touch it."

"Daaaaaaaaaaaad." Cirrus sighed and shook his head.

Cirrus looked at his father for a few seconds to reassure that he wasn't going to suddenly scare him again, but then he just went on ahead to touch the bubble-like thing. After a dainty poke on the clear, soapy substance, the bubble wiggled, jiggled and floated up from blocking the hole. The bubble glistened and rose just a few inches above Atmo's head, so he took a hold of it and started squishing and squeezing it.

"See? It won't pop. This is *The Bubble*, with a capital B. It's *that* important." Atmo said as he gave the Bubble a bear hug. "This is what blocks the doorway between our globe and the largest globe ever. Do you remember what that large globe is called? Think of geography class, boy!"

"U-uh!" Cirrus was thrown off guard from the unexpected question. "I...uhh...I can't remember. I do know that those human things live there though."

"Oh c'mon, now." Atmo snuffled. "It's called Earth. It's the biggest of all of the globes. It is the globe of all globes!"

"But, Dad." Cirrus replied. "I do recall from science class, that there is a globe called Jupiter that is bigger than Earth."

Atmo paused for a moment in bewilderment from Cirrus's sudden educational answer. He placed his hand on his scruffy chin and gave his son a nod of approval.

"Well done." his father said enthusiastically. "but none of this smarty-pants stuff matters at the moment, as long as you stay safe and come back soon is all that is important, okay?"

Cirrus wished that he and his father's conversation would last a lifetime so he would not have to leave Cloudscape Town at that very moment. Deep down, he was still very afraid of leaving the globe. All of the young globelings, including Cirrus, were raised to believe that they were forbidden from ever leaving the globe and only "strong" globelings may leave and return safely. There were many rumors spread about something called *dust* that surrounded the globes and many feared that they would choke and suffocate if it came too close to them. Cirrus unwillingly remembered all of those terrifying gossips and was about to call it quits, but then his father suddenly said something that surprised him.

"I can't believe I'm saying this, but just imagine that you are in one of your video games." Atmo said.

Cirrus took his glance away from the dark hole in the ground and fixed it upon his father, who was still holding the Bubble. After all of the times Atmo had criticized and poked fun at his son's video gaming hobby, he mentioned it as if he was trying to comfort his son in this serious situation. It may seem odd, but Cirrus became enthralled with the thought of pretending that he was in a video game, which would make it seem as more of an adventure that he was familiar with. He was, as a matter of fact, about to head out on a quest in order to save a girl from a villain. *Already sounds like the plot of a video game to me anyway,* he thought.

"The Journey of Super Cirrus." Cirrus yearningly muttered.

"The Legend of Cirrus." Atmo said.

"Super Cirrus Brothers! Well...I don't have siblings." he replied.

"Resident Cirrus 4: The Zombie Cake Plague" Atmo giggled.

"Okay, I think that's enough." Cirrus laughed. He then turned away from his father, looked down the dark hole, and took a deep breath. He stuck one foot inside the hole and he could see that there was a large spiral staircase that led to a light at the bottom.

"Hey, I do remember this place now. So this is the 'swirly-swirl'." Cirrus said in awe. He remembered his dream that he had last night about himself, as a child, sitting on a large, spiral staircase. There was a chiming melody that he remembered from his dream too. "Is this where that random, musical weather comes from?"

"Why, yes." Atmo crossed his arms and smiled. "Music is my favorite kind of weather, especially on a cloudy day when the glitter falls." Cirrus felt at ease when he thought of the weather. As snow, rain and sunshine are to humans, the globelings might have a music storm or glitter shower every so often. They believe that glitter and music box melodies are parts of their weather.

Outside of Cloudscape, that very moment, Destiny had lifted up the globe and twisted the music key at the bottom of the globe stand. She flipped it right-side up and the music began to chime as the glitter fell.

From viewpoint of Cirrus and his father, an assortment of colored glitter arose slowly from the flowery field and the music played very loudly. They both quickly covered their ears in surprise, but smiled.

"My, my! What a coincidence!" Atmo shouted. "It must be a sign, son! You are getting a special sound off for the beginning of your journey!"

Cirrus had a wide grin on his face and was filled with an eager sensation that he had never felt before. As he watched the sparkles of glitter softly soar amongst the air and heard the loud music play, he was so overwhelmed with excitement that he grabbed ahold of his satchel and nodded.

"I guess I should press start to play The Journey of Super Cirrus, huh?" They both laughed as Cirrus stepped his second foot into the hole in the ground.

The Greatest Cake of the Globes

```
HP: 10/10
BP: 10/50
MP: o o o o o o o
```

☆Chapter Five☆

Out Upon the Shelf

In he went, slowly but surely. The music box tune gradually stopped and the globe became quiet once more. Within seconds, he began to show dismay the further he stood on the steps of the spiral staircase. He didn't want to turn his head and show his father his troubled face, but when he did, he saw that his father had a bit of a worried look to himself as well. They both stared at one another for a moment as if they would never see each other again, but Atmo quickly covered his feeling of doubt with a smile.

"Come back quickly, ah?" Atmo said as he held out his hand. Cirrus had never seen his father act so serious. Sure, he can get irritated at his son a bit, but usually he was a big jokester who can always make someone laugh. The calmness in Atmo's voice began to make Cirrus feel troubled. However, he refused to acknowledge his dual thoughts. As afraid and doubtful as he felt, he decided to continue down the globe's steps.

"I'll be back before the dough raises, Dad." Cirrus took his father's hand and strongly shook it. Atmo nodded and gave his son an encouraging smile.

Down the hole Cirrus went. There was nothing to be seen other than the old staircase that he stood on. As he looked downward through the cracks of the steps, he could see a faint light near the very bottom. The staircase was incredibly narrow which made Cirrus feel claustrophobic. Each step he took, he grew more and more uneasy. He turned to look up at his father, but only his silhouette from the light was visible. Cirrus took a deep breath and continued to walk down the steps.

Back in the globe, Atmo slowly nodded to himself and then returned the Bubble back to its original resting place over the hole. He sighed and began to retrace his steps back home through the flowery fields.

"I sure hope you can make it back safely, son. You've already made your mom and me proud." Atmo muttered cheerfully to himself. However, something suddenly struck his mind; something that he wished he could have brought to Cirrus's attention sooner. "Oh, I do hope he realizes that we don't have a working oven to bake this enormous cake with…" Atmo grumbled. He shrugged his shoulders and walked off.

Cirrus was nearing the final few steps of the staircase that had felt never ending. His heart could not beat any faster than it already was, but the time had finally come for him to exit the globe. The light was not as bright as he had expected, but it still had an overwhelming glow. In the floor, on which he stood, was a large opening that allowed the light to flow in. He crouched down on to his knees and held out one hand over the hole. A soft breeze tickled his palm through his glove. It was strangely comforting.

A few moments went by as Cirrus prepared himself to enter the opening. He then spotted a rope ladder across from where he was standing. Hesitantly, he walked over and began to climb down. Instead of entering complete darkness like the hole up above, he was now entering total whiteness. He shielded his eyes from the light by quickly shutting them, but he continued to fumble down the wobbly rope ladder. Closing his eyes had thrown him off balance, causing him to slip and abruptly fall down the ladder. He thought he was done for.

"Yaaah-ooow!" Cirrus groaned as he fell to the ground. He opened his eyes and saw that he had only fallen about a foot from the rope. He sighed and felt his chest to see if the recipe vial was still attached to him; which thankfully it was. He was beneath the globe's base; right underneath the music knob. As he rolled over and got back on his feet, he noticed a bit of a gray powdered substance stuck to his clothes.

"What's this stuff?" he asked himself. He started to brush it off of him, but then he suddenly gasped. "AH! This is dust—the gray powdery material that eats away at innocent globelings if they breathe it in!" Cirrus held his breath as he scurried out from underneath the globe and was frantically stomping and shaking the dust off of his body. His panic steadily dwindled away once he had become mesmerized by his new surroundings.

He froze in his tracks. In that very moment, he had suddenly realized how small he actually was; as if he were just a mere speck in this world. To be honest, he was only four centimeters tall according to human measurements. The shelf he stood on seemed to go on for miles, but it was only three feet long.

Even though he was standing right next to his globe, he still felt that he ventured somewhere very far away and dangerous. He couldn't believe that he lived in a world within a single study room; Destiny's room, for that matter. The walls were light purple and, across the room, little gnome and faerie figurines were lined up along the window sill. *Are those small creatures globelings too?* As Cirrus continued to examine the room, he came to the conclusion that human decor is almost as similar as Cloudscape Town's, but perhaps a little less fluffy and sparkly. A few moments after absorbing the new atmosphere, he slowly inched, or better yet "millimetered", his way further down the shelf to examine the other snow globes. Luname was right; there were six other globes that lie upon the shelf. If doubt and fear were shaped like anvils they definitely just dropped on Cirrus's head. The comprehension of how small he actually was made him dread the thought of even going back home. A human could easily knock over the globe and destroy all of the globelings. He couldn't bear to imagine the shelf falling; destroying all of the other globes with their own worlds within them. He didn't want to admit it, but he was definitely afraid.

The Greatest Cake of the Globes

Thinking that his anxiety levels were at its peak, he decided to go all out and test himself by glancing over the edge of the shelf. He crouched down and began to crawl on his knees. His fingers gripped tightly on the shelf's rim and he pulled himself forward. A scary thought crossed his mind when he realized just how easy it would be to fall and or jump off of the shelf. He could jump if he wanted to, but that's just plain ridiculous.

 He saw the entire floor of the room. The shiny, wooden floor was almost completely covered up by a pink and blue rug. There was a desk that had a small, pink lamp sitting on it. Crumpled up sheets of paper were also scattered all across the desk. However, Cirrus had failed to notice the slightly opened window that was about to give him quite a scare. A faint draft blew in from the window and eventually made its way to Cirrus. He felt the wind lift him into the air, causing him to firmly grip the shelf.

 "AHHH!" he gasped as he was chucked into the air. The wind quickly stopped and Cirrus had dropped onto the ground like a sack of jelly beans. Without hesitation, he flung up from the ground and galloped toward the second globe. He didn't care what world was within that globe; he just wanted to be off of the shelf and away from that scary wind.

Before he knew it, he was already halfway up the spiral staircase in the second globe. For a moment, he stood still so he could catch his breath. A few goose bumps poked their way through his skin as he got a sudden cold chill. He began to shiver as he continued to walk further up the steps and when he sighed, he could see his breath.

"Huh?" he said. He then let out some more of his breath. "Steam? Fog? Is my breath going through condensation?" It was something he had never seen before. The temperature in Cloudscape Town always remained room temperature. He carried on exhaling his breath and watching the vapor as he drew near the entrance of the new world.

"Brr…It's so cold in here." he mumbled. He rubbed his hands together and placed them over his mouth and nose. A light became visible through the steps above. The entrance was just a few spirals away. Cirrus found himself wobbling up the last bit of steps as they were coated in a sheet of ice.

"W-woah! These steps are slick." he stated. Finally he had reached the top. The Bubble that blocked the entrance was frozen. He pushed and pushed until it rolled off at last. One hand rose from the opening and soon the other. He could feel something cold, yet fluffy at the same time. His head surfaced from the hole. There, he was able to see the new world that he was in, and what a wonderful sight to behold!

```
HP: 07/10 -3 heart pts. from wind
damage
BP: 10/50
MP: o o o o o o
```

☆Chapter Six☆

A Silly Boy in the Snow

Cirrus stared in wonder, completely forgetting about the chill in the air. Surrounding him were tall pine trees that were decorated with colorful lights and shiny bulbs. Each time he turned his head, the lights sparkled through each pine needle as if the lights were twinkling on their own. They reminded him of the stars he would see through his bedroom window before bed.

"Never have I seen a Christmas tree so big." Cirrus marveled. He managed to lift himself out of the hole and rolled the icy bubble back on top of it. While he dusted some snow off of his arms, he looked to the distance and was able to see a small village that was also illuminating with holiday cheer.

"Wow, Cloudscape Town never seems this festive around the holidays. Look at all of this white fluff! It must be snow! Like cold clouds." Cirrus chuckled. Snow had never been seen in Cloudscape Town, but everyone was aware that it existed. He marched forward down a path of peppermint and spearmint stones that lay atop a blanket of snow. The ground shimmered with every step he took. The frosty atmosphere started to make him shiver, however, and he regretted not packing his jacket, but he tried to bear with it as long as he could. Those ingredients need to be found; found quickly for that matter.

The further he walked toward the village, he began to notice two tall, skinny figures standing near the entry way. *Those must be globelings.* He felt hesitant about striking up a conversation with beings from another world. *What should I say*, he thought.

Cirrus reached the last peppermint stone in the path. Once he looked up at the two figures, he realized that they weren't globelings at all; they were just wooden soldier statues.

"Oh!" Cirrus exclaimed. "You two had me going there for a second. I thought you were both alive." He looked up and examined the statues for a moment. They both stood completely straight and seemed about four feet taller than him. Glossy paint covered their symmetrical, wooden bodies. Each had different colored soldier attire; the one on the left was painted green while the other on the right wore red. Both had black mustaches and white beards that snuggled around their square teeth.

"But we are alive." a voice said from above. Cirrus gasped and drew back from the green soldier.

"W-wha? Who…" Cirrus glanced up at the soldier and watched its solid, painted eyes blink. He cautiously took a couple steps away from the figures in fear that it may harm him for trespassing.

"Look at you, scaring away the poor thing." scowled the red soldier.

"Look at you, calling him a *thing*. How rude!" said the green soldier.

"Look at you, lacking holiday spirit." clacked the red soldier.

"Look at you, accusing me of lacking spirit." clanked the green soldier.

The wooden men continued to fling words at one another. Cirrus just stood there shivering in bewilderment. He observed how the levers protruding from their backs made their mouths move up and down in a vertical manner. Their teeth clacked together every time their mouths would shut. After a couple minutes of arguing, the clacking began to irritate Cirrus to the point of saying something to stop them.

"Look at you, making me listen to the both of you argue!" Cirrus spoke over their voices. The festive figures became quiet and their heads turned back to the visitor.

"Our apologies, holidaymaker." they said simultaneously.

"Holidaymaker?" Cirrus asked. Never had he heard of such a word.

"A tourist." replied the red soldier.

"Traveler, visitor, guest, sightseer, rubbernecker, caller…" said the green soldier.

"I think he gets it, SpearMint." the red soldier rolled his eyes.

"We are the Nutcracker Soldiers of JingleJangle." boasted the green soldier. "I am the loyal, trustworthy, noble, handsome...SpearMint~. This is PeppyMint. He's made of wood."

"So are you!" PeppyMint whined. "Anywho, we welcome you to our home of holiday splendor. Please enjoy your stay here in JingleJangle." They both held out their cylinder arms giving Cirrus permission to go through. Cirrus suddenly felt at ease once they stopped arguing, but he did think that they were kind of humorous. Before he was able to walk through the red and white swirled gate, PeppyMint stopped him.

"Wait just a minute…" PeppyMint said in a strict tone. Cirrus awkwardly turned around and walked back to the nutcrackers like a scared dog. His face cringed at the thought of him accidentally doing something wrong, but he tried to hide it.

"Y-yes…?" Cirrus asked curiously. PeppyMint then tossed him a velvet, violet cloak along with a pointy, purple hat.

"Bundle up, Buttercup." PeppyMint laughed.

"That was the cheesiest thing I have ever heard." SpearMint grumbled.

"Thank you very much!" Cirrus wrapped the warm cloak around him, placed the hat over his large ears and began to trot towards the village.

All of the houses had pointed rooftops that sat above rounded walls with frosted windows. The more Cirrus looked at them he began to feel as if the houses were actually frosted and that they were made of sweets! *Oh, I sure hope the Poison Prince doesn't want attack this place too.* The flavorsome homes encircled a frozen pond where many citizens were gathered. There were carolers at nearly every door and their voices chimed through the village, spreading wonderful, holiday cheer. As the older globelings walked to and from their homes and little shops, bells jingled while playful children ice skated and mingled on the pond.

At that moment, Cirrus wished that his parents were with him. A family vacation at JingleJangle would be perfect for the holidays, but then, he suddenly thought of Luname. He imagined them together hand in hand—after he had rescued her from the evil prince, of course—ice skating on that frozen pond. Since he was so clumsy, he figured he would eventually slip and fall on the ice. Luname would most likely giggle at him after helping him back up.

"Would that be an appropriate time for a kiss…" Cirrus mumbled to himself. He was lost in his fantasy, but then suddenly got hit in the face with a snowball.

"Woops! Sorry about that mister!" a kid shouted from afar. The kid and a few other children quickly scurried off. Cirrus shook the icy snow off of him; though, since his cheeks were already so red from his fantasy of Luname the snow quickly melted off.

Cirrus thought they hit him with a snowball by accident; so he just shrugged it off. However, he wasn't meant to be the children's target. When he took one step forward, he felt something tug onto his cloak. He turned around and didn't see anything that could have been near him, but then he lifted up his cloak and saw a little boy cowering beneath him.

"Uh…" Cirrus said awkwardly. "Hello there!" The young boy slowly stepped out from underneath his cloak and sighed. He looked as if he was still a toddler since he was so small. His outfit was embraced in reds and greens. He wore a pointy hat, just like the one Cirrus wore, and it nestled on his curly white hair, which looked rather similar to cotton that was about to be blown away by the wind. His skin was very dark in contrast to the paleness of his hair.

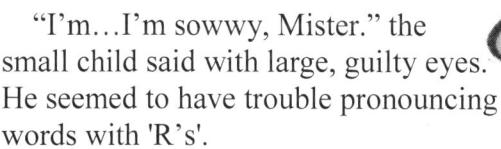

"I'm…I'm sowwy, Mister." the small child said with large, guilty eyes. He seemed to have trouble pronouncing words with 'R's'.

When the boy looked up, Cirrus was able to see his face. He had a plump, red nose and two pink circles on his cheeks, which had resembled Luname's. Cirrus's thoughts of her were quickly interrupted by sudden tears of the little boy.

"Aw, no! It's okay!" Cirrus knelt down to the boy and tried to cheer him up. "It was just an accident. They didn't mean to hit me. It's not your fault."

"Yes it is!" the boy pitifully whined. "They were twying to hit me, but I made them hit you instead. I was supposed to get snowballed."

"Now, I'm sure they were only playing a game. They weren't trying to hurt you on purpose." Cirrus said positively.

"Yes they were…" the young one cried. "All of the other kids are mad at me 'cause I'm going to wuin Chwistmas 'cause Santa Cwause is going to choke on the cookies I made him 'cause I put too much cinnamon in them and I don't have any milk for him to drink and I don't have monies!"

"My my my, what a fast talker you are!" Cirrus said. He could barely understand the little boy's mumbled speech, but he understood the gist of it. "Don't worry, though. Santa will still like your cookies and he won't choke."

"But there is too much cinnamon!" the boy groaned. "Santa needs to dwink milk after eating the cookies because his mouth will be too dwy to swallow them!"

"I see…" Cirrus pondered. He thought about the time his cakes were too dry to swallow and his gut shivered. "Everything will be fine, silly." The little boy stared up at him in awe. His pale, blue eyes suddenly seemed to light up.

"You know my name?" the boy asked.

"Huh, your name?" Cirrus became confused.

"My name is Silly!" the boy said in a chipper voice. "You must be one of Santa's elves! That's why you know my name!" Silly had a smile that spread eagerly from cheek to cheek. The situation felt a bit uncomfortable for a short moment, but Cirrus didn't want to deny what made the little boy finally smile.

"T-that's exactly right, Silly!" Cirrus said as he exaggerated his voice. He stretched the tips of his round ears to make them look pointed. "See? I *am* one of Santa's elves and he sent me here to help cheer you up."

"So, you can help me get some milk for Santa?" Silly asked as he tugged on Cirrus's velvet cloak.

"Is it Christmas time already?" Cirrus asked. He looked down at his wrist, as if he were wearing a watch, but then quickly put his arm down as he realized that he did not even own a watch. *Why would me looking at a watch answer my question about whether it was Christmas time or not*, he thought, but then quietly laughed to himself.

"Chwistmas Eve is on the twenty-fourth of every month and that's tomorrow!" Silly said. Cirrus wasn't surprised to hear that the globelings here celebrate the holidays every month. It was a Christmas globe, after all. He was about to accept Silly's request, when suddenly he remembered that cinnamon was one of the ingredients that he needed for the cake recipe, as well as milk. He quickly thought of a plan.

"I'll be sure to bring you some of the freshest milk there is out there, but do you think you could do me a favor as well?" Cirrus asked kindly.

"What is it, Mister Elf?" Silly asked.

"When I bring you the milk tomorrow night," Cirrus began. "do you think I could have some cinnamon?"

"Oh! Yeah!" Silly jumped. "Anything to save Santa! We have lots of cinnamon at home!"

"Great!" Cirrus laughed. "Sounds like a plan."

Silly ran up to Cirrus and hugged him tightly. A child had never hugged him before and for that, he already began to feel as if he was doing a great deed for someone. His heart warmed and he jolted with motivation.

"Silly, I'm going to have to leave now," Cirrus leaned down to him and began to whisper. "…but I promise I'll be back tomorrow. Don't let those other kids be mean to you. Just be confident in yourself, okay? Tell them that Santa will give them coal instead of presents if they are mean to you."

"Heeheehee, okay." Silly playfully whispered. Cirrus turned away from the town and started walking back to the nutcrackers' entrance. He and Silly shared a parting wave goodbye, and then Silly trotted his way back into his warm home. Forgetting that he was wearing the purple hat and cloak, Cirrus walked past the nutcrackers.

"Hold up there, Buttercup!" PeppyMint exclaimed.

"Leaving already? You just got here!" SpearMint asked.

"Oh, I-I'm sorry. I, uh, want to go tell my parents about this place. I'll be back tomorrow though." Cirrus declared as he took off his hat and cloak. He handed them to PeppyMint.

"Hey!" SpearMint whined. "How come you gave him both your cloak and hat?"

"Because he likes it when I call him *Buttercup*." PeppyMint boasted.

"That's not fair!" SpearMint groaned. "Fine, I'll call him Sir Cornelius the XIII. That's a much better nickname, if I do say so myself."

"Whaaaa?" Cirrus was baffled.

"What an awful nickname. Buttercup suits him." PeppyMint growled.

They continued to speak nonsense to each other yet again. Cirrus rolled his eyes and sighed. He snatched his hat and cloak out of PeppyMint's spherical hand while he wasn't looking.

"My name is Cirrus!" he broadcasted. "Not Buttercup, not Sir Corn-something the whatever; just Cirrus." He handed his pointed hat to PeppyMint and then handed his velvet cloak to SpearMint.

"There, now you both have something of mine." Cirrus crossed his arms. The nutcrackers both looked at one another and nodded.

"So we do." they both agreed.

"I've got to go now. No squabbling, okay? It's the holidays!" Cirrus smiled and walked off. The two nutcrackers shook hands and promised not to squabble anymore…at least while Cirrus was around.

The Greatest Cake of the Globes

*Side quest Unlocked:
Search for milk for
Silly.

HP: 07/20 +10 max HP
from entering new world
BP: 10/50
MP: . o o o o o

☆ CHAPTER SEVEN ☆

ENTERING A DREARY PLACE

After Cirrus had exited JingleJangle, he could feel his whole body thawing from the chill of winter, like an ice cube getting comfy in a hot tub. Out he crawled from beneath the globe and was once again on the shelf. He made sure that there was no wind to propel him through the air like last time. Everything seemed to be safe, so he decided to make a run for it. At that very moment, however, Destiny made an entrance into her study room.

"Eck!" Cirrus screeched. "Is that a…human?"

He hunched down so she wouldn't see him, which seemed pointless for there was no way he could have been seen by the human eye from such a distance anyway. He began to think about all of the stories he had heard about humans when he was younger. There have been so many rumors that humans were horrifying giants that destroy the homes of globelings. They take hold of the snow globes and deliberately smash them for enjoyment. The more Cirrus observed Destiny, however, he found himself questioning those statements. A cheerless woman was all that Cirrus could perceive. He watched as she sat down at her desk and stared at a blank sheet of lined paper. Her sighs were long and desperate as the white paper was illuminated by her desk lamp.

"I don't even know…" Destiny mumbled. "I can't…"

Cirrus tilted his head in concern. The more he looked at her the more he felt sorry for her. Something was obviously troubling the human. Suddenly, another human walked in; it was Zachery. Cirrus decided to listen in on their conversation.

The Greatest Cake of the Globes

"Would you like me to make you something to eat while you are brainstorming?" Zachery asked as he poked his head through the crack of the door.

"Nah…I'm fine. Thank you, though." Destiny quietly replied. "I doubt I'll be able to brainstorm anyway."

"Why do you say that?" Zachery pouted.

"My creativity is long gone. I can't think of anything to write about or how to even begin writing. It's hopeless…" Destiny sighed as she took off her large, violet-rimmed glasses and began to rub her eyes. Zachery entered the room and gently ran his fingers through her hair.

"If you keep this up," Zachery said. "…you *will* end up making yourself sick."

A feeling of déjà vu whacked Cirrus in the chest. He remembered his mother saying nearly the same thing to him; warning him about stress causing sickness and all. At the time, he just felt sorry for himself and was too stubborn to acknowledge his parents' kind words.

"I just wish that I could just write a story." Destiny replied. "A story with meaning…with morals, and have a unique, unexpected adventure of some sort, but my imagination just isn't the same as it used to be when I was little."

"You will overcome this soon. I'm sure." Zachery said cheerfully. "It's just little 'ol writer's block. Don't push yourself, okay?" He kissed her on the cheek and was able to get her to smile again; just for a short moment. After that, he left the room and softly shut the door behind him. Destiny folded her arms on her desk and lightly nestled her head over them.

Now that she wasn't looking, Cirrus stood up and swiftly ran to the next snow globe. While trying not to be distracted by the human's distress, he briefly examined the globe before he entered it.

The second globe looked more aged than the others around it. It was decorated with rusted, antique borders and faded, ceramic flowers. The entire globe was faded of color, save the violet gems that bordered the base. He eventually found his way in and started walking up the customary spiral staircase that each globe seemed to share. This time, however, the stairway was completely pitch black; as dark as a starless sky. Cirrus couldn't even see the slightest bit of what was in front of him. The steps creaked and the hand rails were unstable. Every wooden step was on the brink of collapsing. After a few moments of fidgeting to find some light, he groaned.

"Come one…Come on…" he said in a shaky tone. "Where is the light to the entrance? I can't see a thing!"

BONK!

The top of his head had suddenly hit something. He cringed back and held his head in agony for a few seconds, but he made a speedy recovery as he pushed up on the ceiling as hard as he could. Out he popped from the ground like a mole. He was holding the entrance-guarding bubble above his head, but something was unpleasing about it. This Bubble wasn't clear and colorful like the others; it was murky and frail. Unexpectedly, the bubble crumbled in his hands, causing dust to fall on top of him and land in his hair.

"Oops..." Cirrus coughed. After shaking the dust off of his hair and finishing off a couple of sneezes, he explored the new area that he had entered. The trees were all dead and the grass was entirely lifeless and dry while dark gray clouds patched up all of the blue in the sky. The atmosphere was completely dull and unwelcoming—but the strangest aspect of this new world was the loss of color. Every inch of the area was black, white, and gray. Not a drop of color in sight.

"Huh...going from JingleJangle's winter wonderland to a place like *this*?" Cirrus said. "What an unhappy place. Where have all of the colors gone? What possible ingredient could I find here?" He plucked the cap off of the vial around his neck and took a glance at the recipe.

"DrearyDrough. This has got to be where I am. This place is so...*dreary*." He continued to read the ingredients. "Blueberries?" he laughed. "Where in the stars will I ever find blueberries here? They definitely won't be blue. That's for sure."

Cirrus felt surprisingly underwhelmed. This world was nothing. After only a few minutes of being inside DrearyDrough, he was already beginning to feel lazy and demotivated. Everything that surrounded him was so gloomy that it made him feel gloomy himself. He wondered if the Poison Prince had his way with this world. However, something caught his eye out of the blue (or is it *out of the gray*?). Through the maze of tree branches, there seemed to be an old building of a sort just a little ways from where he was standing. He shook off the depressing aura and scuttled through the trees. There was a cake to be baked and a town to be saved; no time to wallow in self-pity!

As he ducked underneath each withered tree branch, after getting nicked in the face by some thorns, he was able to get a better look at the Victorian-styled home. It was quite clear that time had aged the house to a great extent. Cirrus carelessly walked through the wooded area thinking it was an abandoned building when he suddenly spotted a man sitting on the porch of the eerie house. He jumped behind a tree in case the man saw him, but fortunately he didn't. He debated walking any further.

From what he could see, the man was covered in a black cloak which almost appeared gray from the amount of dust that was caked onto him. His legs were long and bent. They looked like sticks that have been recently scorched by a campfire. No matter how long Cirrus stared at him, the man did not budge an inch. Was he a statue just like the nutcrackers from earlier? But, they were alive by the magic of cheer and holiday spirit. Cirrus wondered if there was anything joyful keeping that man alive.

Just then, the man had let out a small whimper while he picked up a few items from behind him. They were tiny, glass jars. He held them in his arms and began to cry. Cirrus was tempted to leave the globe, but the sound of the man's sobs made him think otherwise. Before he knew it, he was already near the porch, standing in front of the upset man.

"E-excuse me..." Cirrus spoke softly.

"EYAHHHHH!!!!" the man screamed in horror, causing Cirrus to scream just as loud and fall to the ground. The glass jars shattered and a gray, thick liquid poured out of them, which seemed to be paint. The man stumbled up the porch steps and quickly ran into his house like a startled mouse—the door slammed shut. Cirrus remained sitting on the cold ground in a daze. He scooted his foot away from the paint that inched toward him and noticed the sharp, broken glass scattered all around him. He caused that man to break his belongings and could not help but to feel responsible.

The Greatest Cake of the Globes

"C-color..." a gentle voice said. Silence was louder than the voice. The front door squeaked and only the man's large eyes could be seen from the darkness of the house. "Such vivid, wondrous colors embrace you."

Not knowing what to reply, Cirrus became a bit shaken and gave the man a forced smile. Surely, an apology was in order for scaring the poor man and causing him to break his jars.

"I'm really sorry...for breaking your jars of paint, Sir." Cirrus spoke with guilt. "I didn't mean to scare you, really."

"Why are you here?" the man somberly asked. "As you can well see, there is nothing here for you but the lifelessness that surrounds us."

"I'm sorry I..." Cirrus felt timid. "I'm sorry for causing you to drop your paint. I really am. I really didn't mean to scare you like that." He didn't know what else to say and he just felt like he was repeating himself.

"Those paints are not of use to me anymore." the man said in a monotone voice. The front door leisurely opened a bit more and the man continued to stand in the shadows. In moment's time, he stepped out.

Gradually, the dim light from behind the clouds revealed the man's features. He stood at the same height as the doorway. As a matter of fact, he had to duck below the doorway to get through. He seemed nearly eight feet tall in comparison to Cirrus. His body was incredibly thin and had long, frail arms. Scruffy, black hair fell passed his chin; almost to his shoulders and his eyes were large and blank as if he had seen a ghost. His uneasy appearance made Cirrus wonder if he was among the living.

"Their colors have gone; gone far away, just as my spirit; just as my happiness." the man said as he pulled out a paintbrush from his pocket. He held it out in front of him and widely opened his eyes. "This paintbrush symbolizes my own likeness. With a variety of color and a touch of inspiration, this paintbrush is the key tool for making a masterpiece…however…"

Suddenly, he dropped the paintbrush onto the ground and his body soon followed. His back bent and his head went limp.

"Without color…without inspiration…it's nothing but a dried up stick with no purpose—as am I."

Cirrus was still sitting on the hard ground, confusingly staring at the man's poetic body. He could barely understand what the man was talking about, but he did figure out that the mysterious fellow had to be a painter at least. Several seconds passed in the awkward silence that Cirrus was accustomed to. He continued to feel tongue tied.

"I'm really… sorry to hear that, Sir." Cirrus stood up and tensely burrowed his foot into the dirt.

"Lorne." the man stated. "My name is Lorne. What do you go by, dear boy?"

"Um…I'm Cirrus." he replied as he placed one hand behind his neck to calm his nerves.

"Please come in, Cirrus." Lorne said as he stood up and bowed, giving Cirrus permission to enter his home. "I must treat you to some tea for having frightened you."

Cirrus felt highly uncomfortable—more uncomfortable than he had felt in a while. *Shouldn't I be the one treating Lorne to some tea; not the other way around*, he thought. However, he still needed to find those blueberries around there somehow. They just had to be there. No one could deny the legendary recipe of The Greatest Cake of the Globes. Seriously, the recipe was written in gold ink; that had to mean something.

The Greatest Cake of the Globes

Cirrus quietly stepped in. He walked into the house a few feet in front of Lorne. The house was dimly lit and Cirrus could barely see the interior around him. All of a sudden, the door noisily creaked and shut behind him, leaving complete darkness to befall all around.

"Oh, I do apologize. One moment." Lorne said as a slight scraping noise was heard. He had struck a match against his cloak and lit a portly candle that sat upon a small, wooden table. With the candle lit, Lorne noticed that Cirrus was cowering in a corner by the door. Cirrus quickly stood up and cleared his throat, trying to keep his cool.

"Don't be ashamed. I am the same way. That's why I do this." Lorne carefully placed the large candle on top of his head. It fit around his head like a cozy, top hat.

"That's actually a pretty good idea!" Cirrus smiled.

"I fear the darkness…and I find comfort in candlelight…" Lorne admitted as he adjusted his candle-hat. "That is why I decided to create a candle that I can wear on my head so the light could follow me everywhere I go. However, my candle is nearly at its end. I will be in darkness forever in due time…"

"Oh…" Cirrus didn't know what to say. Lorne's face remained in an unemotional void.

"Come now. Warm up by the fire place in the foyer while I prepare some tea." Lorne said as he led the way through the shadowy corridor.

Ciara Jackson

```
*Side quest Unlocked: Find Blueberries
 in the dreary world .

HP: 07/30   +10 max HP from entering new
world
BP: 10/50
MP: . . o o o o o
```

☆ CHAPTER EIGHT ☆

FOR LORNE

Cirrus was led into a dark room that was illuminated by the glow of the fireplace—the fire a ghostly white. Lorne stepped in front of him and started moving things about. He took a puffy, silk pillow off of one of the couches and began fluffing it, causing dust to flutter everywhere and itch at Cirrus's nose. He plopped the pillow down on the floor beside the fireplace and grabbed a blanket from a chair. He coyly glanced over at Cirrus.

"Here. Sit." Lorne politely demanded as he patted the pillow. "Sit here and let the warm fire do what little comforting it can."

"Uh..s-sure…" Cirrus walked over and clumsily sat on the cushion, trying to avoid eye contact with Lorne. There was something about that man's eyes that made him feel even colder than he did in JingleJangle. A blanket was carefully wrapped around him by Lorne. "Uh…Thank you." Cirrus said respectfully.

"This fire no longer gives me comfort." Lorne said as he dusted some dirt off of the blanket around Cirrus's shoulders. "I'll return with tea momentarily." A few seconds later, Lorne was gone and Cirrus was all alone in the dark room. He wondered if he was more afraid when Lorne was next to him or when he was alone. It made him feel bad that he thought that way about that stranger, but he just couldn't help but feel intimidated. His mind began playing tricks on him; instead of Lorne returning with tea, he imagined him returning with a knife…or even a hatchet. *He's going to kill me and chop me up into little, itty-bitty bits*, he thought. He continued torturing himself with sick, morbid thoughts until Lorne had finally returned with tea.

"For you." Lorne spoke softer than air as he held out a chipped tea cup. Cirrus flinched back thinking he was going to be hurt, but then accepted the cup in relief. The man took off his candle-hat and sat it on the nearest table. He then fetched a cushioned stool that was next to the couch and sat it next to Cirrus—*very* close to Cirrus. He took a seat and turned his wide eyes to his guest for several moments, examining every inch of Cirrus's attire in amazement, but then quickly turned away.

"Agh, I-I apologize." Lorne placed his hand over his eyes. Pain rose in his voice. "I shouldn't stare at others. It's just...your colors...such stunning shades of purples and blues."

"My colors?" Cirrus asked as he blew into his tea to cool it.

"Yes. It's been nearly twenty years since I've last seen color." Lorne sipped his tea. A thin stream of black liquid ran down his chin. Cirrus sipped his tea as well.

"Twenty...YEARS?!" Cirrus swallowed hard. His voice cracked from the shock of how thick and bitter the tea was. The consistency was of a rusty-like syrup that had gritty sand bits settled at the bottom—the sugar? It can't be! He quickly tried to cover up his coughs of disgust so he wouldn't seem rude. "So, I take it that you have seen it before? Color, I mean." Cirrus asked while covering up his shriveled face.

"Yes." Lorne answered. "Oh yes...b-but pardon me. I must ask why you are here. I don't see why anyone would want to come here."

"I...well, it's rather hard to explain." Cirrus said as he grimaced from the scent rising from the tea.

"I've got time if you do..." Lorne softly spoke.

"Oh...well, I, uh, where do I even begin?" Cirrus thought for a moment. "I guess you can say that I'm from another globe on a quest to gather ingredients for a cake recipe, b-b-but before you say anything, I will be able to save my whole town if I succeed!"

"A cake can save a town?" Lorne seemed baffled.

"It's really not easy to explain. You see, there is this girl that I like back home, who is the mayor's daughter, and she is having a cake competition for her birthday in which I...uh...*entered.*" Cirrus started confusing himself.

"You must be quite the baker to enter such an important contest." Lorne sipped at his tea again.

"Eeeeeyeah..." Cirrus felt even more embarrassed. He knew he was lying to himself and also began to stretch the truth in order for Lorne to believe him—an explanation with no evil video game characters involved. "Well, I found out that one of the contestants plans on poisoning his cake entry and making the whole town get really sick!"

"Absurd!" Who would do such a thing?" Lorne scowled. A new emotion formed on the man's long face that Cirrus wasn't used to.

"I know, but that's why I'm in search for the greatest cake recipe out there. If I win, then the town will choose my cake instead of his. That's why I'm here. There is an ingredient that I need somewhere in this globe." Cirrus popped the recipe out of the vial and pointed to the words DrearyDrough on the small sheet of parchment.

"Oh, is there anything I can assist you with? What's the ingredient?" Lorne asked with interest.

"It says blueberries." Cirrus said confusingly as he rolled the recipe back up. The man didn't reply. Cirrus frowned whenever he saw Lorne's face, though. The tall man's eyes were even wider than before, but then they immediately closed.

"No, I'm sorry…" Lorne held the tea cup close to his face. "Blueberries have never grown here in DrearyDrough."

"O-oh…" Cirrus sighed and placed his tea cup down. He tightly wrapped the blanket around him more. "I hope I can find them somewhere else then. I trusted this recipe…but it looks like I better leave soon if they aren't here. I'm running out of time." Cirrus began to wriggle out of the blanket in order to stand up.

"Wait!" Lorne raised his voice. "That girl you mentioned…excuse me for asking, but do you *love* her?" He inched closer to Cirrus and showed great interest.

"Luname?! Uh…" Cirrus blushed and his heart fluttered. "I've only known her for a little while…but…"

"She is important to you, nonetheless. Correct?" Lorne asked as he nodded his head anxiously.

"Well, everyone is important…I guess what I'm trying to say…" Cirrus fumbled with words in a shaky voice. For some reason, he was starting to feel strangely comfortable around Lorne. Then, the more he talked about Luname, it hit him. He really did like her. It wasn't just a simple crush, but he still didn't want to believe his feelings. He didn't want to get his hopes up. After all, who knows if he is even going to succeed on his quest?

If he couldn't defeat the Poison Prince in the video game, how in the world was he supposed to beat him in real life?

"She…" Cirrus fiddled with his fingers. "She is the only one who I've felt comfortable talking to in a long time. She is really kind and doesn't think that I'm awkward or unusual…or maybe she does, who knows?" Cirrus slumped back down onto the dusty cushion in front of the fire. He let out a lengthy sigh and curled up into the blanket. Lorne seemed concerned and placed his cup of tea down onto the floor. He leaned over to give Cirrus a comforting pat on the shoulder, but then quickly drew back when Cirrus began to speak once again. "Honestly, she probably just feels really bad for me. The only emotion she most likely feels toward me is pity. I mean, come on. Why would the daughter of the mayor have any interest in talking to me? Yeah, right. I just hope that we can be friends if I can save her and my town." Cirrus closed his eyes. There was a brief moment of silence, but Lorne slumped down in front of the fireplace and stared deeply into the silver flames—eyes glistening like sequin.

"Think upon…the happy side…Little Primrose." Lorne whispered. His eyes closed and a sudden tear slid down passed his quivering lip. Sobs began to bubble up his throat and he immediately fell into a shaking fetal position.

"Ahwah?!" Cirrus yelped as the blanket fell off of his shoulders. "Are you okay?! Did I say something wrong?!" Lorne sat up and attempted to console himself to hide away his tears, but that quickly backfired. His body became weak and he started shaking profusely.

"I, ah, please, d-dear boy—hold me, p-please!!" Lorne demanded in between breaths. He crawled on his knees over to Cirrus like a sad child wanting his mother to comfort him during a storm. Cirrus, although terrified and confused, cautiously wrapped his arms around the tall man and firmly squeezed him.

His chest pressed hard against Lorne's and he could feel the man's heart jackhammering out of his chest. The man's cries became louder and more pitiful with each spasm of his throat. Whatever was happening—it was happening way too fast; Cirrus didn't even know what to say or think or do. The once silent room was then filled with Lorne's sobs echoing off of the walls, his loud cries muffled from Cirrus's shoulder.

Roughly five minutes after the tearful event, the grown man's cries had died down and he remained locked in Cirrus's arms, panting slowly. Cirrus could feel that his shoulder was soaked in tears, but he did not seem to pay any mind. He maintained a strong embrace around Lorne and gently swayed him side to side like a newborn. It seemed to be the only thing he could do for the man at the time.

"I'm...terribly sorry...that you had to see me in such a sorrowful state." Lorne sniffled, wiped his face, and sat up straight. "You handled it in a very calm manner, though...and I thank you."

"N-no problem." Cirrus delicately smiled. He still felt shaken from that whole ordeal.

"Please..." Lorne said as he stood up and placed the candle-hat back on his head. "Follow me and I will explain everything."

"S-sure." Cirrus nodded. He followed Lorne up a couple flights of stairs and through twists and turns of different rooms. Every room was just as dark as the other.

"Hey, um..." Cirrus whispered from behind.

"Yes?" Lorne stopped.

"Would you mind me asking...why is it so dark in here?" Cirrus asked.

"Once, the sun would shine throughout all of the windows and flood the halls with a creamy light, but without it, only candles are able to illuminate my home." Lorne turned away and continued to walk.

"Where did the sun go?" Cirrus sounded befuddled.

"...In due time." Lorne replied as he opened a tall, lopsided door that lead to a bedroom.

As the door opened, Cirrus expected to see something amazing, as if it were to explain the very meaning of life, but no. The room was just as dark and dull as the others. Nothing was special in there for all he knew.

"True beauty..." Lorne whispered. The corner of his mouth slightly lifted. Cirrus wondered if that was the man's way of smiling. Suddenly, he became greatly curious as to what could possibly make that gloomy man smile.

"I can't see anything." Cirrus shrugged.

"If darkness swallowed beauty, would you still believe it was there though you could not see it?" Lorne widely grinned and stared off straight ahead. He walked as the flame from the candle-hat gently flickered each time he took a step. The further he walked away, however, the more Cirrus could see something large on the wall opposite of him. It was a painting of a woman.

"Oh, how beautiful!" Cirrus said in awe. Lorne lifted a match from his pocket and let the flame from his hat ignite it. He then lit a candle that sat on a table below him, causing a chain reaction of other candles to catch fire. The candles' domino effect lit up the entire room allowing each detail of the painting to be seen.

The portrait of the woman was very well-painted and it almost took up the entire wall. She wore a shoulder-less, silk frock and had a primrose blossom in her hair. Her bangs were straight and rested above her eyebrows. She appeared to have very large, round ears which Cirrus found to be adorable. The whole portrait was black, white and gray; matching the rest of the scenery in the globe, but suddenly a glimpse of color in her eyes had caught Cirrus's attention.

"This is a portrait that I painted of my dear wife long ago." Lorne said as he grazed his hand across the bottom of the circular frame.

"Y-you?!" Cirrus clapped. "You painted that? What a spectacular gift you have, Lorne! I'd kill to have as much skill as you-"

"NO!" Lorne snapped and turned to Cirrus. "No need to say something so blunt and ludicrous! Killing won't cause you to gain the artistic ability that I have acquired throughout vigorous practices over my lifetime!" The tall man stomped around furiously and spoke fast.

"Lorne, Lorne, Lorne! It was just a figure of speech; a way of expressing something....I'm not going to kill anyone!" Cirrus said in a cold sweat and cowered to a corner. The man's anger ceased.

"I...I'm sorry once again." Lorne slapped his palm over his own face and turned away. "I'm overly sensitive when it comes to...love and death." He turned and threw a steady gaze upon the painting. Cirrus could feel his stomach turn for he could sense that something terrible must have happened to the woman in the painting.

"The colors that I used to paint my beloved wife have faded over the years. The colors within this globe have faded. The light has faded. My body has faded." Lorne explained as he walked closer to the painting. "The only color that remains now is in her violet-blue eyes."

"Did…did she?" Cirrus asked as he bit his lip. He couldn't bear to ask the full question.

"…Years ago…" Lorne closed his eyes tightly. "No, I mustn't. Do you really want to listen to a poor, pitiful man's banter?"

Cirrus grabbed the nearest stool and sat it close to the array of candles. He sat up straight with eyes completely focused on Lorne, similar to a student preparing to take down notes from a teacher's lecture. Lorne softly smiled, but then took a deep breath.

"Years ago, my wife, Viva, and I made a wonderful living here. Each day the sky was bright and blue. The grass and trees bustled with soft evergreens. Our house was surrounded by Viva's garden that flourished with a rainbow stream of flowers, fruits, and vegetables. She was a florist, after all. Whenever she would tend to her garden, I would paint her. I would paint her kind face; her beautiful soul lit up each canvas." Lorne paused for a moment and his smile vanished. Cirrus could only assume that the talk of happy times were over.

"One day, I became very ill…" Lorne's voice fell deep. "I was bedridden for weeks and showed no sign of recovering. I was sure it was the end for me, but I was content. I had Viva by my side and that was all that mattered, but one morning she came to me with the news of her sudden departure. *'I'm leaving the globe, Darling.'* she said. *'I must go find medicine for you.'* I begged and begged her to stay, but my precious flower wouldn't take no for an answer. I began to weep, but she cradled me to her bosom and said *'Think upon the happy side, Little Primrose.'* That was what she used to call me…Little Primrose." His head dropped. "Those were the last words that I heard from her…and then after she had placed a yellow primrose blossom in my hair, she left. Weeks later, I recovered on my own. She never returned…and that was twenty years ago." Lorne placed both of his hands on the painting and clutched his fingers tightly. He held back his tears. Crying once in front of a guest was more than enough.

"However…" Lorne sighed. "I am certain that you are curious about the remaining colors in her eyes."

"Oh…I…you don't have to tell me anymore if you don't want to." Cirrus said. Truthfully, the curiosity was eating away at him.

"I'm afraid that I fibbed to you earlier." Lorne admitted. He knelt down and opened a hidden door from the wall below the painting. Cirrus stood from the stool and tried to catch a peek at what he was doing, but it was too dark to see. Once Lorne stood up, green stems and frilly leaves poked out from around his shoulders. He was holding some sort of plant, but Cirrus couldn't quite tell what kind it was. The shrub swayed and ruffled as Lorne turned around, revealing the mysterious plant.

"A blueberry bush!" Cirrus gasped.

HP: 07/30
BP: 10/50
MP: ● ● ○ ○ ○ ○ ○

☆Chapter Nine☆
No Time to be Snoozing

Lorne held the blueberry bush close to his chest. The plant lavished with plump blueberries that were a delicious shade of indigo. He plucked one of the berries off of the stem and squished it between his fingers.

"Look how ravishing. You see? " he asked. "The liquid from the mushed berry emits a bluish-purple color. By mixing the blueberry juices with white paint, I am able to create the perfect color for Viva's eyes."

"Ohhhh, it all makes sense now." Cirrus spoke as if he solved a mystery. "That's a plant grown by Viva and that's why you didn't want to tell me about it."

"Forgive me..." Lorne softly apologized. "But, I do not know if I can give these to you."

"What? You don't have to even think about giving them to me. I couldn't take those." Cirrus felt sympathetic.

"It is still amazing that this plant has yet to die. This is the only color I have; the only thing living in my world." Lorne gently ran his fingers through the leaves.

"And it is your wife's plant too..." Cirrus said compassionately.

"That is true, but you can save many people from harm with the help of these blueberries...including the one you love. I just don't know how I can bring myself to part with these." Lorne moaned with sincerity.

"Lorne..." Cirrus smiled. "It's okay. I don't want to make you unhappy."

"It is time that I add another coat of paint to my lovely wife's eyes." The tall man stared deeply into the painting.

"That is perfectly fine!" Cirrus brightly said. He could tell that he was feeling more at ease around Lorne. He didn't seem to be as afraid of him anymore. "I'll tell you something, though. How about I come back here tonight?"

"What? You want to come back here?" Lorne asked timidly.

"Sure! I'll leave right now and explore another globe and then I'll come back tonight to visit you again. Would it be alright with you?" Cirrus stood up and adjusted his boots.

"Why, yes it would, but..." Lorne fumbled with his black, straw-like hair. "Wouldn't you rather just go back home until the morning and restart your journey from there?"

"Nah, I don't want to go back home until I have all of the ingredients. Tonight will be fun. We'll have a sleepover!" Cirrus laughed and backed up toward the door.

"A sleepover?" Lorne sounded confused.

"You'll see." Cirrus waved to Lorne and started to walk out the door.

"You will...you will come back?" the man slightly smiled.

"I promise. We're...friends now. You won't be alone anymore." Cirrus gave a comforting grin and waved as he left the room. Lorne's eyes began to shine. An enormous feeling of happiness swam within his mind. He turned to the painting and sniffled.

"Viva, I...I think I've made a friend." he chuckled to himself in disbelief and had a stunned smile across his face.

As Cirrus exited the house, he felt really bad for leaving Lorne alone. He couldn't imagine how it felt to be isolated for twenty years, especially in a cold, colorless world like DreayDrough. Cirrus understood what it was like to be lonely, never having friends to talk to and all, but he still had his parents and the whole town around him, despite him never socializing with any of them. At least he had the comfort of color all around as well.

While being lost in his thoughts, Cirrus reached the bottom of the spiral staircase and exited the globe. Before he crawled out from underneath the base, he took a deep breath and double checked to see if the humans were around yet again.

"Humans aren't that scary." he said to calm his fear. "They all can't be destroyers…right?"

He quickly scurried down the wooden shelf hoping the humans wouldn't see him; in which, again, was highly unlikely. However, they were not in the room at the time, making things feel much easier. He looked at the clock next to Destiny's desk.

"Seven O'clock?!" he gasped. "What have I been doing? I don't even have a single ingredient yet!" There were four more globes to explore and he was nowhere near finished with his quest. He jolted to the next globe without even taking the chance to examine it. Up another twisted staircase he rushed; filling his mind with motivational words; *Do it for mom and dad, do it for the bakery, do it for the town, and do it for Luname!* He had to say those words over and over again to feel worthy. He frantically ran up the stairs full of confidence, but then suddenly…*THUD!*

"OW!" Cirrus gasped and rubbed his thigh. He ran too fast and tripped. "Of course I would trip UP the stairs. I guess it is probably best to approach a new world slowly…" He nodded off the pain and paced himself up the remaining steps. At that moment, the air felt warm and smelled fresh. He reached the top and moved the Bubble out of the way. Something was strange about that Bubble too. It felt prickly, like straw. When he propped himself out of the hole, he realized that the Bubble was actually covered in hay. There were hay bales resting all around him, but the sudden strong sent of fresh air and food delighted his nose.

"Wow, something smells wonderful!" Cirrus sniffed the air. A warm breeze made his pale purple hair tickle his cheeks. The air smelled of fresh chamomile flowers and firewood. It reminded him of his favorite hot tea he usually drank as he played video games back home; a pleasant memory indeed. As he looked around, he saw a large, red barn surrounded by hay; lots and lots of hay and grass. Across a stone bridge, there was a small cottage that had smoke puffing out of the chimney. He caught another whiff of that smell again.

"Someone must be cooking." he wondered. He saw a few farm animals sleeping in the barn as he walked passed it. There was a cow, a few chickens, a horse, and two pigs. He thought they looked so cute sleeping. It must have been nap time for the farm animals.

"I bet this is the place where I get the milk, butter, and eggs." he said and trotted along the bridge. He checked the recipe again to make sure he was in the right place.

As he walked across the bridge he began to notice something strange. Something was not right, and then it hit him. There was absolutely no sound coming from anywhere or anything! He stood still for a moment to listen, but he couldn't hear a single thing; not even the wind or the water below him. *How odd*, he thought. He then hopped off of the bridge like a bug. There was no thud as he landed either; no sound of crunching grass and hay as he stepped on it. The cottage could be seen from a better view now. The cobblestone, faerie-tale home gave off a warm and comfortable feeling; the same feeling you would get as you cuddle underneath a handmade quilt along with some feather pillows. Cirrus felt his eyes become heavy the more he stared at the cottage. This place definitely had to be O'Cottage.

"Oh, no no no" he yawned. "No time to be snoozing! Not yet." He walked up to the front door and gently knocked. His knuckles made no sound as they clonked against the wooden door. A few seconds passed without anything happening. He knocked again, a bit more rough this time; still no sound. He knocked for a third time, no luck. The aroma of delicious, homemade cooking suddenly turned into an awful smell of burnt toast and sauerkraut. Yuck, not a pleasant scent at all.

"Hello? Excuse me!" Cirrus cleared his throat. "I'm new to this place and I, uh, have a question or two…hello?" No one seemed to be home, but then the door suddenly cracked open. Cautiously, he poked his head through the door and looked around inside. No one was there, but he saw a large puff of black smoke coming from another room. Something smelled horrible in there.

"Ah! Hello?! I see smoke! Hey! Is everything okay in here? Can you hear me?!" Cirrus quickly ran into the house and followed the trail of smoke. It led him into the kitchen where he saw a big, cast-iron kettle shaking and liquid bubbling over. Fire flakes were spitting uncontrollably out of the fire pit, burning patches of the wooden floor around it, but yet no sizzling sound was heard. When he turned his head, he saw two globelings slumped over the kitchen table; not moving an inch. *Oh my goodness, they are dead!* The very thought made his stomach turn. Truth be told, they weren't dead, they were just taking a nap; a *very* deep nap. Cirrus, on the other hand, didn't know what to do and began to pace around the kitchen.

In due time, he came across a steel hook he could use to latch on to the handle of the boiling pot. He grabbed the hook and lifted the heavy pot away from the fire and tried to lower it to the ground quickly, but carefully. The pot hit the ground a bit roughly only spilling a few drops of burnt soup onto the floor. He ran over to the bucket of dirty dishes and scooped up a bowl of water to pour it over the fire. Slowly, the fire died down. Cirrus felt weak in the knees after handling the pot, but was relieved that the fire settled. Though the situation was very dangerous, he still felt the courage to prevent the sleepy farmers' home from burning to the ground.

Moments after Cirrus caught his breath, a loud snore startled him from behind and nearly scared the wind out of him again. That snore was the first noise that he had heard since he entered the place. He gratefully sighed when he realized that both of the globelings lying on the table were actually sleeping. A stout woman in a torn apron was snoozing the day away while a portly old man with a poofy, white beard was snoring across from her. They were both wearing pointy hats and looked like little gnomes. As a matter of fact, they actually were gnomes! Cirrus took a moment to recollect his senses and lightly tapped the man on his shoulder.

"Excuse me, sir." he laughed to himself. "I was wondering if you could lend me some items by chance? Milk, eggs, and butter are all I need. You must have very special goods here." Silence went by.

"I'll work for it. I'll churn the butter, I'll milk the cow! It's for a good cause, I assure you." He nudged the man's shoulder, poked his nose, and tickled his belly, but the old man wouldn't wake up.

"Is that okay? Are you folks awake? Excuse me!" Cirrus raised his voice louder and louder. He even shook the man and woman to where they almost fell out of their seats, but they still didn't wake up.

"What's going on?" Cirrus groaned. "They are asleep…even the animals are asleep! My voice isn't loud enough to wake them up! What do I do?!" He pulled up a chair next to the sleeping farmers and examined the recipe from the vial necklace. Milk, butter, and eggs from O'Cottage, it said. He was sure he was in the right place.

"I can't just take the ingredients without asking. I just can't. I'd feel so guilty." he whimpered. He felt his stomach growl and make all kinds of demonic noises.

"Oh, just in time. Now I'm hungry." his head drooped to the table. "I guess I should just go back to Cloudscape town and get something to—" he paused for a moment and saw a cabinet. The door was slightly open and he could see a variety of delicious looking breads and cheeses. He wondered if it would be okay if he just grabbed a quick snack. He hesitated for a while because his morals were confusing him. Was it stealing or was it borrowing? Should he reward himself with some food for saving these globelings' lives? He didn't know what to think. Heading back home wasn't an option for him. He wants to have every ingredient with him when he heads back. However, he was going to head back to DrearyDrough to accompany Lorne for the night, but he was certain that he was not ready for Lorne's cooking, especially after tasting that bitter tea.

After contemplating for a couple of minutes, Cirrus stood up and tiptoed to the cabinet. Tiptoe-ing seemed rather pointless since the farmers were so deeply asleep and his feet made no sound anyway. He opened the cabinet door and saw delicious looking foods. There were loaves of wheat bread, jars of various shades of purple and red jams, perfectly whole cheeses, sliced meats and plump fruits. His mouth watered the longer he stared at them. After glancing back and forth at the farmers a couple of times, he finally gave in and grabbed some food. He began slicing the bread and dicing the cheese.

☆*☆*☆

Meanwhile at Cloudscape Town, Cirrus's mother was busily wiping down the bakery counters. Atmo was washing the dishes back in the kitchen when he saw his wife pause for a moment. She seemed to have had a troubled look on her face.

"What's the problem, Hun?" he asked as he wiped bubbly dish soap off of his hands. Stara's eyebrows arched up.

"I have the strangest feeling about Cirrus." she sighed.

"Aw, c'mon now." he patted her shoulder. "Have some faith in the little guy."

"I just have this odd feeling…" Stara spoke. "…that his social awkwardness is getting the best of him and that he's sitting around doing nothing and talking to himself."

☆*☆*☆

Back at O'Cottage, Cirrus was dining amongst the farmers at the kitchen table…talking to himself.

"What a fine jam you have made, ma'am!" Cirrus said as he licked a jam glob off of the side of his lip. He then looked over at the woman and started talking in a high pitched voice as if she were replying to him.

"Why, thank you young man!" the *woman* said. Cirrus then changed his voice to a deeper tone and turned to the old man.

"Hoho, hope yur likin' the cheese, boy, 'cause I made that with the freshest of cow's milk muhself!" the *man* boasted.

"Oh, both the jam and the cheese taste delicious. Thank you!" Cirrus complimented them. After he swallowed the berry flavored bread, he paused for a moment.

"I can't believe I'm doing this." Cirrus rolled his eyes and his head dropped to the table, but then he suddenly shot up. "That's it. Finish eating, head back to DrearyDrough, get a good night's rest and head right out the door to get all of the ingredients in the morning. That's the plan!"

Outside, the sky was painted a pastel pink for the sun was just about to set. Cirrus cleaned up, thanked the sleeping folks for the scrumptious meal once more, and headed out as quickly as he could. He planned on visiting another globe in the morning and, who knows; he might be able to find something that would wake up the farmers if they are still heavily snoozing by the time he returned. Whatever it took to get those ingredients, Cirrus was sure going to try his best.

```
*Side quest Unlocked:
Wake up old gnome
farmers.

HP: 27/40 +10 max HP
from entering new world
+20 HP from eating
BP: 10/50
MP: . . . o o o
```

☆Chapter Ten☆

A Nightmare While Awake

Outside of the globe, Destiny's desk lamp dimly lit the study room. Cirrus crawled out from underneath the cottage globe quietly and noticed that the once cotton candy-colored sky had become a dark blue in a matter of minutes. His heart nearly skipped a beat whenever Destiny had walked into the room, but as the moments passed, she calmly sat at her desk and began clicking about on her laptop. From what he had observed from her, Cirrus figured that she wouldn't do anything to harm him, or so he had hoped. He quickly tiptoed his way back to DrearyDrough when suddenly a voice called out from the shadows of the shelf.

"H-help...help me...!" the voice said. It sounded very weak and raspy. Cirrus looked towards the back of the shelf and froze. A frantic fluttering noise rumbled his ear drums.

"W-who's there?" Cirrus clutched his fists with fright. The voice rose again from the darkness. The buzzing rapidly continued.

"Please...Help!" the voice cracked again. Feeling scared and hesitant, Cirrus rushed into the shadows to help whoever was in need.

"Quick! She's going to get me!" the voice cried. As Cirrus approached it, he could see something of a light brown color. Suddenly, something had flapped in front of him and two giant eyes were staring at him. Cirrus shouted and fell to the ground, shutting his eyes tightly. The giant eyes quickly folded down and disappeared.

A figure turned to Cirrus and faintly apologized. Cirrus peeked through his fingers and saw a moth that had gotten trapped in a spider web.

"I'm so sorry…" the moth whispered. "Here you are trying to save me and I scare you with the pattern on my wings. How rude of me…"

"Huh…?" Cirrus's eyes began to adjust to the darkness. After a few moments, he could see that the fluffy moth had tattered wings, as if he had been struggling to break free for a good amount of time. The moth was out of breath from thrashing about. It was no surprise. A labyrinth of spider web was surrounding the both of them.

"She's going to eat me, small one." the moth spoke desperately. "Please, cut me free! I'm not ready to die."

"Ah! I'll try…I-I mean I *will*!" Cirrus pulled onto the stringy web and noticed that it wasn't breaking as easily as he had hoped. He tried biting the web with his teeth and it ended up being a success. "Yes!" Cirrus shouted with relief. He bit and bit and bit through the web until the moth was free. Several strings fell softly to the ground as each thread was cut. The moth squeezed and twisted his body to assist Cirrus in his rescue. Soon after, the moth was as free as the wind!

"AHOH!!!" the moth shouted and gleefully took flight. "You, little-little thing, have great, big courage! Thank you!" The moth flew off within seconds.

"You're welcome!" Cirrus felt extremely accomplished and had a wide grin on his face. He, the awkward globeling who couldn't do anything right, had saved a life; definitely something good to tell his parents. He took a deep breath, inhaling fresh pride, and began to walk away. However, something didn't seem right.

"Wha…? AGH!" His heart sank as he saw a prickly leg wrapped around his foot. In that instant, he was lifted upside down into the

air, causing his velvet satchel to fall off his body including the recipe vial. The necklace dropped onto the shelf and began to roll to the edge. "NO!" he started wriggling and squirming around in the spider's grasp. The spider let out a wicked groan.

"YOU STUPID THING! YOU FREED MY SUPPER!" the spider growled as she squeezed Cirrus harder.

"I'm sorry!!" Cirrus pleaded. "He was asking for help! I wanted to help someone for a change!"

"WELL, LOOKS LIKE I BETTER ASK FOR YOUR HELP TOO." The spider opened her mouth wide. "HELP FEED MY CHILDREN WITH YOUR FLESH. THEY HAVEN'T EATEN ANYTHING AS SWEET AS YOU IN WEEKS."

That's it! I'm done for! I'm spider chow! Cirrus cringed in terror at the sight of the spider's venomous teeth. She had many eyes with bushels of lashes that surrounded them and they all looked at Cirrus with hunger. If only he was able to escape by pressing the (A) button really fast, but no luck. As Cirrus yearned for video game action commands, a shadow suddenly appeared over them. It was an assortment of rainbow feathers that glided above the shelf. The feathers caught onto the web and swooped the spider away, causing her to drop Cirrus roughly on the shelf. Away the spider went, taking all of the fear with her. Cirrus turned his head and saw a very close Destiny dusting away the cobwebs from the wall. With not a single moment to lose, he fled to DrearyDrough, praising the human with thankful thoughts. He snatched back his belongings and was gone in an instant. Destiny continued to trickle away the dust on the shelf.

As Cirrus reached DrearyDrough once more, he was soon accompanied by a worrisome Lorne. He had been sitting on his porch waiting for Cirrus's return.

"Dear me, Cirrus!" Lorne cried as he stood from the stoop. "What the blazes happened to you?" Cirrus looked down and saw that his cape was torn and that he was covered in dust. He went to explain to his friend what had happened, but his heavy panting got in the way and he hunched over his knees. Lorne patted some of the dust off and helped Cirrus into the house.

Soon enough, the two globelings were back in the room with the fireplace. As Cirrus settled down over the assortment of pillows and blankets on the ground, he could feel one side of his body being warmed by the fire while the opposite side tingled from the cold. He could still feel the spider's webs flossed between some of his teeth. Lorne winced and covered his eyes as Cirrus spoke of his scary encounter with the spider.

"How unsettling..." Lorne shivered. "A spider grabbed you. That chills me to the bone! A nightmare while awake, indeed. "

"The spider said that she wanted to eat me, which I assume makes sense. I did free her dinner after all." Cirrus said in a shaky voice. "I just couldn't let that moth get eaten, though! He was calling me for help. I just couldn't leave him like that."

"So, that spider has been out there for a long time…" Lorne swallowed hard and turned white. "You, you don't suppose that…Viva…"

"Don't, Lorne. Don't think that way." Cirrus sat up straight. "I know what you are thinking and it's not true, okay?"

"Now, that's something that you do not know for sure!" Lorne snapped and held his head. "Who knows what beast could have swallowed up my beloved wife. Why, why, why did I let her go out there? I could have stopped her! It's my fault that she is dead and gone. I shouldn't even be allowed to breathe this very air! I—"

WHAPUFF!

Cirrus had smacked Lorne in the head with his feather pillow. Lorne shockingly gazed at him ignoring the messy strands of black hair poking his eyes. Cirrus stood tall, arm poised in feather pillow attack mode. His face was stern and sincere.

"This air is for everyone to breathe." Cirrus spoke seriously. "Be thankful for each opportunity you get to take a single breath." Lorne steadily gazed into Cirrus's golden eyes, which seemed to glisten from the fireplace.

"If your wife is truly gone…" Cirrus lowered the pillow. "…then learn to breathe for her. Each breath you take is a gift for her. She would want you to be alive." As soon as Cirrus finished his sentence, Lorne felt his heart ache. Seconds go by as he gradually inhaled through his mouth. His body trembled as he imagined his wife's lips pressed against his, as if he were breathing in her breath; her soul. Tears heated the bottom of his eyes.

"Okay, now." Cirrus knelt down and pointed to his face. "Grab your pillow and hit me with it."

"W-what? Why?" Lorne asked astoundingly and wiped his eyes with his sleeve. Cirrus whacked him in the head with the pillow again. "What?! Stop!" Lorne flinched and clenched his crooked teeth as Cirrus continued to pulverize him with the plump pillow. Before the third blow, Lorne lifted his own pillow up to defend himself.

"You gotta hit me, Lorne; or else I'll just keep whacking you with the puffy punisher." *Oh, that sounded terrible.* Cirrus snorted at how much he regretted nicknaming his pillow that, but went along with it. He raised the pillow high above his head, menacingly. However, before he could attack, Lorne swung the pillow passed Cirrus's face. He shook the hair away from his cheeks and jokingly snarled at Lorne. The once dreary man returned the playful growl and continued to hit Cirrus. The two globelings sword fought with pillows as if they were in a theatrical feature of a sort. Nearly ten minutes later, however, they became worn out from their "epic" battle. Soon enough, only the crackle of the fireplace could be heard. Both Cirrus and Lorne were wrapped within the piled blankets. Lorne was barely awake. He hadn't moved that much in a long time.

"I kind of feel sorry for the spider." Cirrus mumbled abruptly, breaking the silence.

"What?" Lorne seemed befuddled. "The spider wanted to eat you and now you say that you feel sorry for it?"

"Well..." Cirrus began. "It was very scary, but I took her food away. She was only trying to eat the moth because she was hungry and was trying to survive. She said she had hungry children too." He thought for a moment. Suddenly, he had the craziest idea that he could, perhaps, share some of his yet-to-be-made cake with the spider and her children. He was sure she would forgive him then.

"I suppose you are right." Lorne yawned and rolled over. "But, enough of the spider. We should get some rest, friend. I'll prepare some breakfast for your early awakening."

"Oh-oh, no thank you, Lorne." Cirrus quickly said. He was too afraid to try any food that Lorne would prepare since everything in the kitchen seemed so bland and colorless. He imagined that the food would taste, well, bland and colorless.

"Are you for certain?" Lorne asked in concern. "Breakfast is the most important meal of the day, you know."

"I'm certain. Thanks, Lorne. Goodnight." Cirrus rolled over and shut his eyes as he hoped Lorne would accept his decision about breakfast.

"Restful night, Cirrus." Lorne closed his eyes as well. Shortly afterward, the room fell silent once again as the two globelings fell right asleep.

After a little while, Cirrus's eyes began to flutter as he drifted into a deep sleep. Thoughts of Luname and his mother and father played through his eager mind. Suddenly, images formed in his mind's eye. He was dreaming.

☆*☆*☆

Flowers of many colors surrounded him as a warm breeze trickled through his hair. A finger or two started to twitch as his arms stretched behind him.

"Ohhh. I need to go get those ingredients. Today is my last day! Upsy-daisy!" Cirrus yawned and bounced up from the ground. He knelt down to touch his toes, but then he tumbled forward and did a somersault. The ground vanished from beneath him like a cloud. He could feel himself falling very slowly, as if he were submerging in water. He still felt very calm, however.

A psychedelic mesh of bubbles surrounded him and linked together to form a spiral staircase. Each time he took a step, the previous bubble would explode into paint, producing a single note of music. A rainbow river of paint dripped behind him as the notes formed a nostalgic melody. Reds, oranges, yellows, greens, blues, violets, and pinks poured from thin air.

The last step produced a sour note and then burst into a black liquid. Cirrus flung forward into the darkness. This time, though, he was falling fast and felt uneasy. He could hear the Poison Prince laughing in his ears. Lorne's cried could be heard from afar.

"Agh!" he shouted as he covered his eyes.

The darkness gradually faded into a shadowy, pink haze. Cirrus's hands frantically caressed the soft, bumpy fabric that was surrounding him.

Was it grass? No, it couldn't have been. It was too dry for grass. He looked around and noticed that he was lying on top of a little rug. He was on the floor of Destiny's study room and could see all of the globes high upon the shelf, including Cloudscape Town. He took a deep breath and stood in a worrisome pose.

"How will I ever get back up there?!" Cirrus questioned his abilities of climbing. That instant, his feet began to lift off from the ground. Bubbles spread beneath them like out-of-control-dish soap and formed into a cloud, lifting him into the air.

A door opened in the room. An eerie feeling came flowing in along with a figure of a young, human boy. Cirrus could not see his face, but the child was still a tremendous size in comparison to the globeling. The boy took a step, climbed up onto a chair, and reached for the snow globes. The Poison Prince was hovering around the little boy. Cirrus froze.

"**Do it**!" the prince demanded of the child. The boy touched and rearranged the globes as he giggled to himself. He grazed his hand across all of the globes, but then stopped on the one in the middle; DrearyDrough. There was a brief moment of ominous silence, but then the young boy thrashed his hand across the globe and sent it soaring to the ground, cracking it into many pieces.

"NO!!!" Cirrus's stomach became sickened. His voice had quickly given out and he could no longer manage to scream. Tears streamed down his cheeks as he thought of losing Lorne. The boy twisted his head like a malfunctioning robot and stared at Cirrus with dilated pupils. He bent backwards and twisted his spine and arms around. His footsteps frantically paced the ground toward Cirrus and stood suddenly right in front of him. The boy twisted his body back to normal and continued to gawk at Cirrus.

"What's going on?" Cirrus wordlessly mouthed. He was startled that he was unexpectedly trapped within a glass ball. His heart raced as he punched and beat his arms against the glass barrier in attempt of escaping, but it was too late. He was in the grip of the young boy. He raised the glass ball in his hand high. Cirrus tried to scream, but not a sound could be heard. The boy let go.

SHATTER**!**

Cirrus woke up in a cold sweat.

```
HP: 40/40     HP replenished from sleep
BP: 10/50
MP: . . . o o o o
```

☆Chapter Eleven☆

The New Keen Cat in Town

Morning soon arrived at the dreary globe and Cirrus didn't quite get the warm welcome of sunshine that he was used to from Cloudscape Town. An annoying, washed out light made its way through the ragged curtains and nearly blinded him. The fireplace had smothered overnight, causing a faint haze of smoke to fill half of the room. Cirrus coughed and groaned as he sluggishly rolled over in the blankets—still on edge after such a bad dream, but when he had realized that it was Luname's birthday, he jolted up from the makeshift bed and gasped. He couldn't believe it was already the day of the cake competition and he hadn't a single ingredient; not a single one! In a matter of seconds, he sprinted through the hallways and galloped down the worn staircase nearly tripping on every splinter. Lorne was steaming water for tea in the kitchen when he heard Cirrus stomping outside the doorway.

"Cirrus, good morning!" Lorne greeted. "I've-"

"No time, Lorne!" Cirrus paced back and forth in the kitchen doorway. "I have to go right away. I'm running out of time! The competition begins tonight!"

"But, Cirrus…I've been—" Lorne tried to speak as he continued to stare out the window.

"I'm so sorry, but I don't have any time to spare for breakfast." Cirrus interrupted.

"I want to give you these!" Lorne hurriedly spoke as he turned to him, revealing a large jar of freshly plucked blueberries. Cirrus had become quite surprised and halted his pacing.

"But...those are your wife's...H-how can I possibly take those?" Cirrus's heart began to warm with thankfulness and guilt.

"Take them. You need them." Lorne walked over and gestured the jar toward the traveler. "Viva would have given you these if she were here now. She would help you save your town. Here."

Cirrus felt overwhelmed with a mixture of feelings. He was happy, sad, thankful, and guilty all at once. He could not believe that Lorne, the depressed, lonesome man without a single friend, would give up such a valued possession. Cirrus would finally be able to have at least one of the special ingredients for The Greatest Cake of the Globes, but then again, he would be taking away the only color that Lorne had—unless...wait. A sudden thought had popped in his head.

"Come home with me." Cirrus stated abruptly without thinking.

"W-what?!" Lorne took a step back and clutched his chest. "How could...how would...I...do you really mean that?"

"For sure!" Cirrus smiled and looked at the jar." You have given me your most cherished item, so I want to give you something that you can cherish forever; a chance to live in a world of color again!" Lorne's words escaped him. His lip began to twitch into a smile. "My hometown, Cloudscape Town, will inspire your imagination just by the sight of all of the colors that will be around you! Next door to my house there is a vacant building that we have been trying to rent out for some time now. Oh, and there is also an art shop right across the street from home." Cirrus boasted with a smile. His words made Lorne's eyes shine like a freshly polished doll.

"An-n-n art shop? This is truly remarkable, dear boy! I..." Lorne calmed his stutters, licked his fingers and pinched the flame on top of his candle hat. "I wouldn't need to keep a light around me at all times, would I?"

"Not at all." Cirrus opened his arms and spun around. "Even at night, the streets of Cloudscape Town glow from the twinkling of the stars! You will love it. That is, if you want to go. I'm not forcing you."

"I will definitely need some time to think." Lorne clumsily fell to his chair. Cirrus helped him sit up safely and agreed.

"I'll stop back tonight before I head back home. Just so you know, I'll always stop by even if you don't want to leave your home." Cirrus placed the jar of blueberries in his satchel. "Thank you again. I can't thank you enough for this. I'll be sure to see you soon." The two globelings shared a parting wave as Cirrus left to explore the next globe.

☆*☆*☆

In Destiny's study room, a clock's pendulum ticked back and forth, intimidating Cirrus's nerves. The ticking reminded him of those count downs in a video game that would instantly cause a game over when the timer would hit zero. He rushed to the next globe in fear that he would get struck with a game over 'tune'.

He entered the new globe by removing the usual Bubble entry way. Birds were chirping as he poked his head out of the ground. A bunch of bushes blocked his view from the new area, so he began to slowly crawl through the leaves. Soft, pastel colors seeped through the bushes the more he wiggled his way around. He then saw a row of cars, about ten, and they too reminded him of Luname. He couldn't seem to get her out of his mind. The cars were each a different color: one was baby blue like her hair, another was the rosy pinks of her blushing cheeks, the one next to that was the soft yellow of her poofy shoes, and so on. He was beginning to realize how much he enjoys pastel colors since he had met her. However, while trying to not get sidetracked, he made his way to the parking lot to examine each car. It was very quiet, so he tried not to make a sound.

As he looked through the first car's window, he saw two young globelings sleeping underneath a quilt in the backseat. They were completely in a deep sleep. Cirrus hopped to the next car only to find another sleeping couple in the backseat. The third car also had a snoozing pair of teens. He began to worry the more he saw everyone sleeping in each car. He stopped by the last car on the hill and banged on the window.

"Don't tell me that everyone in this globe is asleep too!" Cirrus loudly groaned. All of a sudden, a young, tough looking man abruptly sat up in the backseat.

"Hey, hey, woah, woah! I'm gettin' some backseat-bingo heeah!" the man said as a brown haired girl straddled him and kissed his cheek. He slicked back his greasy hair and lunged toward the window. "You cruisin' for a bruisin' pal?!"

"Ah! N-no I'm not cruising!" Cirrus instantly blushed. "I didn't mean to bother you, ack!!" He quickly ran down the hill away from the parked cars, passing a poorly crafted sign that said *Jukebopper Lover's Pointe*. He was so embarrassed that he did not even pay attention to where he was heading. Despite how hard he was trying to focus on his surroundings, he could not get the image of the teens taking part in some naughty love time. With his mind being elsewhere…

CRASH!

Cirrus had collided with a local paper boy riding a bike. The boy had flung off his bike and had landed on top of Cirrus, whose cape was tangled within the bike's wheel.

"Oww…" both of the globelings whimpered. The boy gasped and quickly helped Cirrus back on his feet.

"Gee whiz, I'm sorry, sir!" the teen boy apologized and fiddled with his hands. "I'm such a spaz. My mind was completely not focused on what I was doing."

"Heh, I can relate…" Cirrus chuckled to himself, finally forgetting about the lip-smackin' whoopie he witnessed seconds earlier. He was surprised on how much older the boy sounded compared to his looks.

"Aw, I done gone and tore your costume all up!" the teen scratched at his freckled nose. Cirrus was a bit confused. He wasn't wearing a costume, but he realized that his clothes were a bit more vibrant compared to all of the chalky pastels around.

"Oh, this? Don't worry about it." Cirrus shook all of the dirt off of his pants and cape.

"You must be a new keen cat in town, huh?" asked the boy as he flicked dirt off of his freckled nose. "…and there I went crashing into you. Let me make it up to you by treating a new fella like you to some breakfast."

"A keen cat…?" Cirrus muttered to himself. "Oh, no no, that is quite alright. You really don't have to. Thanks, though!"

"It's no sweat, friend. See that diner off yonder?" he asked as he pointed down the road to a small building with a big sign in the lot. "I also work there. My pops owns it. Daddy-O, we call him. I'll let you in on some breakfast before it opens. What do you say?"

"Well, uh…" Cirrus hesitated, but his stomach announced its opinion with a loud gurgle.

"Golly! I'll take that rumblin' as a yes indeed!" the boy laughed and led our hero to the diner.

Cirrus seemed a bit regretful whenever he had stepped into the diner. Again, he was about to partake in a leisurely meal while Luname could be being tormented by that dastardly prince. The teen went behind the counter and started turning on the lights. A glowing, neon sign reflected on the black and white checkered floors and caught Cirrus's attention. The sign read "We have Malt Milkshakes." *Malt milkshakes?* Cirrus secretly pulled out the recipe from the vial and it had one hundred malted milk balls listed. He wondered if malted milk balls were used to make those milkshakes. However, before he could say anything, the boy began to speak.

"You're in a hurry. I'll make some blueberry waffles and eggs real quick like!" the boy said as he ran his hands under some soapy water and rushed back into the kitchen.

"How did you know that I am in a hurry?" Cirrus asked curiously. He could hear eggs cracking and sizzling in the back.

"You are all dressed up!" shouted the teen. "Figured that you were heading out for a date or somethin'."

Cirrus paused for a moment and stared at the freshly cleaned counter. He thought again of his parents and of Luname once again. He still felt reluctant about the whole cake competition ordeal. If only he was just going to a date.

"Aw, I'm sorry. I didn't mean to sound nosy or anything." the boy said as he brought out a plate of steaming breakfast. The plate clanked on the marble counter.

"Oh! That's alright." Cirrus muffled. "That was fast. Looks delicious!"

"No sweat. It's on the house. It's the least I can do for ridin' my bike into you. My name is Russell, by the way." he explained as he pinned his name tag on his shirt and placed a white paper cap on his red hair. Cirrus returned his name with a mouthful of waffles.

The two sat and chatted a bit as Cirrus finished his breakfast. They talked about cooking, cleaning, and other happenings of owning a family business. He eventually spilled the beans to Russell about his search for the ingredients, leaving the teen quite puzzled.

"Sounds like you are in quite a pickle!" Russell scratched behind his ear. "I really wish there was something I could do."

"Well...there is something I was meaning to ask-" Cirrus was suddenly interrupted by a loud ruckus outside the front door. Russell looked at the clock and noticed it was one minute past opening time.

"Oh my gosh!" Russell ran and unlocked the entrance with haste allowing a crowd of colorfully dressed teenagers to swarm to the jukebox. Loud rock and roll music started to play as the globelings shook their hips to the rhythm. Cirrus was thrown off guard by how quickly everyone began to dance. Their feet tapped, florescent jackets flapped, and skirts twirled to the uplifting beat. One girl, however, sat down next to Cirrus on one of the glittered stools by the counter. Cirrus really did not know how to strike up a conversation with her, so he was relieved when Russell spoke to her first.

"Howdy, Miss Marsha." Russell winked and nodded. "Why aren't you dancing?"

"Ohhhhhhh....." she let out a long sigh and twirled her blonde hair. "Curtis was supposed to treat me to breakfast this morning, but he hasn't called me or nothin'! But I'm hungry now so he will have to deal with it."

"Don't worry. He is probably just a bit late." Russell thought for a moment. "Would you like for me to go ahead and treat you to a maltshake?"

"Oh, how I'd love one! You make the best maltshakes, Russ. Thank you!" Marsha sat up straight and dusted off her striped blouse as Russell blushed and hopped back into the kitchen. She turned to watch the other teens dance and just happened to notice Cirrus sitting next to her.

"My, my, my! Ain't you a decorative character?" Marsha exclaimed. "Is the Sodapop Bash a costume party too?"

"Oh, no ma'am. I'm not from around here. I'm from another globe. See, this is how I normally look." Cirrus smiled embarrassingly.

"You mean you didn't turn to dust once you left the globe?" Marsha asked shockingly. Cirrus felt quite relieved knowing that he wasn't the only one who was taught to believe that dust meant doom for all globelings. He couldn't help but chuckle.

"I guess not." Cirrus grinned. "...but it still can be very dangerous out there. Like, just yesterday there was a giant-"

"Sausage!"
"Waffles!"
"Eggs!"

Suddenly, all of the teens interrupted Cirrus by shouting their breakfast orders to the kitchen. Russell zoomed to the counter, handed Marsha her whipped cream maltshake, and frantically wrote down everyone's orders. Marsha blushed and gleefully took a sip.

"I hate to ask this fella, but..." Russell leaned to Cirrus. "...do you think you could help me with the orders? Figured you'd have skill with it, owning a family business and all. My pops isn't here just yet and there are way too many customers to handle!"

"Oh, uh...okay!" Cirrus agreed and he and Russell made their way into the kitchen, finally escaping the roar of the crowd. Just as Cirrus finished removing his gloves and washing his hands, a loud, familiar voice shouted from the counter. Cirrus took a look through the window and saw a man with his arm around Marsha. He appeared to have similar features to the tough guy in the car from earlier, though he was dressed in a fitted sweater vest rather than a leather jacket. Cirrus was certain that it was the same guy, however.

"I'd like to place an *ORDER*, PLEASE!" the man demanded in a pungent tone as he kissed Marsha's forehead and held her like a trophy. She giggled and shuffled in her seat. Russell ran out and wrote down his order as quick as he could.

"Speed it up a little, freckles!" the man snorted.

"Oh, Curtis. Hush!" Marsha huffed.

Russell tried to ignore the man's cynical name calling and headed back to the kitchen. Cirrus tapped him on the shoulder.

"Who's that guy with Marsha, if you don't mind me asking?" Cirrus questioned. Russell took a moment and sighed.

"Oh, that's just her boyfriend…that jug-head." Russell rolled his eyes. "Aw, I guess I shouldn't make a big deal about it. I'm just a jealous fella at the moment."

"Ah. I shouldn't have asked." Cirrus apologized.

"It's just…" Russell slowed down his pace. "Today is the long awaited Sodapop Bash. It's a yearly event where everyone gathers to the jukebox and dance the night away with their friends and their lovers…but not me. Marsha was going to be my date. Well…if I asked in time, I reckon."

"That guy is dating Marsha?" Cirrus confusingly asked.

"Yeah. He asked her before I could. His name is Curtis. He always knew that I liked her. My longtime friend gone bad." Russell shook his feelings away and continued to cook.

"But…I saw him playing bingo with another girl this morning." Cirrus announced.

"Playing bingo? That ain't really a bad thing…" Russell seemed puzzled.

"No! I mean…bingo…car…back seat…Ah! He said he was getting *back-seat-bingo*, that's it!" Cirrus imitated kissy faces.

"What?!" Russell gasped. "In a car at Jukebopper Lover's Pointe?

"The hill with all of the pastel cars filled with rebellious teens experimenting with each other's bodies? Yes. I saw him in a green car with a brown haired girl. At least, I *think* it was him. Looks identical, really. That's why I was running this morning. I accidentally walked in on them *doing things*." Cirrus crossed his arms. Russell fell silent and his face flushed with red.

"What's it mean to bruise a cruise…?" Cirrus asked as Russell stomped out to the counter.

"Oh, I'll show ya the meanin' of cruisin' for a brusin'." Russell grunted and rolled up his sleeve. "…with Curtis as the example."

"Ah! Don't be hasty! I could be mistaken!" Cirrus begged and followed him out.

The kitchen doors swung open and, within seconds, Russell was standing eye to eye with Curtis.

```
*Obtained Blueberries

HP: 40/50 +10 max HP from entering new
world
BP: 20/50
MP: . . . o o o
```

☆Chapter Twelve☆
The Clock is Ticking

"Enjoying your maltshake that I made for you, Miss Marsha?" Russell asked as his eyes remained glued to Curtis's.

"What?!" Curtis turned to Marsha and snatched her maltshake out of her hands. "Freckles is the one who treated you to this? I thought you bought it yourself."

"He kindly offered it to me and I accepted it! I have a mind of my own, ya know." Marsha replied. At that moment, Curtis stood and tipped the maltshake upside down over Russell's head.

"Curtis! No!" Marsha exclaimed. He had expected to drench Russell in ice-cold, chocolate goop, but nothing dripped out.

"That's why they are known as the thickest maltshakes around." Russell winked. That instant, he pulled out a can of whipped cream and sprayed it all over Curtis's hair and face.

"And now to top it all off!" Russell tossed a cup of rainbow sprinkles down Curtis's head. The teens started an uproar of laughter.

"Russell!" Marsha cried. "What do you think you're doing?!" Curtis wiped the cream off of his face and shook it off of his dirty, blonde hair.

"You got somethin' you wanna say to me, freckles?!" Curtis snarled.

"It's *Russell* and as a matter of fact, I do!" he brought forth Cirrus to the crowd's attention. Cirrus's heart began to tremble like crazy.

"My pal here caught Curtis swingin' with another girl this morning up on Lover's Pointe!" Russell announced. Gasps filled the room.

"Don't listen to him, sweet cheeks." Curtis said as he folded his arms across her waist. "You are the only girl for me. Why would you believe this stranger anyway?!"

"Why would you say something like that, Russell?!" Marsha spoke furiously. "Curtis loves me and he would never do that to me."

"He's just mad 'cause he ain't going to the Sodapop Bash with you, girlie." Curtis boasted. He held her tightly and stroked her hair.

Cirrus could have sworn that Curtis was the one that he had seen earlier, but something was telling him that he had caused too much trouble and that he should keep his mouth shut. Arguments gave him hives!

"You have no right to listen to a meddler!" Marsha said to Russell and she pointed at Cirrus. "He could be lying!"

Russell had lost his words. He knew she was right. He shouldn't accuse Curtis just because of what the new guy said, but there was a part of him that wanted to believe every word that Cirrus said. Just as he was about to back down and apologize, he caught a glimpse of Curtis flashing a devilish wink, as if he were gloating about getting off the hook. Russell lost his cool and took action. His arm tensed as he punched Curtis right between the eyes. The teens lunged back and the room was echoing with "oooooh"s. Curtis grabbed Russell's shirt collar and pulled him over the counter, causing both of them to fall to the floor in a tussle. They punched each other, tossing back insulting words to one another. Cirrus started to panic and just wanted to leave.

"Look at what you've caused!" Marsha sneered at Cirrus and slapped him clean across the face. Cirrus hadn't been slapped in years ever since he was caught sticking his fingers in the frosting of a cake display as a toddler; and he only had his hand slapped, not his face! Tears formed in his eyes and his throat became tight. Thankfully, the commotion ceased once a large, curly mustached man in an apron walked in.

"WHAT IS THIIIIIIS?!" the man howled. Everyone silenced as the music was only heard playing.

"Pops!" Russell gasped as he stood up and wiped blood from his nose. Curtis stood up holding his mouth and grabbed Marsha by the arm. The two of them dashed out of the diner, leaving behind a shaken crowd. Russell's father looked around and saw whipped cream and sprinkles scattered across the floor, and, boy, did he look angry!

"Did someone not like their dessert?" the big man cheerfully chuckled. "I hope you knocked him a good one, Russ!" The tension in the air seemed to die down once his father started cracking jokes. The teens found their way back to their seats and patiently waited for breakfast. His father began to help prepare the meals while Russell explained what had happened. Cirrus sat down by the counter and rested his head on his folded arms. He remained quiet, but Russell came out from the back and gave Cirrus a comforting pat on the back.

"I have to leave." Cirrus muttered. "I'm just going to go home."

"Aw, it's alright, you know." Russell said. "Curtis is definitely up to something. You are telling the truth. I know it."

"Marsha slapped me!" Cirrus whined. "That was the first time I've ever been slapped in the face by a girl before. It hurt my feelings; hurt them bad! It made me feel like I can't do anything correctly, especially for the girl I like back home."

"Don't give up now 'cause a girl slapped ya. You know, you can do everything you think you can't." Russell spoke. "That's what my pops taught me. I used to be an extremely slow cook, always breaking things and causing a ruckus, but now I'm as quick as can be because I didn't give up! You need to gather those ingredients! Now, what was it that you needed from me? Cuz' I'll gladly help."

"You still want to help me after I caused so much trouble?" Cirrus asked as he shot up from the counter as Russell nodded. "Thank you so much. Well…I guess if it's not too much…I need to borrow one hundred malted milk balls, please!"

"Woah now!" Daddy-O snorted from the back. "Surely not!"

"Why not, pop?" Russell asked curiously. "He needs some help."

"Is your hat on too tight? Tonight is the Sodapop Bash!" he explained. "We need those maltballs for the shakes, son. You can't just up and give away our entire supply!"

"But—" Russell stuttered as the music from the jukebox began to skip. Everyone in the diner mutely stared at the machine as the lights flickered. The gears from within the jukebox started to shake, causing it to short circuit. Sparks flew from the inside and the jukebox abruptly shut off. One of the teens stepped forth and examined the beloved music player.

"Eh?! It's not working at all!" shouted the teen in a shrill voice. Several gathered around in a panic and started muttering amongst themselves. Russell's father squeezed through the group to get a better look.

The Greatest Cake of the Globes

"Say it isn't so!" a girl shrieked. "The Sodapop Bash is a goner!"

"Now wait just a gosh darn moment!" Daddy-O huffed. He pulled out a screwdriver from his apron and unscrewed the front of the jukebox. He knelt down and began to fish around inside for the cause of the disturbance. "Let's see…Ah hah! This is the only thing that broke off. Looks like we need to find a replacement."

As he stood tall, he held out a gear and sat in the palm of his hand. It had snapped off one of the mechanisms from the interior of the jukebox. It would not fit back inside because half of the gear was chipped. Cirrus climbed up onto a stool so he could see over the crowd. Russell's father made eye contact with Cirrus and smiled.

"Say…" he said as he strutted to Cirrus. "You still need those maltballs, don't ya?" Of course Cirrus agreed, but something was telling him that he was not going to obtain those maltballs as easily as he had hoped.

"Well…hm…" the man mumbled as he stroked his mustache. "There is another globe right next to this one that is full of clocks and mechanisms. Some say it's the home to clocks and time itself! If you can find a gear that looks like this and bring it back to us before tonight, I will gladly give you the maltballs; and, heck, I'll even throw in a little consolation gift!" He genuinely winked and handed the broken gear to Cirrus.

As he examined the gear on his white gloves, Cirrus immediately agreed and promised that he would bring it back that evening. An extreme rush of motivation filled his heart causing him to dramatically stand on top of the counter.

"Attention rebellious teenagers!" Cirrus announced as he flung his cape behind him. "I, Cirrus of Cloudscape Town, will acquire a new gear that will repair this jukebox, allowing you all to have the greatest Sodapop Bash yet!"

A roar of cheers and whistles arose from the teenagers as Cirrus stood. Never had he been praised like that before. He felt as if he was finally a hero; as if he were in a role playing game; a knight, perhaps, who was about to embark on a dangerous quest in search for a rare and forbidden item in a new land. It was definitely an exciting moment for him. He smiled proudly for the first time in a while.

"Son…" Russell's father spoke.

"Yeah, pop?" Russell asked.

"Get your friend off of the counter."

After that moment of satisfaction, Cirrus proudly marched away from the diner as Russell, his father, and the other teenagers waved vigorously. Cirrus made his way back to Lover's Pointe within minutes. He took a glance back at the diner from afar as the wind blew through his hair. The wide smile he had before gradually faded. He then thought he should not bask in pride already; he hadn't accomplished anything yet! At that instant, after he made sure that no one could see him, he rapidly exited the globe and stomped down the twirling staircase.

"Oh no, oh no, oh no!" he panted. "Why do I keep agreeing to these *side-quests*?! I'm not going to have enough time!" As soon as he crawled from beneath the base of Jukebopper, Destiny's cuckoo clock had just chirped nine times. He was relieved knowing that it was still early, but the clock was ticking!

Just as he was about to enter the next globe, which seemed to appear quite dirty, a familiar, dark cloud formed in thin air right in front of him. Cirrus stopped dead in his tracks as a hologram of the Poison Prince's face blocked his path. His mouth curved into a wicked smirk.

"SO, NEED I ASK HOW MANY INGREDIENTS YOU HAVE FOR THAT DISTASTEFUL CAKE?" he cackled.

The Greatest Cake of the Globes

"I…I have…" Cirrus stuttered and his heart thumped. "O-on hand…I have only one."

"How delightful!~" the prince jeered. "Only one! Only one! Your time runs short, my sweet friend. Luname will soon be my bitter half, hahaha!"

"I won't let you do this, Poison!" Cirrus declared. "I'll save her and everyone else I've met along the way!"

"Ooooh~ You sound spunkier than ever. I like that." he dauntingly moaned. "You'll never find all of the ingredients in time. So, be sure to have your precious Luname become as cold as a rock after I am through with her." The more the prince spoke the more Cirrus had become enraged. He would not stand for it! The prince was stalling his time even more and, rather than having his threats pile over him like icing on a cake, he decided to ignore him and barge through his cloudy image.

"Don't doubt me!" Cirrus yelled as he ventured to the next globe without looking back. "I'll save everyone! I'll make my parents proud to have me as their son! I won't let Luname down! I'll show myself what I am capable of and take you down once and for all—in *real* life this time!" Within minutes, he had already made it inside the new globe.

```
*Side Quest Unlocked:
Replace broken gear
for Jukebox.

HP: 40/50
BP: 20/50
MP: ● ● ● ○ ○ ○
```

☆ CHAPTER THIRTEEN ☆

TICKS, TOCKS, AND APPLESAUCE

Back at the entrance of the new globe, Cirrus began to have a very difficult time breathing the further he walked up the spiral staircase. His lungs were beginning to feel like water balloons that were filled with acid. The air thickened with a musty, smoke scent that made him start to feel light headed. He covered his nose and mouth with his purple cloak and forced himself up the stairs. A little bit of thick air wasn't going to slow him down.

In due time, he had made his way to the top. The entrance wasn't a vast landscape like the others, however. This one was enclosed in a dark, narrow alley. A dense fog hugged the brick walls that surrounded him and made him wonder if this globe had also fell victim to the Poison Prince. Reluctance began to rear its ugly head when he took his first step. He walked slowly down the alley as his hand glided across the bricks, which had left a chalky, gray powder on his gloves. Paying no mind to the rocky splinters he received from the chipped wall, he focused on what seemed to be a noise in the background, but it did not sound natural at all; it sounded more like metal clanking and scratching together. The sound became more apparent the further he walked—like butcher knives ice skating on stone. It was such an eerie noise that it actually sent chills up his neck.

Once he reached the end of the alley, through the misty air, he could see enormous sky scrapers. They looked as if they literally were scraping the sky from their height. These buildings, although tall and broken, were actually clock towers. Their exteriors were completely made of clock faces and gears. Some clocks had numbers, some had roman numerals, and some even had symbols. The largest of the clock towers had the face of a sundial, but it lacked a shadow. The noise he heard came from

The Greatest Cake of the Globes

the various sized pendulums swinging from each clock tower—some clanking into one another and some bashing into walls. The constant orchestra of ticking and tocking made him feel more aware of what little time he had left, almost as if the ticking he heard was a time bomb strapped to his chest. He quickly pulled out the gear from his satchel and examined it yet again. To be honest, he had no idea where to even begin searching for a spare gear. After a moment, he took another quick look at the treasured recipe.

"This must be TockTick. Tocks and ticks are all I hear." Cirrus muttered to himself. He continued to read the recipe and was suddenly baffled. "What? A golden apple? Here?" The gear was starting to seem like an easily obtainable item compared to a golden apple.

"YOU THERE!" a shout came from afar. "Get back to work, fool!"

"Ah, wha?!" Cirrus gasped and turned around several times, but could not pinpoint where the angry voice was coming from. He stood still and breathed heavily while answering to the fog. "I-I-I don't work here!"

"Is that so?" the voice echoed. "It must be him." Two figures appeared out from the hazy path. Their pace quickened once they had caught a glimpse of Cirrus, which caused his heart to leap. They began to run toward him as if he were some sort of escaped convict. He took off like an elephant at a mouse parade. From what Cirrus had seen of the figures, they were wearing elaborate gas masks shaped like deer heads, antlers and all, and were wearing long, maroon cloaks. One of them shouted from afar.

"Get him! Get him! Take him to the factory before it's too late!"

"Agh!" Cirrus gasped as he took a sharp turn behind an abandoned building. "What do I do...?" Between his quick breaths, he noticed a slightly opened door about three stories high on the building across from him. He ran to the building and up the rickety fire escape he went. The harsh creeks of each step immediately caught the masked men's attention.

"Over there!"
"Quickly!"

"No!" Cirrus stomped up the staircase with even more force. In a matter of seconds, his foot broke through one of the steps and almost caused him to fall. The metal that broke loose from the steps slammed against piles of brick and steel on the ground beneath him. Alas, another sound that made him completely noticeable.

Without a moment to lose, he regained his balance and rapidly tumbled through the door, shutting it behind him. While trying to catch his breath, he examined the room he had entered. It was a small, bright and shiny room that almost looked like the walls were entirely made of solid copper and gold; it definitely contrasted the faded atmosphere of the world outside, although it was covered in cobwebs and grime. He turned his head slightly to the left and—*AH*!

Cirrus's poor heart could not take much more of these startles. His wandering eyes had come across another hooded figure standing right next to him; but wait, it was not a figure at all. He swallowed hard and inched his way closer to the figure. It was only a costume! It was a long, golden cloak with an owl-faced mask accent, but rather than a gas mask, it appeared to be a simple carnival mask. At the spur of the moment, a flicker of light flashed from a window and grabbed his attention. He crawled to the window and peeked through, then saw something very odd; very peculiar. His eyes widened as he overlooked a stadium sized factory with thousands of workers standing ear-to-ear along conveyor belts. Each globeling wore similar uniforms to the guards that chased after him and to the one hanging in the room; long cloaks equipped with a gas mask, but this time they had on black cloaks with sheep-faced masks.

Their hands danced through the broken metal that was sprawled across the conveyor belts. Each globeling assembled the gears and gadgets that passed them within seconds. They must have been extremely knowledgeable of what they were making. Cirrus made his way through the doorway and walked down a set of steps on the side of the room which were luckily hidden in the dark. However, he still ducked between each railing in fear that he would be seen. Oh, what luck, though! There was a door that was opened near the bottom of the staircase, so what else was he to do besides make a run for it? Fortunately, no one was in there. All he could see was a long, narrow room with steel walls filled with coat hangers, all empty—save one. There was still a cloak and a mask hanging from one of the hangers. Cirrus hadn't paid much attention to how badly his chest hurt and struggled with the urge to cough, but he held it back in fear that he would be spotted. He cleared his throat quietly.

"I wonder if that would help me breathe…" Cirrus whispered to himself. Within seconds, he had acquired completely new attire. Though it was not high on his fashion list and was entirely too big, he still felt pretty cool; kind of like a mysterious merchant from a survival horror game.

As a few moments passed after wearing the sheep mask, Cirrus could breathe clearly now. He also had thought up a plan that may help him get out of the factory without being caught. Perhaps he could sneak by the globelings while in disguise. *Could that possibly even work? Who knows?* He began to doubt himself…but what if-

BASH!

Uh oh, no time to think; time to act! The guards in the maroon cloaks found their way into the golden room upstairs by kicking the door. Without thinking, Cirrus clenched his teeth and ran into the crowd of workers, squeezing into a vacant spot between two of them. He thought he blended in quite nicely, despite being a tad bit shorter than the rest. The guards rushed down the steps, frantically searching for the "fool". Their muttered groans and insults had practically been spit upon the backs of the workers as they scurried through the aisles.

"He's not here." a deer masked guard sputtered.

"Search another building." the other squawked. "We mustn't let him continue this rebellion or else *they* might find out."

Cirrus began to wonder about this *secret*, but he didn't want to worry too much about it or be involved. As the guards left the room, he took another deep breath—the gas mask was helping him breathe a lot better than before. He had almost forgotten about the polluted atmosphere, running for his life and all. Several clock faces and clock hands passed down the conveyor belt within seconds. Ah, that was what the metal was; they were assembling various clocks. Not much of a surprise, really. His eyes scanned the metal parts in search of that certain gear he needed for the jukebox.

"Mech, I can't believe that you are actually here." a woman suddenly whispered. Cirrus looked to his right and saw one of the tall sheep-masked globelings facing him. He looked down and saw that there was a name printed on his arm that said "M1642". He didn't know what to do.

"Did it finally fall?" she asked again. Cirrus twitched and picked up the items on the revolving belt, pretending that he knew what he was doing. He had no idea who or what she was talking about.

"Mech, did the golden apple fall?" she said more clearly as she leaned down to him. Golden apple, she said. Those words made Cirrus quiver. That was the ingredient he was there for, after all, but he continued to try to avoid talking to her.

"Wait a minute..." she said in a deep voice. "Did you get shorter?" She reached down and lifted his mask, revealing his lilac hair. She gasped and began to say something, but Cirrus immediately hushed her as politely as he could.

"Please, please!" he whispered anxiously. "I need your help. I'm not from here and I'm awfully confused."

"Who are you? Why are you even here?!" she seemed aggravated. A couple of workers from afar started to complain because the woman had missed her assigned job at the conveyor belt.

"I-I need that golden apple!" Cirrus worriedly spoke.

"What...?" she said in awe. "Quickly, come this way." She grabbed his hands and dragged him away from the workers and led him through a dark pathway. Unfortunately, they didn't leave the room unseen.

The new room they entered was cold and it smelled musty of dirt. The mask surprisingly allowed the smell to seep through and was making Cirrus feel a bit dizzy. A small window near the ceiling allowed a ghostly light to leak on to the hard, stone floor. The light landed on the woman's sheep mask, causing the bronze to sparkle. She grabbed Cirrus's arm forcefully and grunted.

"Why do *you* need the golden apple?" her throat snarled. Cirrus felt shaken.

"M-ma'am..." Cirrus stuttered as he tried to loosen her grip on his arm. "It's very important. I need it for a cake recipe so that—"

"A cake recipe?!" she gripped harder. "The golden apple used for a cake?! Are you trying to make a fool out of Mech?"

"If you would let me explain—"

"Why are you wearing Mech's uniform anyway?!" she barked. "You better not have hurt him!"

"I don't even know who this 'Mech' is!" Cirrus quietly exclaimed. He started to cough through his words. "All I know is...is that...(cough) is that I need that apple (double cough) and this!" Cirrus reached for the broken jukebox gear that was in his satchel and rapidly showed it to the provoked woman. She cocked her head to the side once she was able to get a look at it.

"A quartz crystal gear…" she said in awe. "Such a rare piece. It's been years since these gears were ever in use."

"Oh…" Cirrus felt disappointment tickle his nerves. "So, there must not be any more around then." He coughed nearly three times more. The woman stared at him in silence for a moment.

"There is only one gear like this left…and it's…" the woman paused as her firm grip left his arm. She stood tall. "I don't understand you." She said deeply. "Nor do I trust you or know who you are, but I have the strangest feeling that you and I could help each other." She noticed that Cirrus was beginning to tremble. The air was making him sick.

"Come now." she demanded as she lifted up the window near the ceiling. "I'll help you, but you must explain to me why you are here as I lead you to someplace…forbidden." Cirrus did not like the sound of that, but he had no other choice. The woman swiftly jumped through the window like a cat, while Cirrus the turtle just jumped up and down, failing to climb through on his own. After a few awkward grunts and slips, he was lifted through the window by the assistance of her arm. At least no one saw them escape, or so he had thought. The same pair of eyes from before watched them from the shadows.

Outside again. Same scenery; the white haze of fog and emptiness. Cirrus tried to ignore the unpleasant environment while he explained his purpose for coming to the TockTick globe. They walked and walked and walked; for a good fifteen minutes actually. It felt more like an hour to Cirrus, or was it thirty minutes? He couldn't tell. It was rather ironic to be in a place where time was such an important aspect, yet one could not even keep track of it. The further they walked, the less they could hear the chattering of the factories from below. All he did was speak of his quest, his home life, while occasionally turning around to make sure they weren't being followed, and would longingly talk about Luname and how much he admired her. The

The Greatest Cake of the Globes

woman never spoke a word, not a word the entire time. She rarely nodded and looked around, but hadn't a single response to anything that Cirrus had said. He turned back once more to see if he could hear the factories from afar, but nothing rang to his ears. They must have walked pretty far away. Once he turned back, the woman's figure faded into the fog within seconds.

"Ehah! Wait!" Cirrus felt a chill glide up his spine once the thought of being lost in a hellish cloud of nothingness that had crossed his mind. *Not here! I must not get lost here!* His footsteps became louder as he ran through crunchy, dead grass. She could not be found. "Please! Wait!" he called out as he frantically shifted his body in search of her. He ran a bit further before the long garments he wore became entangled underneath his boot, causing him to fall head first onto the ground.

His gas mask chucked itself off of his head and rolled several feet away from him. There was an intense pressure in his upper nose that made him even dizzier. A hot liquid quickly followed the pain and trickled down his nose. It was bleeding; though wasn't a bad nose bleed, it was enough to cause great discomfort. Without thinking, he wiped his bloody nose on his gloves, his *white* gloves. He felt extremely stupid. *That is definitely going to stain*, he thought. Strange that he would worry about staining his gloves at a time like that. After his nose regained some feeling, he limped his way through more fog in search for his mask. The air stung his nose which made him sneeze and cough even more; even his eyes started to burn and become full of sour tears. His eyes could barely stay open.

Cough. Cough. Heavy cough. A hoarse cough. Sniffle. Grunt. Cough. Poor Cirrus! He shut his eyes tightly and continued to walk straight and, within moments, he could breathe. He could breathe without pain! The grass beneath his feet didn't crunch anymore. The air no longer burned his throat or stung his nose. Besides the iron he could smell from his nosebleed, he could also smell…leaves, trees and possibly even flowers. *Could it be?* He slowly opened his eyes, blinked a few times, and saw a clear image: a vibrant blue sky with fluffy clouds. Ah, those wonderful, familiar clouds that he was used to! He saw an absurdly large tree, leaves in as many shades of green anyone could possibly imagine. Flowers, lots and lots of dandelions, yellow ones and the ones that spread their seeds through the wind, the ones that look like bubbles in a field. Even if they were technically weeds, they were still flowers in Cirrus's eyes. Finally, he saw the woman, her long cloak still draped over her, but her gas mask was off. She was standing near a man lying underneath the tree, who was as still as the tree itself. So many questions filled Cirrus's head. *Where am I now? Where did this tree come from? How come I can breathe clearly now?* But for some reason the only thing he could seem to ask was:

"Is he...dead?"

She stood faced away for a moment, but then turned to Cirrus.

"No. No, he is just sleeping." she faintly smiled and turned back to the man.

Cirrus was thankful that the man was alive. He wouldn't have known what to do if he was dead. Strangely, however, the woman's appearance caught his attention immediately. She was a very unique looking globeling; the most unique of all in Cirrus's opinion. Her tired eyes were large and a bright hazel that was surrounded by long, dark eyelashes. Her nose was small and also had a very petite mouth. Short, blonde hair stood straight up from her neck and pointed outward like a wizard hat. Even her ears were pointed; like an elf! Cirrus felt like a fan boy. She looked like she could be a customizable character in an RPG, except Cirrus, being as indecisive as he is, would take forever on choosing her class, stats, and abilities. *Would she be a soldier or a warrior...? A cleric? Maybe even a magician. Who knows!*

A few seconds later, Cirrus had wiped away his gamer thoughts and began focusing on his real adventure. He sniffled a couple of times as he walked closer to the woman, who knelt down to the man on the ground. The man had long, black hair that looked very soft. A small braid twirled its way passed his dark, caramel skin. He was rather well-dressed in a cream colored blouse, a brown vest that was decorated with gears, and loosely fitted trousers. He sure did look a lot more comfortable than the workers down in the polluted city.

"Mech…Mech?" the woman tapped his shoulder gently. Mech's eyes twitched and his slow breathing pattern was interrupted.

"Ahwah…I…I can't go down yet...mmn…" he mumbled and slowly peeled his heavy eyelids open.

"I know, I know." She agreed as she looked up to the tree above them, eyes searching the leaves. "It still hasn't fallen." Cirrus's eyes joined the gaze up at the tree and he saw the large, golden apple twinkling as the sunlight touched it.

"Ah! There it is!" Cirrus stood beneath the tree and praised. "That's what I need! Yes!"

"Oh, no. I'm sorry, stranger." Mech apologized as he squinted and firmly blinked. "You cannot have that apple until it falls on my head."

"Wha?" Cirrus looked back and forth from Mech to the apple. "That apple is huge! It's like…well, it looks like it's the size of a basket ball! That could really hurt you if it falls on you."

"Please, Mech. See. He agrees. That's what I've been trying to tell you. He's right." she pleaded. "You need to come back down soon. The workers are furious with you."

"My dear friend, Loroli…" Mech smiled; a dimple carved itself in his left cheek. "I've told you many times that this apple will change our lives once it falls on my head."

"Huh…" Cirrus felt awfully confused. "How will an apple falling on your head change your life? There will only be blood and applesauce left once it hits your head."

"Time explains a lot, my friend." Mech took a deep breath. "This apple will help me prove the truth. Now, I wait." Mech closed his eyes and fell into a deep sleep.

```
HP: 20/60 +10 max HP from entering new
world    -20 HP damage
BP: 20/50
MP: . . . . o o
```

☆Chapter Fourteen☆
A Face Without Time

A soft wind trickled through Loroli's golden hair as Cirrus's eyes intriguingly searched the sleeping man beneath the tree. It seemed like the appropriate time to do so since Mech wouldn't catch the outlandish globeling staring at him. His chest dropped and lifted so tenderly like a slumbering baby in his mother's arms. Everything Mech was wearing seemed clean and new, except one accessory—a golden pocket watch that seemed to be rusted shut. He wondered why it was dirtier than the rest of his accessories.

"I need help getting him back down to the factory." Loroli sighed. "He is so stubborn and won't tell me what he is planning. I worry for him..."

"Uh...I don't suppose you want me to knock down the apple, do you?" Cirrus asked tensely while he swayed his hips nervously.

"If it were possible, I would seek your help." Loroli answered. "Unfortunately, it is too high up to climb. I just don't know..."

The tree was nearly one hundred feet tall and there were no low branches or knotholes to help support a climb. He knew it seemed impossible to get, yet he couldn't bear to give up. After all, he had come this far and he still only had one ingredient in his satchel. He looked Loroli in the eyes and his gaze proved that he would help her in some way. Her small lips curved and quivered into a smile. She smiled so uneasily as if she didn't know how to.

"Thank you." She stood, looking back and forth between Mech and the apple. Her mouth returned to the frown. "The sooner it falls, the better."

"Won't you feel bad bringing him back to that horrible environment down there?" Cirrus asked, hoping that he didn't insult her. Her eyebrows twitched.

"I..." she hesitated. "It's what he is supposed to do. It's what we are *all* supposed to do. If he doesn't work, time will soon stop. Others will bring him harm if he keeps refusing to work."

"How come you all work so much?" Cirrus asked feeling a bit nosy. "Wait. Did you just say that time will stop?"

"Of course." she said frustratingly. "If we stop working, time will stop and we will be frozen in place forever, never able to move or work again."

"That..." Cirrus held his head in confusion and uncomfortably chuckled. "That...wait...what? No, no that doesn't happen. It doesn't make sense."

"Do you mock how I was raised?" Loroli asked with frustration in her voice. "How *we* were raised? We were raised with the knowledge that a person isn't worthy unless they dedicate their life to work. Don't think I'm a fool."

"No, it's not like that!" Cirrus made clear. "I've just never heard of such a thing. Work is great and all; it makes you feel accomplished and you always gain experience whether it's good or bad, but you need to experience yourself every once in a while, you know? Find out who you are and what you like."

"Huh? What do you mean?" Loroli asked.

"Um...like..." he thought for a quick moment. "Oh, sort of like, what do you want to do with your life? I was taught to do whatever makes you happy. What makes *you* happy?"

"What's...'happy'?" She tilted her head to the side. A small laugh had escaped Cirrus at the thought of her joke of a response, but then realized that she was serious. His smile fell clean off his face.

"Y-you...you don't know what happy is?" Cirrus swallowed hard. His gut wretched as he watched Loroli shake her head *no*. *How, how can someone possibly not know what happiness is?* Pity began to overwhelm him. Never until then did he realize how thankful he was for knowing happiness.

"Happy...happiness." Cirrus wondered. He had never thought about how that word could ever be explained, so he decided to make it as direct as possible. He pointed over to Mech and kept a steady eye on Loroli. "Mech. He makes you happy. I saw you smile at him earlier."

"Mech makes me happy." she repeated. "I don't understand."

"Being around Mech makes you feel good, safe and..." the last word escaped him.

"Warm." Loroli added.

"Yes!" Cirrus agreed. "He makes you feel warm and ticklish. That's happy." Loroli touched her cheeks and rubbed them.

"My cheeks feel really warm when I'm around him and my heart beats faster. Is that happy?" she asked while she continued to rub her cheeks.

"Hm, that sounds more like *love* to me." Cirrus winked and smiled. Love; that word seemed to confuse her as well. "Oh, love is like a step up from happiness. It's when you are really *really* happy with another person no matter who they are." he explained as he thought of Luname. His smile was cornered with blushing cheeks.

"I like that thing your face is doing." Loroli smiled. "I've seen Mech do that too."

"Huh, what's on my face?" Cirrus wiped his nose, thinking that his nose was still bleeding.

"Your mouth is tilting up on both sides." she said. "How are you doing that?"

"Oh! That's called smiling!" Cirrus's eyes widened. "You are smiling right now!"

"I am?" Loroli opened and closed her mouth, wrinkled her nose and stretched her mouth from side to side. She smiled, and then frowned; smiled, frowned. "I like how this feels. It feels nice and...happy!"

"That's good!" Cirrus exclaimed. He felt like he was playing a game of emotion-charades. Without knowing, his throat began to choke up as if he were about to cry, but he held back his tears. He just could not believe how much she has missed out in life without knowing happiness and love; oh, how he took those feelings for granted! "Now, since you know what happiness is, why do you want Mech to come back down to work?"

"Well…" Loroli blushed more. "When he works, his assigned area is right beside me. We build clocks together."

"Ah, now that makes sense!" Cirrus nodded. "You want him back down not for conformity, but for happiness. He will be beside you, working with you. That is what you desire, Loroli. You want to be with him, not for him to spend the rest of his life working non-stop." She remained silent for a while, but then continued to smile.

"I'll do it." Cirrus agreed once more and patted her on her shoulder, as tough as that was since she was nearly three feet taller than him—though not as tall as Lorne— and then grinned vigorously. "I'll help you and Mech be together."

After a few moments, they began to venture back down the hill; back down to that chattering town, filled with empty feelings and forced labor. Cirrus checked his gas mask nearly three to four times to make sure that it was on tight. He didn't want that horrible pollution to cloud his lungs even more. Come to think of it, he wondered why the environment was so polluted to begin with. A tickling sensation had started to form in his chest which made him lose concentration. He felt a coughing frenzy about to arise, but he tried to breathe softly to maintain it.

Loroli was walking beside him rather than ahead of him that time. Though, he couldn't tell if she was still smiling or not since her gas mask shielded her face. He could only hope that she still was.

"What is your name?" Loroli asked. She broke the silence.

"Cirrus O'Zone." he replied proudly. Hm, that was odd; he admitted his last name to someone. Having to say his full name had always made him feel uncomfortable. O'Zone was the name that everyone could see from the main street of Cloudscape Town. It was the most colorful and well known shop sign on the block. He feared that if anyone were aware of his last name, he would give his parents' bakery a bad image; so he always kept it hidden. Even his name tag had his last name blocked out. With that said, perhaps Cirrus was beginning to feel a bit more confident in who he was and finally showed pride toward his family name. It felt exciting to him!

"Thank you, Cirrus." Loroli said. He could hear her smile from her voice. Just then, the clanking noises of the town quieted and a voice suddenly echoed through the town. A roar from a crowd soon followed, and it didn't sound like a good roar either.

Loroli and Cirrus quickly made it down to the town and hid behind a large piece of abandoned scrap metal. He wanted to ask her what was going on, but judging by the way she was shaking, he assumed she was just as clueless as he was. A small hole in the metal had given Cirrus a fish-eye view of the crowd that was gathered in the middle of the road. The fog made them hard to see, but he could tell that they were the workers from the factory. Their sheep masks and black cloaks gave that away.

"We have ourselves a non-worker!" a deep voice shouted. The two men with the deer masks stepped forth. The angry voices of the crowd grew louder.

"The traitor still has not returned to our aid!"
"He will cause our demise!"
"WE WILL FREEZE!"

"QUIET!" the other deer masked man bellowed. The crowd's screams fell too jumbling mutters. Cirrus finally asked Loroli if she knew what was happening, but she remained without a word. Her breath was rapid causing Cirrus to feel frightened, but he continued to listen.

"There is a globeling among us who is destroying our society..." said the deer-faced man.

"And we all know who that is!" the other deer masked man said in a shrill, mocking voice.

"He sits and watches and laughs in our faces, spits on our beliefs and feasts on our sweat!" the other continued. He yelled and flailed his arms; the draped, red sleeves of his maroon cloak swirled through the fog. "Why should we tolerate such upheaval?! When one refrains from their work, then another will, and then another and you all know what happens after that!"

"We'll freeze..." Loroli whispered.

"WE'LL FREEZE!" the crowd chanted. Cirrus shook his head with shock and uncertainty. He began to believe that the globelings in the town of TockTick were brainwashed with habitual customs of saying "we'll freeze" when asked that question. He suddenly remembered the old rumor he was taught from back home: 'leave the globe and you will turn to dust' they all said. How stupid and childish that sounded to Cirrus now!

"Time will stop!" deer-mask number two barked. "We must all remember what happened to the great Golden Owl. His heart stopped beating as soon as his pocket watch stopped ticking. Look above, my people! It has already begun!"

The mass of workers' heads circled to the enormous clock tower. Cirrus found the clock through the small viewing from the hole and saw nothing out of the ordinary at first, but then the crowd shrieked in horror, causing him to study the clock even further.

The Greatest Cake of the Globes

"NO!"
"IT CAN'T BE!"
"NOT YET!"
"WE MUST MAKE MORE CLOCKS!"

"Oh no…" Loroli held her hand to her mouth. She was terrified.

"What?!" Cirrus shifted his feet in the dirt. He felt like a bomb was about to drop or something. "What's going on?!"

"The great clock tower…" Loroli's voice cracked. "It no longer tells the time!" Cirrus quickly took another peek at the tower. It was true; time could no longer be read on the clock tower, but that was only because the clock's face was a sundial and all of the pollution was blocking out the sun.

"The sundial…" Cirrus whispered to himself. Suddenly, it hit him. Of course the tower wasn't telling time! It's because…"There is no sun!" he announced and stood up on his knees. He took Loroli by the shoulders and shook her, trying to shake some sense into her. He tried to talk quietly, but his discovery was making it difficult not to raise his voice. "No sun! You need the sun to have the sundial tower tell you time!"

"W-what?" she asked fearfully.

"The fog!" He smiled as if he had just solved a murder case. "The pollution! It's blocking the sun, don't you see? The more you all work in the factories, the more smog you produce! Everyone just needs to stop working for a while! You won't freeze; time won't stop! I promise you!"

"But, that's what The Deer Lords taught us…" Loroli spoke, but the deer-masked men interrupted.

"The Golden Owl would not have wanted things to end up this way!" both of the deer men said. "Unite again in one hour, and we will find the traitor before he causes our demise! Let us find M1642 and punish him for what he has caused!"

The crowd roared much louder. At that moment, Cirrus became furious. He had never been so angry, not ever since that one time he went an entire six hours without saving his video game and the power went out during an electrical storm. His mage had gained so much EXP, too. What a shame. Gaming tales aside, he was in super-serious-Cirrus mode now. Try saying that three times.

"I'm going." he said sternly as he ripped off his mask and cloak without a care in the world. The gold in his eyes were brighter than ever. He held out his hand to Loroli, who was still quivering on the ground, and waited for her to return the handshake. "I'll be back within one hour and I assure you, I will help put an end to this madness. I will make the golden apple fall, and perhaps cause the 'Deer Lords' and their corruption to fall with it." Loroli nodded and grabbed his hand. He had the most firm, trustworthy handshake that she had ever felt.

"You are the happiness we all need." she said. Then, within seconds, Cirrus had disappeared into the fog. Loroli stood quietly and made sure that no one could see her. She sighed and tried to quickly think of a plan to save Mech. Unexpectedly, from within the shadows, a pair of hands grasped her mouth and pulled her away.

Her figure faded in the fog, away from sight.

The Greatest Cake of the Globes

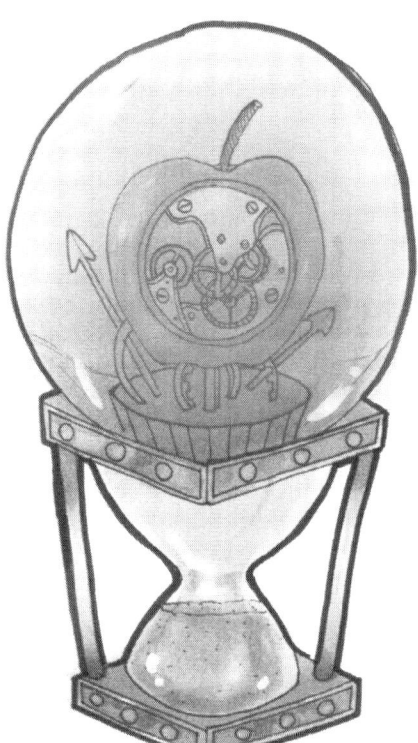

```
*Side Quest Unlocked:
Make the Golden Apple
fall from tree.

   Status: POISONED


HP: 10/60    HP
gradually decreasing
BP: 20/50
MP: . . . . o o
```

☆ Chapter Fifteen ☆

The Withered Flower

The rage that clouded Cirrus's mind made him exit the globe in full storm. The smog kept him hidden from the riot, thankfully allowing him to escape without being seen. His escape could have possibly been the only benefit from the pollution. The air felt lighter once he reached the bottom of the spiral staircase and quickly left the globe. To think that he actually felt more comfortable on the shelf, the shelf that he had feared for years, rather than being inside that globe. He took a deep breath and exhaled relief, but when he looked up his breath was nearly taken from him again. A huge face of a human was completely taking over Cirrus's standpoint. Large, green eyes were examining the snow globes on the shelf. Cirrus scurried underneath the base of TockTick yet again; feet shuffling as fast as they could.

"Hey, honey?" the voice rumbled Cirrus's ears for being so close. Zachery began to poke at TockTick. "One of the snow globes is getting kind of murky-looking."

"What? Which one?" Destiny asked from the kitchen. A cabinet door shut. She walked in shortly after and headed over to the shelf with Cirrus still hiding underneath the base. "Aw, the clock globe. How did the water get so dirty? I don't even know how to clean snow globes." Destiny and Zachery both faintly chuckled.

"Look it up on the internet?" Zachery suggested.

"I suppose." Destiny shrugged. She started to walk out of the room when she had suddenly stopped at the doorway. Cirrus took the chance to make a run for the final globe, but he continued to curiously listen to the two humans.

"You feeling okay?" Zachery asked quietly. He slicked his brown hair behind his ears.

"I…" Destiny hesitated. "I think I may stop attempting to write stories." Her head dropped down and she leaned on the doorway's frame. Zachery never would have expected her to say such a thing.

"You've wanted to be a writer your whole life." Zachery explained. "Why now? Why would you want to give that up now?"

"I just…" Destiny tried not to get flustered, but her head was filling up with so many emotions that she couldn't tell which one to show. She adjusted her large, purple glasses. "I feel like I've lost my touch for storytelling. I don't think I've written anything decent for a long time." She had Zachery's arms wrap around her tightly.

"What about the little girl who found a mystical sketchbook that made her drawings come to life?" he mentioned. "What about the angel who could grow up? What about the creatures from the sea or the elves and the zodiac beasts? Or the one about a man with the mannequin who could sing? You don't realize how many will go untold if you go and give up."

Destiny felt like crying. It surprised her to hear her husband's memory of her childhood story plots! It gave her just a twinge of hope, but still she remained unmotivated. A smile was shown just to keep Zachery satisfied. Cirrus saw them take each other's hands and share a kiss. They left the room as their three little dogs trotted behind them. *Poor lady*, Cirrus thought. Out of all of the globelings he had been helping with their troubles, he wished that there was some way that he could help Destiny too. But, how silly of him; how could he help a human? That's impossible.

He turned to the final globe and took a deep breath—ah, what a joy it was to breathe clean air. As he walked closer to the globe, his disbelief suppressed his deep coughs. This was it: The last globe. The final world. The boss stage. The time-to-rescue-the-princess stage. *Let's hope she isn't in another castle.* Cirrus, despite feeling weak, marched forward. Even though it had only been a couple of days since he had left the bakery, he felt like he hadn't been home in a lifetime.

This globe's exterior looked enjoyable, however, which eased Cirrus's nerves. It bustled with plastic flowers, glass mushrooms and ceramic waterfalls. Vines twisted and twirled around the glass bulb and out from the flowers came sculpted butterflies and bubbles. In he flew like a bee that had just found a fresh pool of pollen. He glided his way up the familiar swirling stairs and felt a sudden flash of whimsy overcome him. The stairs had seemed to be lifting him, guiding him toward a beautiful place that smelled of lilacs, lavender, maple trees and honeysuckles. The frustration that clouded his mind from TockTick melted away. His eyes closed, but his feet still skipped up the stairs with delight. He coughed, but didn't pay any mind to the pain in his chest until he took a deep breath afterward—something didn't feel right. He breathed in heavily again—no, there was still something wrong. His pace slowed as soon as he caught a glimpse of the entrance. His feet became heavy; his heart a pounding drum; his breathing—stopped.

He collapsed.

"Mom...

Dad...

Luname...

Silly...

Lorne...

Russell...

Sleepy gnome couple...

Loroli...Mech...

I couldn't do it."

Nearly a half hour had passed. Cirrus could feel something tickling his face, but could not see a thing. Birds were chirping, or, wait, were those crickets playing violins? He couldn't tell. Hopefully it wasn't night time already. A trickling spring could be heard as well. He struggled to open his eyes, but it felt like something was pinching his eyelids together.

"Heeheehee!"

"Teehee!"

"Hmmhmm!"

"Ah!" he gasped. There were sounds of squeaky giggling all around him. He wiggled his head and felt grass blades tickle his ears. The giggling sounded further away now. A strong numbness stung his throat despite a pleasant taste in his mouth. The taste of smoke no longer smoldered his tongue, but something rather sugary-sweet glazed his taste buds. He flung his body upward, still unable to see, licked his lips and groaned.

"He's awake!"

"He's not dead!"

"Let's keep squeezing his eyelids!"

"Hey, no!" Cirrus rubbed his eyes and blinked rapidly. "Who's there?"

"The kind one helped you."

"She healed you all up!"

"She did a good job, indeed."

"The kind one?" Cirrus stopped rubbing his eyes and tried to maintain a steady stare. His vision was like an unfocused camera floating in water. He could see vague colors and lights, but everything else remained hazy.

"You had a lot of smoke in your lungs."

"Very dangerous!"

"Smoking is bad for your well-being, you know."

"I don't smoke!" Cirrus stated irritably as he fumbled with his necklace to confirm that he still had the recipe. "Am I in FaeAway?" His only response was of giggling. Solid shapes were beginning to form in his vision. He was sitting alone in a round patch of grass that was encircled by flowers, mushrooms, trees and saplings of all shapes, colors, and sizes. The tree canopy shook in the light breeze and the sunlight twinkled on each blade of grass. Cirrus slumped over and took another deep breath; his body felt like he had just taken a nap in an iron maiden. He clutched his chest and whimpered again.

"You'll feel better soon!" said the little voices harmoniously. Just then, three tiny faeries flew from the petals of roses and tulips and danced around Cirrus's head. One had pink hair and the other two had yellow and blue. Their dresses matched according to their hair color, or was it that their hair color matched according to their dresses? Too cute, nonetheless!

He watched them sway in the air as a path of glitter sprinkled from their feet. The pink faerie chuckled and pluckled— oops, *plucked* a berry from a tilted labyrinth of vines. Each of the faeries took a bite and serenaded Cirrus with mmm's and yums. They flew back to the plant and plucked a couple more berries and offered him a bite.

"Have a frazwick berry!" offered the pink faerie.

"You shall be full with just one bite." said the blue faerie.

"It's a great diet food!" the yellow faerie flexed her muscles.

"Oh! Well, if it's alright with you, then thank you!" Cirrus, being rather hungry, reached for the berries when suddenly a twig had snapped behind him.

"Don't!" a voice demanded from afar. The three faeries grouped together and sighed.

"Aww, we're sorry." they whined. Quickly, they snatched the berries from Cirrus's palm and gobbled them up. A tall woman approached from the shade of the trees—her eyes covered with straggly hair.

"I'm sorry for any trouble they may have caused you. Judy, Carol, and Terry can be a nuisance." she said deeply. She carried a small basket filled with flowers and sat them beside Cirrus. "You must never eat a bite of food that a faerie offers you here, or you will never be able to return home." she said blankly.

"Oh, uh, they are fine, really." Cirrus said. He started to stand up, but the woman stopped him.

"Lie down." she commanded gently. Her voice was soft, yet it echoed through the forest. He did as he was told. He felt obligated to listen to her. There was something odd about the woman the more he looked at her, but he couldn't quite tell what it was. Her hair was a rusted copper that fell to her knees and stuck to her face.

Whenever she would blink, her bangs would catch on her eyelashes—which irked Cirrus a little. Her skin was glazed like porcelain; an overall appearance of sepia—she looked like a timeless photograph. The shoulders of her dress swelled like deflated balloons and her dress was ruffled as if they were wrinkled rose petals. She was like a withered flower that needed warmth and water.

"Who…" Cirrus began to ask.

"I'm in need of removing your shirt." she spoke and began fiddling with her basket.

"Ah?!" he gasped. "W-why, if I may ask?"

"Your chest is in pain both in and out." she explained as she pointed to his neck, which was blanketed in a rash. He looked down his shirt and saw splotchy, red marks on his chest. He gasped.

"What is that?!" he asked worriedly.

"It is just an allergic reaction to some chemical or smoke that you aren't used to." said the woman. "You've been playing around in a toxic area, haven't you? I've already given you sweet nectar to heal you from the inside. Just lie down." Cirrus hesitantly removed his dirt and blood-stained gloves. He unhooked his cape and it draped to the ground. His shirt was removed eventually after continuous thoughts of someone looking at his frail body. If he were any more embarrassed, his face would be more red than the rash. The recipe vial was removed from his neck and he placed it safely on top of his cape.

The woman lifted a mortar and a pestle from her basket of plants. She picked several flowers, placed them in the stone bowl and began grinding them up. Cirrus stared at the sky all wide-eyed and pink-faced as he silently listened to the mixing of the herbs. The three faeries hovered around him and observed his face, making him even more uncomfortable. Suddenly, a soft paste was spread across his chest and surprised him with a burning sensation.

"Agh..." he cringed and bit his lip.

"Shhh, lift up and breathe this in deeply." she told him as she handed him the bowl and helped him sit up. He held the bowl to his nose and inhaled. It smelled of mint and honey and left a soothing coolness through his throat. He exhaled pleasure.

"Mmm, this stuff smells really nice!" he smiled. "What is it exactly?"

"It is a blend of chamomile petals, eucalyptus leaves, sapling root and honeysuckle nectar." she explained. "It will burn for only a little, but it will help settle the swelling."

"Ahh....w-wait." he looked down at his necklace. "Honeysuckle nectar! Is there any more of it here?!"

"I'm afraid that I used the last I had of it on you, dear boy." she apologized and brushed her hair behind her ears—her very large, round ears. "I'm sure I can find more around here somewhere. Why? Are you in need of some?"

Cirrus's eyes were as big and bright as a moon at midnight. Something had struck his attention. Those ears looked awfully familiar. Sudden realization swirled in his head. He sat in silence and scanned the woman frantically, curiously. He wasn't sure. Should he ask? It had to be. No. It can't be...could it?

"You...just called me 'dear boy'..." Cirrus thought out loud. He stood up, still shirtless, and circled the woman. "You are very knowledgeable of plants and medicine." He glared at her inquisitively. "You also told me not to eat the berries...because I will be *stuck* here." He stroked his chin. "And your adorably large ears...Is it possible?" He asked as he tapped his foot.

"What are you saying?" she asked confusingly. She embarrassingly covered her ears with her hair.

"You must be Viva!" Cirrus declared and pointed at her as if he was accusing her of a devious crime. He smiled sinisterly.

"Yes, that is my name." her violet-blue eyes flickered.

…

"…*what*?" Cirrus asked.

He stopped his detective act and lowered his skinny arm.

"You are right. My name *is* Viva." she looked around. "How did you know? Did the faeries tell you?"

"I-I-I…" he was at loss of words. He was just playing around—only joking! He saw her violet-blue eyes—the same color of blueberries. He didn't think she was actually…her! Not even the paleness of his body could hide the amount of goose bumps he had bubbling up. "Oh my…"

"Whatever is the matter?" Viva asked as she stood up straight.

"V-VIVA?! *The* Viva?!" Cirrus shouted and wrapped his arms around her. It hurt his chest, but he didn't care. "I was only making ignorant assumptions but oh my goodness you are alive you are alive it is you!!!" He spoke so fast that Viva could barely understand him.

"Don't touch her like that!" shouted Judy as she shook her yellow hair.

"You'll squeeze all of her kindness out!" Carol said as her face got as pink as her dress.

"Let her go, Mr. Squeezie-squeeze-a-lot!" growled Terry as her blue dress rattled around her feet.

"What are you saying?" Viva asked as she tried to pry Cirrus off of her waist.

"Lorne! You *are* Lorne's wife!" Cirrus exclaimed and burrowed his head into her bosom. "Oh, I can't wait to tell him

The Greatest Cake of the Globes

and bring you back to him! He is going to be ecstatic!" His feet danced. Viva went still.

"L-Lorne…" Viva muttered. Her eyes became dark and crystallized. "That…that is cruel of you. He has been dead for nearly twenty years…"

"No, Viva!" Cirrus shouted happily. "He's alive and well! I saw him yesterday in DrearyDrough. He tries to paint, but he just can't without you! Little Primrose is alive!"

"Little…Prim-" Viva's knees buckled and she fainted to the ground. Cirrus knelt down and fanned her. The three faeries became furious and fluttered angrily around him.

"What did you do to her?!" questioned Judy.

"You hurt her!" exclaimed Carol.

"She is not allowed to see him!" said Terry.

"Huh, why not?" Cirrus asked worriedly.

"She stopped you from eating those berries for a reason, you know." the three faeries said.

```
*ACHIEVMENT UNLOCKED: Viva found alive!
HP: 50/70    HP gradually increasing +10
MAX HP from new world
BP: 20/50
MP: • • • • • o
```

☆ 145 ☆

☆ CHAPTER SIXTEEN ☆

To Others, a Weed; To us, The Queen

"She made that mistake twenty years ago." Terry sighed. Cirrus's hand hovered over Viva's face for a short while before he touched her. Cirrus brushed her hair out of her face and tried to shake her back into consciousness. Viva's hair weaved between the grass and flowers on the ground as she was still out cold.

"We feel really bad now." said Judy. "We were only trying to help her…but now she can't leave. We forgot about the rules."

"I don't understand!" Cirrus shouted. "What does eating a berry have to do with being trapped here?!"

"Dummy! Don't you know your faerie lore?" Carol began. "Our food is magic. If you eat anything in the faerie realm, you are trapped here by magic. It is a binding spell."

"Sounds more like a curse…" Cirrus sighed and rubbed his forehead. "Who made up such a stupid rule anyway?!"

The three faeries gasped and stomped their feet in the air. "If you have something to complain about, Lil' Purple-head, then you go and speak to the queen and king at the Castle of Fae." At that moment, Cirrus felt a tug on his shoulder.

"It's no use." whispered Viva. Her eyes glistened in the sunlight. "I've tried before, but after a while I had given up for there was no purpose after Lorne's death."

"Well, your purpose has come back!" Cirrus sat her up and helped her regain balance. "Lorne is alive and I am going to take you back to him. Faeries…" he looked at them sternly. "Take me to the Castle of Fae." he demanded. The faeries looked at one another, shrugged, and then flew off. Cirrus and Viva, both hand-in-hand, followed.

Moments later, they all arrived at the mystical castle. Though, to Cirrus's surprise, it was not like any castle he would have imagined; no stained glass windows that told ancient stories, no crystal walls or marbled towers; it looked more like an oversized cottage held together with vines and cobblestones. Wide tree branches poked their way through the cracks and twisted into circular forms as rope swings dangled from each twig. The kingdom looked more like a pixie's playground. The faeries flew ahead and left a trail of glitter to sprinkle on Cirrus's pointed nose. He continued to follow them, but his arm had tugged since Viva had stopped behind him.

"Again, this is pointless…" she sighed. "I will never be able to escape. I ate those berries and broke the rules. This is my punishment…"

"Well, it is not fair to you." Cirrus crossed his arms. "You had no idea that you were breaking a rule so-"

"I didn't feed myself." Viva quietly interrupted. Cirrus's became perplexed as she began to explain.

"I came here in search of medicine for Lorne. I'd heard rumors of another globe that bustled with plants and herbs that were sure to cure him. However, when I left DrearyDrough, I was captured by a nasty spider and was trapped in her web for days. I was able to escape thanks to a rainbow feathered cloud that swooped over us and carried her away…"

Thank goodness Destiny's family dusts a lot... Cirrus thought to himself.

"That was my chance to finally come here and gather some remedies. I was famished and weak from the spider's poison and lack of food and water…that I actually had passed out. I was dying, Cirrus. The three little faeries that you had just met were the ones who saved my life. They fed me and nurtured me back to health, but then…I was told of the consequences."

"So, it was their fault then!" Cirrus exclaimed irritably.

"Shh! No, don't be so harsh on them. They saved my life. They only did it to save me." Viva pleaded. "I would have died, so I am forever grateful to them. I, myself, was convinced that Lorne had succumbed to his illness after the weeks I had been gone, and I knew for a fact that he would have wanted me to live rather than to die for his sake." Cirrus stood in guilt for a moment.

"Lorne told me that he could never leave DrearyDrough because the memory of you was too precious to part with." Cirrus said gently. "Your house…his portrait of you; that's what keeps him there."

Judy, Carol and Terry returned and circled Viva and Cirrus several times. "You have been so kind to us!" they all said in harmony.

"You've taken care of the royal garden!" said Judy.

"You've helped nurture the ill!" Carol explained.

"And, you've made a lot of us happy!" admitted Terry. The three faeries began to braid Viva's worn hair and stuck tiny primroses in-between each knot.

"Let's give it a shot, Viva. I'll help you. I'll do whatever it takes." Cirrus said as he held out his hand. Viva's face began to glow and she gladly accepted his offering hand.

As they walked along the cobbled rocks, through the willow tree's vines and toward the castle gates, Cirrus told Viva and the faeries of his adventures so far during his search for the mysterious ingredients for The Greatest Cake of the Globes.

A few moments later, faint strumming of an instrument could be heard through the castle walls. Cirrus paused before he entered the door.

"What's the matter?" Judy asked. "Afraid of music or something?"

"No." Cirrus answered. "I'm just a bit confused as to why the door is…sparkling?"

"Eh, just go through it. It's a magic door, of course." Terry demanded. "You'll go right through it like a ghost! Be quick about it."

Cirrus faced the door in awe and curiosity. He watched the colors on the door swirl and mend together, forming shapes like glittered stars, squares and triangles. He imagined what it must feel like to have those colors coursing through him when he passes through the aura. *Will it feel like water, like air, like magic, or like nothing?* He took a step back, took a deep breath, and charged toward the door.

BONK!

Viva crossed her arms and looked at the faeries with displeasure. "You trixie things…" Viva said. The three of them giggled and apologized. Cirrus shook his head and rolled his eyes at the faeries.

"Just turn the doorknob, you simple bimble." The faeries began to laugh again. Cirrus didn't realize how annoying something so cute could be. Anyway, he looked below him and saw two spiral doorknobs and felt like a fool. He sighed and continued forward, hesitant to disrupt anything on the other side.

"Wait." Viva warned. "I had almost forgotten. Today is the Merry Masquerade of Fae and Mystic Folk. Try to make your way passed the dancing beings…for they are quite lively and they may not stop for anything." Cirrus looked a bit confused, but nodded his head and pushed the door open.

Booms, bangs, balloons and bubbles bustled about the ballroom…it was 'B'eautiful! Confetti trickled on the floor, covering the claps and clacks of the dancers' feet. Everyone seemed to have on elaborate costumes and festive masks that complimented their outfits. Faeries, gnomes, witches, wizards, elves, kobolds; such a variety of magical beings all together in one room. Oh, and how they dance in such a harmonious rhythm! Each being seemed to have their own style of dancing that they were accustomed to. The elves eloped in calm sways alongside the flute. The witches and wizards waltzed together to the strings of the violins. The gnomes were doing jazzy, disco pelvic thrusts. Viva wasn't kidding on how lively they were, indeed!

While trying to avoid disrupting the dancers, Viva concealed herself behind the twisted tree trunk pillars that encircled the ballroom. She wanted to sneak passed the dancers unseen. Cirrus followed close behind her, not really understanding what the big deal was about being seen, until he felt a tug on his cape and was pulled to the dance floor by a bouncy, bubblegum colored witch.

"Cirrus!" Viva shouted, thus revealing her hiding place; and, just like that, was swept away into the bustling crowd along with him. A tall, Elven man held her closely and spun her in circles to the rhythm of the harp. A diamond crested mask covered his eyes and when he smiled his teeth had a shine that was brighter than any crystal. Viva struggled to escape the elf's fanciful embrace, but he was not letting go. The music had made everyone in the crowd spellbound with pleasure. Even if she were to ask them to stop dancing, chances are they would not stop, for the music was just as potent as a witch's broth. Speaking of witches, Viva was able to catch a glimpse of Cirrus, who was being dragged along the floor by the happy-go-lucky witch.

The moment felt like it would never end. Viva thought of Lorne. She thought of him strongly; so much that her heart began to ache. The embrace she would much rather be in would be Lorne's. Her heart pounded and became furious when she looked at the grinning Elf. She clenched her teeth, bit her lip and screamed as loud as she could.

"I DON'T HAVE TIME FOR DANCING!!!!" her voice shrieked throughout the ballroom and echoed off the walls, causing the minstrel and his fellow band members to stop the music. The crowd instantly froze in place as if someone had just paused a film. Viva broke loose of the Elf's grasp and rushed to Cirrus, who was lying underneath the skirt of a flower goddess. She pulled him halfway out of the dress and sighed. His face was red and his eyes were wide.

"I've seen many a goddess panties and I am not as ashamed as I should be." Cirrus muttered to himself while he remained in a daze. Viva sat him up and gently slapped his cheeks.

"We will have none of that." Viva said sternly. "We must get to the throne room!"

They made their way passed the motionless dancers and glided up the center steps. A melody played for every step they took; the staircase rang like a glockenspiel with their footsteps chiming like sporadic raindrops. At the very top of the stairs in the ballroom there was a grand waterfall that curtained the entryway to the throne room. Cirrus stopped yet again before walking through.

"Ah hah, so passed this waterfall is the throne room!" he stated with poise.

"Yes. Just through there." Viva replied. "Let us go. I must see Lorne." She and the faeries passed through the falls first. Cirrus nodded and smiled. He knew *just* what to expect. The waterfall was *magical*, it was *mystical*; other waterfalls would drench you as you walked on through, but, no, not this one. He marched on through expecting to come out the other end as dry as sand on the moon.

~~~SPLOOOSH~~~

He was soaked head to toe as well as Viva and the faeries.

"Hey!" Cirrus groaned jokingly, for the water was of no worry—it just was shockingly cold. The faerie trio immediately shushed him. Once he had swooped his wet hair out of his eyes, he was inside a dark forest. However, he was still indoors, yet trees and plenty of other greenery thrived within the room. The ceiling was sheltered by a canopy of tree leaves and branches that were illuminated from the sparkle of stars. The room was dimly lit with a blue aura, and a soft chirping symphony of crickets and bullfrogs could be heard. *Was it not just daylight moments ago?* Cirrus started to worry if he was losing track of time once again.

Viva continued on ahead in silence. Cirrus could tell that her desire to see Lorne was giving her the courage that she needed. He fed off of her bravery and followed close behind her. They walked through the swaying branches of willow trees—which just happened to be the hair of tree spirits that smiled when Cirrus walked by. Moss and ferns blanketed glowing mushrooms that were beds to many small creatures. The faeries flew ahead and pulled back the last of the willow branches as if they were curtains, revealing a large statue of a man sitting in the middle of a shallow pond.

"Woah…" Cirrus said to himself under his breath. "Is that a statue of the king?" He started to walk and follow Viva, but the faeries denied his passage.

"Viva must go first. She will wake them." they whispered.

Viva slowly walked into the pond. It was cold, but she didn't pay any mind. Her dress became even heavier in the water, which reached only to her knees. The statue of the king held out his hand as if he was offering a gift. A single weed was growing from the palm of his hand—it was a seeded dandelion. She approached the statue and breathed deeply. The faeries whispered behind Cirrus.

"Speak to the Earth, cast the internal wind."

Cirrus watched as Viva blew the dandelion's white seeds of fluff into the air. The seeds looked like ballet dancers twirling in the wind—*pop pop pop*! They turned into bubbles and popped into notes of music. The statue's eyes opened to reveal a golden light. In an instant, the whole room lit up like a summer day. The light was so bright and sudden, that Cirrus could almost feel his pupils shrinking to the point of non-existence. The dandelion floated above the king's hand and twisted into the body of a woman. The faeries spoke again with more excitement.

"To others, a weed; to us, the Queen!"

"Good day, Queen Taraxacum—good day, King Radian!" They shouted as they flew toward Viva with glee. The king, still giant and golden, stroked his brow and yawned.

"Oh, dear me!" he spoke in a deep, yet pleasant voice. "My darling! We have overslept…and on the day of the Merry Masquerade of Fae and Mystic Folk too."

"All is well, my sweet." The queen smiled and flew to the king's face and kissed his nose. She was but the size of his nose as well. "Oh! Why hello there Viva, and, oh look! Cirrus is here too, my love!" The queen gestured for Cirrus to come forth. Viva turned her head to him with confusion. He was terribly puzzled as well, but he began to walk closer as his heart pounded.

"You, you were expecting me?" he asked timidly, but rather than panic, he was too busy observing the remarkable appearance of the king and queen. She wore a crown that replicated the head of a seeded dandelion. Her eyes were round and almost tired looking—her nose was large and long, yet pointed so thin. Her shoulders were decorated with the petals of a yellow dandelion, and her dress looked as if they were made of leaves that faded from green to red. She was practically a flower, or perhaps she was! The king looked like he had just bathed in the sun; his eyes were small and golden; dark pointed ears poked out from his white hair. His skin shimmered with a tan glow. He looked at Cirrus and Viva with steady, glossed eyes.

"Oh, how silly of me." the queen spoke to the king. "He still doesn't know." She smiled and playfully rolled her eyes.

"What? Did something happen?!" Cirrus began to question them frantically.

"Easy, easy!" King Radian spoke. "It's not bad at all. It's actually quite good." The queen flew down in front of Cirrus's face.

"You are the one who was chosen to find the ingredients to the legendary, extraordinary, rare, and deliciously sweet Greatest Cake of the Globes, are you not? We were told you would come by a dear friend of ours."

"Ah! Yes, I am! Cirrus O'Zone, ma'am!" Cirrus blushed and was filled with delight. "That means you must know a lot about this magical cake, being a faerie queen and all. Do you know anything else about it?"

"Well…" The queen hesitated for a moment, yet looked Cirrus right in the eye and spoke. "I do know of one thing about the great cake that you may not."

"Y-yeah?" Cirrus leaned closer to her. She spoke softly.

"It doesn't exist, my darling."

The Greatest Cake of the Globes

```
HP: 70/70      HP restored
BP: 20/50
MP: • • • • • • o
```

☆Chapter Seventeen☆

The Royal Faerie Proposition

"W-what?" Cirrus asked as he clutched the recipe vial. "What do you mean it...doesn't exist?"

"It's just as I said, my dear." stated the queen. "There has been no such thing. That vial you hold—the recipe—it was made up."

"B-but it can't be fake!" Cirrus laughed. "This is the only thing that is able to stop the Poison Prince from destroying my hometown and how I will be able to save Luname! Besides, every ingredient that is listed in this recipe exists in every globe! How can that be fake? It is correct down to the very last detail!"

"Ah, the Poison Prince." the queen sighed whimsically. "Is that what he is calling himself these days?" The room became silent for a moment as Cirrus's lips searched for words. He didn't know what to think; he didn't know what to say, but then the queen broke the silence.

"The Poison Prince is merely one of the contestants in the cake competition, don't you know? Who you may ask?" she grinned blissfully. "Why, his name is Nimbus—one of my pupils from years ago, and he is the brother of the person who had written the recipe. Do you have any idea who wrote the recipe?" Cirrus lifted his eyes, which were near tears, and waited for her to say that his mother wrote it, or his father, just to mess with him. If anyone would make a fool out of him by having him partake in a false quest, it would be his parents, but it was the brother of the person who wrote it. Cirrus did not have an uncle the last time he checked, so that ruled them out for sure. *Who could it be?* He would not be mad at the person who wrote it, for they must have had some reason for doing such a thing, but why? The queen mentioned a man named Nimbus—who had stood next to Cirrus during the announcement of the cake competition. Though, he barely remembered the face.

"No, no. 'twas not your parents." the queen hummed. "It was your Luname, darling. She did it all for you."

"W-wha?!" Cirrus's whole body felt like it was crumbling into blushing bits of rocks. Why would she even go through that much trouble?

"In all honesty, Cirrus…" spoke King Radian. "Can't you see? She really admires you. She likes you. She's seen the way that people have treated you and she put you up to a challenge. However, she did not think you would go through with it. A quiet young man who feared his own voice, never able to be comfortable with himself around others—" Cirrus interrupted the King's words by stomping in the water.

"I'm still going to collect the ingredients that it asks for." Cirrus sternly declared.

"Even though it's just a stupid, fake recipe?" the faeries asked and mockingly giggled.

Having heard the faeries accuse the recipe as being *stupid* caused Cirrus to feel frustrated. The "stupid" recipe was the one thing that was able to push him out of his comfort zone. Luname created the recipe, for that matter. She was the reason he was able to leave Cloudscape Town to begin with. She was the reason that he could finally prove to himself that he was useful.

"I could just give up and go home empty handed if what you say about Luname is true and that the Poison Prince is a fraud, but I will not. This recipe is not a fake to me. It's physically written here in this vial and it is one of the best recipes I've come across." He examined the vial on his dirty glove. "There is no way that I can mess this up. It was written for me. It's basically the recipe of my life. The places I've seen and the globelings I've met; I wouldn't have been able to meet them if it wasn't for this recipe. I would have never been able to get to know them or realize that each of them have their own problems; some even worse than what I thought I had…and now I have the chance to help them! I can help them and do something great for once. Such as Viva…"

"Viva?" The queen turned to Viva and flew around her, stroking the wrinkles in her dress. "And how is it that you intend on helping her?"

"By setting her free." Cirrus raised his head with dignity.

"That cannot be. I am sorry. She broke a rule many years ago and a lifetime here she must remain. Even so, our powers have—" The queen quickly sighed and tapped her fingers. She looked back at her husband, who had raised one eyebrow. The queen blinked slowly and slightly returned a nod to the king. Cirrus took a firm grip on Viva's hand to reassure that he was there for her and the queen looked back at Cirrus with wide eyes. "There is nothing we can do…" she said regretfully. "But, there is something that *you* could do."

"Anything!" Cirrus cried.

"Though it may be a dangerous proposition…" King Radian muttered.

"Please, tell us!" Cirrus's heart anxiously fluttered.

"Very well." said the queen. "Bring happiness to the human woman beyond the globes; for she is our caretaker. Our worlds are powered by her joys and motivations and her recent lack of ambition has caused our own magic to wither. If you make her feel at ease, her energy might just be what we need in order to gather enough power to mend Viva's spell."

"I've seen her several times on my quest so far. She is called 'Destiny'. I was afraid of her when I first saw her, but I soon realized that she and I are merely the same. She is a writer, from what I could tell, but I don't think she believes in her ability to create stories, just as I never believed in my ability to bake cakes or socialize with others."

"Well, there you have it." the king applauded. "You already know what is troubling her. Now, you just have to answer her calling the best way you can."

"We will grant Viva her freedom and we shall also give you an item that could aid you on your quest." added the queen.

Wind chimes and the trickling of pond water played through Cirrus's mind as he thought. He looked at Viva and saw the guilt in her eyes. She did not want him to do something so drastic for her, yet she couldn't bear to hold him back from her one chance of freedom. He turned his head back to the king and the queen who were patiently waiting for his answer.

"I'll do it." Cirrus nodded valiantly.

"I-I…" Viva tried to speak, but she couldn't bring herself to words.

"Let me do this. I will reunite you with Lorne. I just have to! You're his love; his life! He is my friend. This is what I want to do." Cirrus stood and splashed about the water laughing—his cape soaked and clinging to his body. "Ahh, I feel great, completely different about myself! I am not as useless as I may seem. I will free you and I will help everyone from the other globes!"

"Cirrus! T-thank you, thank you so much…" Viva cried happily for the first time in twenty years. A glimmer of purple lit up her eyes.

"I promise! I promise I will make everything right!" Cirrus closed his eyes and spun around joyfully. The queen held out her hand and flicked her wrist, causing Cirrus to disappear into a cloud of puff and glitter. Viva gasped.

"Don't be alarmed dear." the queen laughed. "I just helped him get to his destination a bit faster."

Ciara Jackson

The same cloud of glittered magic formed outside of the FaeAway globe and popped our hero onto the corner of the shelf; a little too close to the corner, but he was still cheering with pride and didn't realize what the queen had done. Oh—OH! Too close! He felt the ground suddenly vanish from beneath his feet. He opened his eyes and saw that he was dangling in midair. He had fallen off the corner of the shelf and his cape was the only thing keeping him from falling to the ground. He gasped as if he had just been splashed with some ice cold water and he quickly grabbed for the corner, but he was not fast enough. The cape had slid toward him and off he plummeted to the ground. Luckily, a light switch had broken his fall, but the force of his body weight caused the switch to, well, switch! The ceiling light suddenly went off and, just as a child goes down a slide, Cirrus slid off of the switch and began to fall once again.

"NO!" he shrieked with regret. Even in his last thoughts, he thought of nothing but Luname, his parents, Lorne, Viva, and the others—never will he be able to prove his potential to them just because he slipped off of the shelf. He was going to keep falling—fall to his doom on the ground and his body will be swept up like a dust bunny during spring cleaning. He was going to die with guilt and anger toward himself.

The ground neared. His torn cape flapped frantically around his head. There are no reanimation elixirs where he was going. As his eyes tightened shut and his mouth clenched, he prepared to feel everything around him just…stop; which suddenly did. Everything stopped. That was peculiar. His back had hit something abruptly, but he could still hear his cape flapping. Was he still falling? What's taking so long? Well, his questions would be answered if only he would open his eyes.

"I'm so sorry that I didn't help you out earlier, little thing!" a ragged voice said loudly. Cirrus gasped and finally opened his eyes. That flapping he continued to hear wasn't from his cape; it came from the same tattered wings with the eyeball patterns on them from before.

"Moth?!" Cirrus caught his breath and let out a huge laugh.

"That's me!" the happy moth replied. "I was so distracted by that darned light when you were being pestered by that spider. Heck, you were almost a goner again if it weren't for you turning off that ceiling light! It almost distracted me from saving you from your fall, too!"

"Oh!" Cirrus held on the moth and laughed out of pure awe and amazement. "Yes! Thank you! Thank you!"

"No problem!" the moth chuckled. "I shall return you to your shelf home, fella."

"Oh, wait!" Cirrus thought for a moment. He looked on Destiny's desk and saw the same blank sheet of paper still untouched. An idea had struck him. "Would you mind taking me down to the human's desk first and then back to the shelf?"

"Of course not. I'll fly right on down there now." The moth didn't hesitate to agree, which was certainly a surprise for Cirrus.

The Greatest Cake of the Globes

"R-really?" Cirrus asked again to make sure. "You don't want me to obtain some sort of precious gem or rare item before you take me to my destined area?"

"What are you talking about? Can't a fella just be nice?" the moth laughed.

"I suppose you're right!" Cirrus shrugged and nodded. He tried to focus on his objective rather than acknowledge his fear of heights, but something still made him feel uneasy the closer he flew to the desk. Something wasn't right. Next to the sheet of paper was a clear container that he had never noticed before. It seemed like it had some sort of broken knickknacks in it. He really didn't think much of it until they were about to land. When they flew above the container, he saw what looked like broken glass.

"…W-what is that?" Cirrus muttered to himself as he felt his heart sink. Just as they were landing, he quickly turned to the shelf and noticed that six out of seven globes remained. There was a noticeable gap between O'Cottage and JingleJangle—he knew which globe was not there anymore which caused his heart to melt in pain. That was DrearyDrough in the container. DrearyDrough had fallen off of the shelf and had broken into tiny pieces.

```
*Side Quests Unlocked: Free Viva. Bring
happiness to human. Reunite Lorne and
Viva.

HP: 30/70 extreme HP drop from
heartbreak
BP: 20/50
MP: • • • • • o
```

☆Chapter Eighteen☆

A broken Unbroken Promise

The moth had barely mounted his feet on the desk before Cirrus flung his body off of the insect.

"What?! No…no, no…!" he shouted and nearly tripped on his own feet when he ran to the container. "Lorne! No! Lorne! It's me! Cirrus!" His fists pounded on the wall of the container in hopes of breaking it, but he only rattled the glass bits inside.

"Lorne, are you in there? I found her! I found Viva!" His shouting began to fog up a small section of the container in front of his face, but as he wiped it away with his sleeve, he saw Lorne's candle hat. It sat on its side beneath a pile of rubble with its rim crumpled; no flame to be seen. At that moment, the moth walked over slowly and cleared his throat.

"Oh…Did a friend of yours live there?" the moth asked sympathetically. Cirrus didn't say a word, but his quivering lip and glossy eyes answered the question for the insect. "I see…That globe took a nasty fall not too long ago. A little human boy climbed up on a chair and picked it up. Then, before you knew it—dropped it. Boy, did he receive a scolding from the human though."

"B-but why?!" Cirrus fell to his knees and began pounding ferociously on the wall. "This can't be happening! She is alive! I told her that you were alive! I told her that you *are* alive! Lorne! She is waiting for her Little Primrose!" Cirrus's voice cracked horribly and he clenched his stomach. Loud sobs were muffled by his stained gloves.

"My, my…" The moth took a few steps back and tried to give Cirrus some space. "My condolences."

"I was going to do something really great." Cirrus lifted his head and tried to hide his quivering mouth. "I was going to reunite you with your love. I was going to make you happy. How am I supposed to tell her that you are…that you...are…" The room was silent for a few more moments. The faces of everyone that Cirrus had met on his journey patched his memory. There was still so much that he hadn't accomplished. There were still so many people that he needed to help.

"I'll still free her…" Cirrus stood and regained his balance. His vision was warped from the amount of tears he had covering his eyes. "I'll free her for you, Lorne! I'll save Loroli and Mech from the pollution of their cruel society. I'll give the teens of Jukebopper their music. I'll help little Silly have a wonderful Christmas. I will make my parents, my town, and Luname proud just as I had intended to do before this happened." He stood up as straight as could be and marched over to a small bottle of ink that was next to the desk lamp. He sprinted toward it, still in tears, and slammed into the ink bottle as hard as he could; causing it to rattle. He ran once more and eventually caused it to tumble over. Some of the ink had puddled on the corner of the blank paper. He dunked his gloves in the ink without a care in the world and began sprawling large, curved lines all over the top of the paper. After a few minutes of running back and forth from the ink glob to the paper, he was able to write a little message for Destiny.

"Gather the pieces of your life and make your story."

He wiped his face, which left several smears of black ink under his right eye, and stared at the large sheet of paper. *This should make her happy*, he thought. Suddenly, he heard footsteps coming from the other room.

"Oh! Quick, boy!" the moth gasped. "She's coming! She'll be bound to turn on that light, so I better get you back up to your shelf before I get all hypnotized and junk again." Cirrus was swooped up by the moth without warning and was quickly carried back to the shelf. He thanked the moth and bid him a farewell before he hid underneath the base of FaeAway once more. Destiny had entered the room and flicked on the light and there went the moth to the ceiling, clanking against the light bulb.

"I'm still so upset about that snow globe." she sighed. "I've had that one for so many years."

"Well, your cousin is bound to learn a lesson or two when his mom hears about what happened!" Zachery said from the kitchen.

"Oh, I'm sure!" Destiny agreed. The spilled ink on her desk caught her eye as she went to dispose of the broken snow globe. "Oh, shoot." As she went to clean up the mess with some nearby napkins, she saw small words that were written out on the top left corner of the paper.

"Hmm. Hey, hun? Did you write something on my paper in here?" she questioned.

"Huh? Not that I recall. Why?" Zachery replied as a tea kettle could be heard whistling in the background.

"Just checking! Richard probably got a hold of my pens too. The little sneak." Destiny laughed and rolled her eyes, but then squinted closer to the words. "Gather the pieces of your life and make your story? Huh…." she read aloud. She thought about it for a moment. A five year old surely wouldn't write something like that, but wait—along the words were tiny footprints that seemed to have walked off of the paper.

Destiny had hiccupped a few laughs thinking that the footprints were just a part of her imagination, but the closer she examined them the more she realized the undeniable shape of boots. Sadly, the tiny ink prints had abruptly cut off. Pity, she thought. Now she had no way of finding the small creature that made those prints—but suddenly her curiosity reached its peak once the broken snow globe in the plastic container began to chime once again.

The Greatest Cake of the Globes

She quickly circled around the container and lifted the shattered base off of the globe only to find that the music knob had broken off as well. How was it still playing? No more than a malfunction surely. The melody was beautiful, yet heartbreaking to hear. The sound of the chimes struggling to play one last time; such a helpless tune. It could have made some of the toughest people shed a tear. The music began to sound strange, however, as if the tune was becoming jumbled up with another sound. Her right ear picked up a slow beat while her left ear caught on to a faster rhythm. When she turned around, all of her snow globes were dancing with glitter as if someone had shook them.

Cirrus felt a little uneasy once he noticed Destiny walking closer to the globe that he was hiding under. Soon enough, her face orbited around each and every globe. However, once she had reached the last globe—there they were: the tiny inky footprints. Her mind began to wander. Did they belong to a small creature that lived in one of the snow globes? She stopped for a moment and blinked continuously. Those footprints were real; small, but real. There was absolutely no way of denying it. After staring at them for a few more moments an idea had sparked in her head.

"Gather the pieces of your life and make your story..." Destiny whispered to herself once more. That's what the small message said on her desk, but what could that mean? The message, the footprints, the snow globes and the music—perhaps those were the pieces that needed gathered in order to create her story—but wait, that's it! "What if a little being actually *did* live in a snow globe and is the one who wrote the message?" Destiny thought. Suddenly, her heart flickered and she shot straight up. "Zachery! I think I've got it—an idea for a story!"

Footsteps quickly thudded on the ground from the other room and then Zachery stormed in. "Really?! Do tell!" Zachery grinned. Destiny quickly scurried in to the living room to tell him of her plan. The excitement in her voice reassured Cirrus that he had completed the task of making her happy. Within seconds after she left the room, the same puffy aura formed around him and transported him in to the royal faerie throne room in an instant. As he stood on a single stone surfacing the pond, he was welcomed with claps and cheers from the king and queen—even the three annoying faeries were celebrating.

"You did it, Cirrus!" the queen exclaimed. "You made the human happy." Having heard that, he did feel a little bit of satisfaction. He finally felt like he did something right, but he still couldn't feel happy for himself. The smile on his face faded once he had laid eyes on Viva, who was holding a wicker basket and bouncing with delight. He knew that the stars in her eyes would soon dim. Lorne was gone, after all, and she doesn't yet know.

"Our magic alone would not have inspired her." the king added. "The synchronization of the globes' music would have only frightened her. A haunting she would have thought of it, but thanks to your message, she believes it to be something much more imaginative."

"And as promised, Viva will be free to go." the queen gestured a smile. Viva took a sudden deep breath and looked at the queen; her eyes questioning if she was actually telling the truth. The queen replied with a soft nod.

"Cirrus!" Viva cried as she splashed through the water to embrace her savior. She had almost knocked him over once she reached him, but she held him with such gratitude. "Thank you."

The Greatest Cake of the Globes

"But wait!" the king's voice rattled the trees. "A gift to *you*, Cirrus." A ball of light sparked in front of Cirrus's face and had burst into sparkles revealing a golden brooch. It fell into the curve of his palm.

"The Baker's Brooch—made from a fragment of a fallen star; a brooch of passion, hope and love, meant to belong to a strong baker. You know this item well." the queen explained. "Use it when your heart needs to communicate the most. Use it to inspire and heal many who are unable to hear the sound of life."

"The legendary Baker's Brooch...right here in my hand." Cirrus closed his eyes and held it to his chest. The queen smiled and lifted her hand after bidding them farewell. She then transported Cirrus and Viva to the shelf.

"I wonder if he even realized," the queen began. "...that he has been obtaining his own magic with every new world that he entered." She and the king both quietly laughed.

Viva's and Cirrus's figures formed in front of the FaeAway globe. Our hero stood and fell emotionless, for he knew what he needed to tell Viva. He firmly gripped the brooch in his ink stained gloves and, before he could say anything, Viva was already twirling along the shelf.

"Ah!" Viva gasped in awe. "It's been so long since I've seen the shelf and the room of the human. This is wonderful! Please, I cannot bear it any longer. Take me to Lorne, my hero!" Cirrus's heart felt crushed after being called a *hero*. She took his hand and started to skip down the shelf, but his stillness tugged her back. "What is it?" she asked in concern. His face remained blank for a few seconds, but then his eyes began to speak for him.

"I..." he whimpered. "I can't..."

"You can't?" Viva smiled. "Can't what, dear?"

"I can't take you to DrearyDrough." he muttered softly.

"What do you mean? It's right down the sh—" Viva's words stopped suddenly when she noticed that her home was no longer on the shelf. She saw an empty space where it always stood—faint dust surrounded a clean circle imprint. Her mind flooded in disarray. "I-it's gone...why...?"

Viva returned to Cirrus in a subtle panic. He fell to his knees and began to shake. The struggle to hold back tears was useless; his hands went numb, his body trembled, his lips quivered—he couldn't hold back his desperate sobs.

"DrearyDrough...fell." his voice shook.

"No..." Viva quietly gasped.

"It fell! It fell off only moments ago!" Cirrus's throat crackled with pressure. "Lorne fell with it! He's gone...he fell...he's...!" He pointed to the box on Destiny's shelf. That contained the globe's broken remains. Viva stared at the box while Cirrus smothered his sobs in his stained hands. She could see bits and pieces of what she used to call home sprawled across the box—gone, broken, smashed. She slowly walked over to Cirrus and sat down beside him.

"You did everything you could..." Viva somberly spoke. "You freed me after all—"

"No!" Cirrus interrupted her unintentionally. "He was alive today! *Today!* I only saw him this morning! I had you two so close together—so much that it hurt—and now I can't even do that right. I couldn't do what I wanted to do and I can't bear it! This was the one thing I was going to do right for you both!" Viva grabbed him and held him tightly to calm him down. He was so overwhelmed with emotions and could not to do anything but cry.

"I understand. I understand. Shh.." Viva rubbed her hands frantically down his back—patting him like a scared child. "I've made peace with Lorne's death for nearly twenty years now. I'm not feeling too much different..." She firmly embraced Cirrus and his sobs became louder.

"You cry just like Lorne used to..." Viva smiled as a tear rolled down her flushed cheek. She swayed Cirrus slowly back and forth. "He always wanted someone to hold him while he cried."

```
*Side Quest Achieved: Freed Viva. Made
human happy.

*Side Quest Failed: Reunite Lorne and
Viva.

HP: 30/70
BP: 20/50
MP: . . . . . . . *MAX MP*
```

☆Chapter Nineteen☆

The Heart's Storm

After several moments, Cirrus's tears began to fade. Viva, with her arms still embraced around him, whispered softly into his ear.

"Go help the rest of them." she said; her eyes calm and glassy. "They need you as well."

"I..." Cirrus lifted his head and squeezed his eyes together tightly, releasing what little tears that he had left. "Why? Why should I even try? I have only one ingredient for that stupid fraud of a cake recipe and for what? No one in town is in any danger to begin with! The town isn't going to be poisoned at all. So why even bother?"

"Cirrus..." Viva looked at him straight in the eyes. "You are the only one who will be poisoned if you give up and go home now." He stared off to the side. "You will be poisoned by guilt, regret, and embarrassment for not satisfying what you really desire and that's making you and your loved ones proud, is it not?"

"O-of course it is..." he whispered. "I just can't do anything I set myself out to do. I want to help people, but I can't. I want to bake delicious food for our bakery shop, but I can't. I want to talk to people and not be afraid, but I can't!"

"You are talking to me now." said Viva. "Are you afraid?"

"Well, no, but at first-" mumbled Cirrus.

"I bet you were afraid and very nervous to talk to Lorne at first too, but now you would give anything to talk to him again, wouldn't you?" Viva asked calmly. "What about Luname? I bet you felt very anxious around her as well. You consider them two of the most important globelings in your life now, don't you?"

"A-ah..." Cirrus was at a loss of words for a moment. He could feel his heart fluttering just by hearing their names. It wasn't the nervous fluttering he was used to either. It was more of an excited flutter; for love and for friendship, not for fear.

"There is nothing wrong with you, dear." Viva placed her hand on his. "To feel helpless is something we all feel from time to time. Think of how I feel about Lorne; how helpless I felt back then; not being able to retrieve medicine for him. All I can say for you now is not to dwell in self-pity for long…for it may have dreadful effects on you later on." She sighed heavily and stroked her own cheek, reminding Cirrus of her shallow, pasty skin and ragged appearance. "Don't lose your color like I did."

Viva was right. He remembered the portrait Lorne painted of her and how happy she looked. He closed his eyes as the frantic clacking of Destiny's keyboard tickled its way through his ears. As he looked over to the human, he watched as her hands swept over each key with such eagerness. Not too long ago, Cirrus could relate to that so called "destructive" human with the lack of confidence in oneself, but now her face smiled like he'd never seen before and he yearned to feel the same.

"Inside the star beats the heart." Cirrus mumbled Luname's words as he looked at his brooch. He understood now. The brooch was shaped like a star with a heart carved in the middle of it. "I won't give up. Those globelings will be helped and that cake will be for sure baked!"

"Go to them, then." Viva's eyes smiled. "I'll wait here and watch over your two ingredients."

"Two?" Cirrus questioned. I've only received the blueberries from Lorne."

"Yes, the blueberries, and the honeysuckle nectar that I gathered for you while you were out." Viva lifted the floral, wicker basket from behind her. "It's more than a thank you gift." He looked in the basket and saw several jars of golden, honeysuckle syrup lying next to the large container of blueberries. He felt overwhelmed with gratefulness, but there was a job that was needed to be done fast. He returned an appreciative smile, shared a parting wave and entered the base of the TockTick globe. Hopefully he still had time to help the others!

☆*☆*☆

After several moments, Cirrus was near the entrance of the world. He could tell he was getting closer just by the unmistakable lack of fresh air. However, he retrieved the gas mask that he left behind as soon as he reached the top of the spiral staircase. The ticking and clattering of the industrial machinery was surprisingly quiet this time around, but he was welcomed with an even louder racket: an angry gathering of workers. The environment was still as clouded with pollution as ever, but that did not stop him from hearing the barbaric protests that the workers were shouting.

"HE WILL REGRET IT!"
"WORTHLESS!"
"LAZY GOOD-FOR-NOTHING!"
"WE ARE GOING TO FREEZE!"
"THIS IS ALL M1642'S FAULT!"

M1642? Oh no, that's Mech's number! These workers were still upset with him not being on the job and in fear that time will halt if everybody stops working. Cirrus's heart raced as he watched the crowd goose-leg march out of the city as if they were in an army. Hundreds of globelings were gathered in anger and he knew that they were all capable of doing something terrible if this wasn't stopped soon. What is one globeling supposed to do? Cirrus felt like his stomach was on a roller coaster, front seat and all. Without hesitation, however, he concealed himself from the crowd and quickly ran through the dense fog in search of the giant tree before they find it first.

Mech continued to sleep beneath the golden apple on the tree. Loroli's shoulder gently held Mech's head. She looked around cautiously, wondering what was causing the vague sound of crunching dead leaves from the hill. Suddenly, muffled chanting arose from the fog.

"...We will freeze..."

"...We will freeze...!"

"...WE WILL FREEZE...!"

The parade of thuds and stomps became louder until a single figure could be seen standing in the fog. Loroli had hoped it was Cirrus's return, but of course when she saw the antlers she knew exactly who it was and her head felt heavy with fear.

"Give him to us, L1463!" the voice spoke hoarsely.

She gripped Mech in fear and began to shake him awake. What good that did. He let out a few soft moans and squeezed his eyelids tightly, but he instantly turned over and burrowed his head playfully under her arm.

"Mech! They're here!" she whispered loudly. When she looked away, however, Mech opened one of his eyes and gave her a smile—then closed his eyes once more.

 The figures emerged from the fog and several hundred others followed shortly afterward. The two hooded, deer-masked globelings stood before the rest of the crowd with a powerful presence. Each crowd member wielded large, sharp tools and gears as weapons. The first deer-faced man spoke above everyone else.

"We have had it with your childish rebellion, M1642! What makes you think you were granted lifelong relaxation while the rest of us work to the bone to prevent time from ending?" Deer Face waited for Mech's response, but nothing was replied.

"What is this?" the second deer-face quipped. "You don't even care if time stops, do you? You want all of us to work just so you can spit on us!"

"As long as you are up here wasting precious time," Deer Face scoffed. "There is no doubt that time will stop. We will all pause and live life stuck in a single position for all eternity. Stand up now, coward! Or we will drag you down." he boasted. "Tis what the Golden Owl would've wanted."

"The Golden Owl would have wanted *this*, you say?" Mech inquired like he knew a secret. His head slowly rose above his shoulders as his relentless glare struck the deer men. He turned to give Loroli a quick nod and a wink, but then promptly resumed the unforgiving glance back at the lords. He adjusted his head—making sure that he was still correctly positioned beneath the golden apple in the tree. Loroli regained her stance as well, when suddenly the sky was blanketed in dark clouds.

"Hah! I knew you would give up eventually!" boasted the deer-faced leader. "Have you anything to say before we put you in place?"

"I have only two words." Mech spoke proudly—grasping the pocket watch he wore around his neck. The sky bellowed with the drumming of thunder.

"Are those two words *'I'm sorry'*?" laughed the leader.

"Nah, it's most likely *'I'm a loser!'* No doubt!" yakked the second deer-face.

"That's *three* words, you idiot." the leader whispered.

"Oh..."

Mech smiled and his eyes sparkled with a golden light.

"I remember!" Mech shouted.

The sheep-masked bunch looked around and began to mutter with confusion amongst themselves while the two leaders tilted their heads.

"What are you even talking about?" Deer Face inquired. His voice suddenly sounded less boastful than it did moments ago. The tree had a halo of gray and indigo clouds—wind blowing like a tornado; leaves and dandelion puffs scattering in the air. Where in the globe could Cirrus be at a time like this?

Loroli struggled to keep her balance from the gusts of wind that knocked against her. Mech, on the other hand, remained as still as the tree that stood behind him. The look on his face was clear proof that he would not be taken down so easily.

"This looks familiar does it not?" Mech asked inquisitively, one eyebrow lifted. Before Loroli could question him a blast of wind lunged against her, knocking her into his arms. He held her tightly and gave her yet another wink.

"W-we have no idea what you are taking about, fool!" the leader's words trembled. "Now, it's best that we head back down! There's a horrible storm coming!"

"*Really*, now!" Mech laughs howled like the thunder around them. "It would be a shame if I was tied around the tree during such a storm, wouldn't it, O' Great leaders?"

The two leaders gasped and shook tremendously. "WORKERS! HE SPEAKS NONSENSE! GET HIM!" Within a split second, the mob roared and swarmed toward Mech and Loroli.

⚡ ⚡ *CRRRACKKCHHHH* ⚡ ⚡

A bolt of purple lightning struck the ground right in front of the mob, halting them in their positions. Silence rose for a few moments, but then a figure approached from behind the tree. It was Cirrus! Light illuminated from the brooch that the faerie king and queen had given to him. He held his hand high, trembling from fear with a face full of astonishment. He had been listening since the crowd had made its way to the tree. The insolence he heard, all of the hate and rude accusations—he couldn't bear to hold back his words any longer. His heart wanted to speak and that brooch gave him the power to make them listen.

"You all work every day, every hour, every minute, and every second. If you all stop working and making clocks—even just for a moment—time will stop, correct?" Cirrus asked as calmly as he could. He tried to hold back his stutters.

"What makes you think we will tell you, an *outsider*, anything?!" Deer Face cackled. "Off with you!"

⚡ ⚡ *CRRRACKKCHHHH* ⚡ ⚡

Another lightning bolt made its way in front of Deer Face within a flash. Cirrus disliked the fact of using fear to threaten these folks, but it seemed to keep them from attacking Mech. The leaders cringed and replied quickly. "YES! CORRECT! Time will stop!"

"If this is true, then how come everyone is still moving as we speak?" Cirrus pointed out. The wind blew harder as the assemblage began to quarrel with one another. "All of you are right here, right now—moving! No one is making clocks at the moment and time still goes on!" The workers continued to mutter sounds of realization and awe.

"Be still, all of you!" scowled the leader. "What does he know? Do not listen to him!"

"Well, I do know the main reason this city is so polluted is the fact that all of these clock factories have been spewing horrible fumes and gases out into your atmosphere!" Cirrus exclaimed. "And look! I'm not wearing a mask. Neither are they! This tree produces clean air. Take of your masks and see for yourselves!"

"Liar!" Deer Face yelled angrily. "Your eyes will melt and your lungs will become ash!" The gathering gasped as one of their own suddenly took off her mask. They watched as she removed her sheep designed disguise, revealing pale skin followed by long, dark hair and tired eyes. She took a deep breath and held it.

"H-he's right!" she gasped as she touched her face. "I can breathe! The air...the air is so pure here!" The rest of the globelings were in awe as they too began to take off their masks one by one, dropping all of their makeshift weapons. They took their first breaths of fresh air for the first time in many, many years.

"I've only been here for a short while and I've already gathered that you have all been raised to be hard laborers. You were told that making clocks nonstop would keep you all alive, but why?" Cirrus asked in a desperate voice.

"I have the answer to that." Mech cleared his throat. "It is because everyone here has been brainwashed by our very own Deer Lords, old friends of The Golden Owl!" In due time, Cirrus halted the wind so everyone could hear what Mech had to say. Only the soft rustling of leaves played throughout the field.

"RIDICULOUS!" Deer Face shrieked.

"Let him speak! Let him speak!" the workers demanded. Cirrus locked eyes with the leader and pointed at the brooch, warning him that he can start up that storm again just as easy as he stopped it.

"The Great Owl..." Mech announced. "The Great Owl was our true leader. He was the one that we always looked up to. He made things right. He kept us happy. Yes, happy—a word that we all had forgotten the meaning of long ago. Many years have long passed since he died. You all remember his death, don't you?"

"Yes, he was a great leader!" a voice called out.
"His pocket watch failed him. That's why he died!" another said.
"We must make clocks so our time can continue forever." mumbled another.

"Yes, that's what we were told." Mech said as he tilted his head downward. "But they were all lies to cover up something foul."

"No..." whispered Deer Face.

"The Golden Owl did not die due to a mere stopped watch." Mech fiercely stated. "He was killed! Murdered!"

"NO!" the second deer accomplice bellowed. Gasps echoed throughout the gathering. The two deer-masked leaders turned to one another, frantically waiting for the other to say something.

"We are all ears, leaders! Tell them!" Mech demanded. "Tell them what you did to The Golden Owl! Tell them what you did to my grandfather!"

HP: 30/70
BP: 20/50
MP: • • • • • •

☆Chapter Twenty☆
There will Always be Time

Loroli turned to Mech and could not say a word. Cirrus remained standing in the midst of both sides feeling like he was an extra in a war film. His eyes shot back and forth between the Deer Faces and Mech.

"Man, this is getting way too deep for me to understand." Cirrus whispered to himself.

"What did you say?!" Deer Face's voice clapped at Cirrus, who replied with a frantic head shake to reassure that he had said nothing offensive.

"Your grandfather?" Loroli asked curiously as she tugged on Mech's shoulder. "The Golden Owl...?"

"Yes. The Golden Owl was my grandfather and our two leaders were the cause of his death! I know that for a fact." Mech exclaimed. The assemblage grew restless of all of the sudden confusion that washed over them. The two deer-faced leaders frantically looked at each other and questioned the eyes of every worker. The leader tried to simply ignore their jeers, but unlike before, he could now see their true emotions rather than having their faces shunned beneath a mask. The forlorn stares he continued to receive eventually began to drive him mad.

"NO! He lies! He lies!" Deer Face shouted.

"Listen well!" Mech exclaimed. "They had purposely dropped one of these apples on to The Golden Owl's head and left him unconscious to die in a storm!" Cirrus looked up and noticed the golden apple begin to shake violently from the wind he conjured.

"Impossible! Those apples would not be able to hurt you one bit if it fell on your head!" the second deer face mocked.

"I see." Mech stated tranquilly. He closed his eyes slowly, smiled, and took a deep breath, and at that very moment...

CLONK!!

The golden apple, nearly the size of a large grapefruit, plummeted on to Mech's skull and knocked him clean down. Loroli rushed to his side and lifted his head off of the grass. Mech's body was as limp as an old rag doll and a stream of blood trickled down his nose.

"Mech! Mech!!!" she cried as she shook him repeatedly. He did not move an inch. Thankfully, he was still breathing, but he was out cold.

"The apple knocked him out!"
"Is he dead?!"
"Oh no!"
"It's true!"

Yet again, the crowd became even more furious with questions than before. They were tired of being treated like imbeciles and wanted answers right then and there. Their voices rattled the tree's branches as they demanded the leaders to explain what was happening right away. The deer-faced lords were in no position for any more excuses. Deer Face clenched his fists and threw his hands in the air.

"YES! It was our fault that The Golden Owl died!" Deer Face whined as he fell to his knees in guilt. He chucked his mask off of his head and flung it to the side, causing the antlers to snap in to pieces. He turned to everyone and revealed his face. It was that of an elderly man—a face that has known too much regret, a face that yearned for more time.

"It was an accident. A complete and utter accident..." the other deer faced man said sourly as he also removed his mask. "A selfish one, at that."

Soon enough, two elderly faced men stood before the gathering. One was bald and the other had a scraggly, salt and pepper colored beard. Everyone gazed at their unfamiliar faces.

"Yes...it is true." the old leader regrettably admitted. "The two of us are responsible for his death. The Golden Owl was a great leader, as M1642...o-or *Mech*, said. He was as wise as an owl and was known for his golden attire and kind words. He made our city a place where we never had to work hard for anything. We always had fun. We always played around with friends and family, until one day the two of us became jealous of him."

"He had been growing this tree, you see." the second elderly man said as he held his hand up to the tree. "He worked hard, unlike the rest of us, to grow this tree and we did not like that. He needed to have fun just like the rest of us. Little did we know...he *was* having fun while he was working."

"So, we did something horrible." the old man added on. "One day while he was up here working, we hid in the top of the tree where all of those sparkly apples grew and we thought that it would be funny if we plucked one from the branches and threw it at him—we thought that maybe then he would get the right idea and come spend more time with us."

"The apple clonked him one a bit too hard, though." the old man's voice choked. "So, being the hooligans we were, we decided that it would be amusing to tie him up around that very tree to see how funny his reaction would be when he woke back up."

"Though, it began to storm terribly." the old leader sighed as the strong winds mocked him. "We became so afraid of the thunder and quickly left for home, leaving The Golden Owl unconscious around the tree. Then...the lightning struck and—"

"Then he died from instant electrocution." Loroli suddenly added. "His broken watch had nothing to do with it." She lowered her stance and removed a golden chain from around Mech's neck. She felt the rust crackle off of the chain within her grasp and held it high above her head for the crowd to see. A rustic pocket watch dangled from the chain. "I know what this is. It is The Golden Owl's—Mech's grandfather's watch. I hold it here in my hand, rusted, but unbroken. The watch still ticks. Time is still told. You told us all that he died because his watch stopped ticking, therefore we must make watches in order to keep our time going." She silenced herself for a moment to allow the globelings to try and comprehend the situation. Her eyes met with Cirrus and she quickly glanced over at Mech.

"I now know why Mech needed this apple to fall on his head." she muttered loudly. "He needed you all to see the damage it could do to someone if it was dropped on someone—for proof that The Golden Owl was helpless in his demise."

Loroli gestured for Cirrus to come closer, and he did what she willed. She lifted the golden apple from the ground where it rolled off Mech's head and swallowed hard at the weight of it—imagining how much pain Mech felt when it fell. She handed the large fruit to Cirrus with a nod. "Right after you had left our globe, I was grabbed from the shadows. I had thought it was one of the angry workers, but it was Mech who brought me safely to this tree. I could not believe he had left the tree, but he told me that the strange, purple-haired man would make the apple fall and all would be well again. So, I thank you for helping Mech. Your magic saved us all." Happiness was fighting its way through the worry in her eyes, but before he accepted the apple from her hand, he turned to the once deer lords and walked over to them.

"I know I'm not one you would want to listen to," Cirrus began as he folded his hands together. "But, I've gathered that you two have practically brainwashed these people to believe that they will die if they stopped working even for one moment. You wanted them all to be constantly preoccupied so no one would dare search for the truth behind the death of your leader. This led to some serious issues." The two old men's eyes remained locked on the dead grass, allowing Cirrus to continue. He spoke loudly to the entire group of globelings. "The constant use of machinery from your factories has caused your world to be filled with smoke and pollution. I recommend that you all stop making clocks and, perhaps, plant trees and flowers to help restore your air. This tree is the reason why we can breathe here. Look! The fog is already fading away since you have left the factories."

Cirrus held out his arm and pointed to the fog. As each second went by, the murky fog became lighter and the grass more vibrant. The muddy atmosphere slowly turned green and pleasant as the echoes of astonishment serenaded through Mech's ears. Loroli noticed Mech's eyes rapidly quivering beneath his eyelids, which had become soaked with tears. She knelt down, lifted his head on to her lap and brushed the torn grass flakes off of his bruised forehead.

"I cannot tell if these tears are from the impact of the apple or the amount of relief that is washing away my doubt." whispered Mech as he searched to touch Loroli's face. His eyes remained closed. "I was very young when I saw the two men tie up my grandfather, but I too was afraid to be under the tree during such a storm. I could not gather the courage to untie my grandfather. I felt at fault..."

"Shhh, you were very young and frightened, as you just admitted." Loroli said as she watched sunlight trickle over his brown skin. He wriggled his eyes open, flinching from the light, and smiled.

"I had forgotten what had happened as the years went on," his voice cracked. "But whenever I was able to catch a glimpse of your face from beneath the mask, I remembered what happiness felt like. I remembered the joy that once was. I remembered fun, peace...and my grandfather." He suddenly lifted his chest and let out a howling yell from the pain of his head as he struggled to sit up. Cirrus, the two old men and the crowd gasped as he stood— watching him clutch his head in agony.

"Y-you are alive!" the old man said as if he were happy to see it as such. Mech stumbled away from the tree with the help of Loroli's guidance. He inched closer to the old men, who now wore masks of fear and sadness. Mech stood and observed everyone that encircled him for a few moments before he knelt down and picked two seeded dandelions from the grass. He stood back up, took the two weeds and blew their seedlings on to the faces of the old men. One of them sneezed while the other shook off the puffs from his scruffy mustache.

"This is what I would like for all of you to do." Mech announced as he plucked another dandelion from the ground. "Each of you pick one of these. Dandelions are perhaps one of the most beautiful plants out there—their seedlings will help our land become green again. Take a deep breath… and then blow."

After a few moments of the crowd's hesitation, the globelings gave in to temptation and curiously began picking the tiny fluff plants one by one. Loroli and Cirrus gathered a few of their own as well. Mech stood tall before the old men, giving them a blank stare until, eventually, they too held dandelions.

"Alright, everyone. Now." Mech peacefully commanded as everyone let out huffs of air. The seedlings floated to and fro within the wind. The sky snowed with rebirth—the sky twinkled with renewal. As the puffs waltzed toward the fog, the pollution slowly withered away before everyone's eyes; not entirely, but enough to where the city could be seen at a distance.

"I'm glad that I've finally gotten through to you." Mech said to the old men. They looked at him in confusion as if they were asking where their punishment was waiting for them. Mech quietly laughed. "You aren't forgiven that easily, but rather than lock you two away where time does not matter, we must work together to rebuild our city. We will have days off. We will take breaks when we are tired. We will have fun doing so. Now, go."

Within minutes, the entire group of globelings had hopped and skipped their way down to the city—many laughing and some even singing. The two men left without a word, but their eyes spoke with great apology. They began to plan for the cleanup as they followed the globelings down the hill. Cirrus, Mech and Loroli remained under the tree. Cirrus watched the crowd as they happily ventured away and heard Loroli speak behind him.

"Mech," she happily sighed as she took his hand. "I'm so glad that you are okay. That was—" Her sentence was cut short by a sudden kiss from Mech. She could feel the warmth of his lips coursing through the more he held her. The tips of her pointed ears twitched with exhilaration. Cirrus turned around just in time to catch them lip locked. His foot fidgeted in the grass to distract him from blushing, but he could not resist a smile. Mech let out a small gasp as he pulled away from Loroli, who was left in a warm daze.

"I've been wanting to know what that felt like for years." Mech giggled softly as his hand fell from her cheek to her chin. "It's like I feel extra happiness around you—warmer happiness than usual. I can feel it especially in my cheekbones."

"A friend once told me," Loroli began. "…that the extra warmth we both feel for each other is called *love*." She looked at Cirrus, whose face brightly lit up.

"Ah, yes. Love!" Mech returned a pleased gesture toward Loroli, but then quickly sprang over to the roots of the tree and retrieved the apple from the ground.

"You. You need this now, don't you?" Mech asked as he held the apple like a bowling ball.

"I, yes, I do. If you wouldn't mind." Cirrus responded timidly.

"Don't be so modest!" Mech laughed. "Loroli told me of the challenging quest you bear. If this apple can help you then it must be so!" The apple was tossed in to Cirrus's arms nearly causing him to tumble over. He did not want to tell them that the legendary cake recipe was a fraud, so he just went along with it.

"Wait!" Loroli gasped and snapped her fingers. "I had almost forgotten. Mech." She spoke so quietly that Cirrus could hear the grass growing more than her voice, but suddenly Mech looked over to him and merrily nodded.

"Why, of course he can!" Mech said as he reached for the rusted pocket watch that Loroli held for him. He examined it in his hand for a moment before he had pulled out a magnifying eyepiece and a miniature screwdriver from his pocket. He began poking and twisting the face of the watch with the small tools. Cirrus watched in bewilderment for several short moments when the clock face suddenly popped open, revealing small mechanisms clicking and clacking about. He plucked out one of the larger gears and gently placed it in Cirrus's hand.

"Hey, this is—" Cirrus fiddled around in his pants pocket and pulled out the broken gear he had obtained from the jukebox back in Jukebopper. The two gears were identical despite the chipped section in the piece he already had.

"A deal's a deal." Loroli winked. Cirrus could feel excitement bubbling up all around him at the thought of the Sodapop Bash being saved. Finally, he felt like he was beginning to accomplish the many things he had set out to do.

"Here." Mech said as he tossed the rusted pocket watch to Cirrus. "Take this with you. Keep in touch"

"O-oh, but this is your grandfather's. I can't possibly take this." Cirrus explained as he placed the watch back in Mech's hand and folded his fingers over it. "Don't worry. The gear is all I really need. Besides, you have already given me so much to be thankful for. I'll come back soon, I promise."

"I understand." Mech nodded respectfully as he tucked away his pocket watch in his leather vest.

"I'd best be on my way, though." Cirrus admitted as he adjusted his shoulder and stretched his back. "My time's almost run out." They all chuckled to one another as they shook hands and shared fond farewells.

"Cirrus!" Loroli shouted from atop the hill as our hero paced his way down to the city. He turned to see Mech and Loroli in a standing embrace, waving to him. "Remember," Mech smiled. "There will always be time!"

```
*Side Quest Achieved: Make Golden Apple
 fall.
*Obtained Golden Apple, Jukebox gear,
 and honeysuckle nectar
HP: 30/70
BP: 35/50
MP: . . . . . . .      *MAX MP*
```

☆Chapter Twenty-One☆
Let the Music Play

"Are you sure you do not feel ill?" Viva softly asked Cirrus as he dusted off his shoulders and set the large apple in the basket. The large fruit made the basket seem toy sized.

"Anything but!" he said gleefully—grunting from the sudden weight of the basket when he lifted it. "The smoke in that world was not as bad this time. Everything is all good to go. We can carry on without worry!" He pointed to Jukebopper's retro globe and marched forward. Viva walked quietly behind him without saying much, for she was afraid that her morose voice would dull Cirrus's excitement. Lorne's words echoed through her, after all. She could not help but to feel her body ache with loss once again.

"I just have a few more places to go and we will be ready to head home." he said loudly, hoping for a pleasant response from Viva, but she did not answer. He turned to her—her feet barely lifting from the ground as she walked, and eyes emptier than a starless night. He stopped for an instant allowing her to catch up to him. Once she was close enough, he took her hand and sighed. "Join me when I enter these last few globes. It would do you some good to see these worlds." As much as he tried to hide the thought of Lorne in his mind, sadness still clogged his throat. Viva, still soundless, faintly nodded—agreeing to go along with him.

The two of them barely spoke a word to one another as they arrived in Jukebopper, but Viva's breath escaped in a gasp once she saw the colorful, pastel vehicles aligned in a row on the grassy hill.

"I wouldn't go looking in any of those cars if I were you." Cirrus laughed uncomfortably as he guided her along the dusty dirt path of rocks that led straight to the diner. Shortly before entering the diner, however, a voice had called out from afar.

"Oh, Cirrus! Oh, do please wait!" the voice whined as it came closer. Before he managed to turn around, a girl had flung herself into him and tightly gripped his ragged cape. "I'm so sorry! I did not want to believe it, but it was just as you said!"

"Marsha!" Cirrus gasped as he struggled to twist his body around so he could properly see her. Viva blinked continuously from confusion, but kept quiet.

"I saw Curtis...he was, he was—" her cries squealed through his ears and caused him to cringe.

"He was what? Take a deep breath and tell me what you saw." he asserted quickly as he tried to console the sad girl. Marsha stood up straight and fanned her tears away from her eyes. After a few moments of pitiful sobs and sniffling, she began to explain.

"Shortly after we left the diner, he walked me home and told me how much he loved me and all." she sniffled some more. "But, I felt bad for yelling at Russell, so I decided to come back to the diner and apologize, but when I was walking to the diner I saw Curtis's bike at Holly's house and when I peeked through the window..." Marsha's lips trembled and she scrunched up her little nose. Cirrus, having no idea who this Holly was, still was able to put two and two together. He could only assume that she too had witnessed the infamous back-seat-bingo.

"Say no more." he declared dramatically as he shielded his ears.

"Curtis really *doesn't* care about me." Marsha's pink lips pouted.

"Now, now. Don't worry." he smiled and looked back at the diner's shining door behind him. "There are many others that care about you." Marsha's eyes glistened.

"Russell?" she blushed and stared off to the ground as if she were recollecting all of the kindness she had received from Russell. "Do you think he would want to be my date for the Sodapop Bash?"

"You never know!" Cirrus shrugged spiritedly and flicked his hair toward the diner. "Let's go see, ah?" He was eager to enter the diner and present the priceless gear to Daddy-O. She dried her eyes, stood before the diner door and gently curtsied to Viva and Cirrus as an apology for having witnessed her crying self. She entered the diner first expecting to see everyone having the time of their lives, but there was only a flock of bored teenagers sitting silently at the booths—some were asleep while others were slumped over the tables, guys fidgeted with their greased hair as girls popped bubblegum in their mouths. Marsha saw Russell slowly wiping the counter tops with a downright dull expression.

"Oh, my..." Marsha whispered. Russell met eyes with her, but quickly pulled away his glance. Shortly after Marsha had stepped in, Cirrus flew into the diner and held up the new gear.

"I've got it!" Cirrus exclaimed with the gear glimmering between his fingers. Russell and the group of teens swarmed over to him with gasps and shrieks of joy. The belly of Russell's father busted through the kitchen door and his voice overthrew the others.

"Can it be?!" his voice bellowed with deep laughter. "By, golly! You've done it! This is exactly what we need. Give me a few moments kids." Daddy-O and the rest of the teens horded around the jukebox as he began tinkering with the inside of the machine. Russell gestured for Cirrus, Viva, and Marsha to come take a seat at the counter while they patiently wait for the jukebox's repair. Russell leaned to Viva in concern of her ragged appearance and tipped his hat to her.

"Could I get you anything, Miss?" he asked. Viva looked shocked and fumbled for a moment, but Cirrus went ahead and answered for her.

"I bet she would like to try one of your famous maltshakes." Cirrus said as he looked at Viva, who was tensely blushing. She was both excited and bewildered to feel such a culture shock, but she agreed to the maltshake. "I'll pass on an order though." Cirrus thanked him. "I just hope I brought the right gear."

"Oh, I'm sure you did a mighty fine job." Russell's freckles lifted his cheeks, though he could feel Marsha's eyes on him; making him feel tense. He was about to take her order, but the butterflies in his stomach made him bolt to the kitchen to prepare Viva's maltshake beforehand. Cirrus could see the guilt on Marsha's face. A few minutes later, with Daddy-O still messing around with the Jukebox, Russell strutted out of the kitchen carrying a fancy glass of cold, chocolaty goodness. The whipped cream and the blanket of sprinkles on top sparked vitality in Viva's eyes.

"How beautiful..." she said softly. She watched in awe as Russell plopped a striped straw into the clouds of cream. The sweet aroma of the chocolate beckoned her to take a sip and so she did. Her eyes jolted open once her mouth cupped the tip of the straw. Nearly seconds later, she had melted in her chair from tasting such deliciousness and held her tingling cheeks with both hands.

"Tasty, ain't it?" Russell chortled and scratched at his nose. Viva replied with a quiet, grinning face—her eyes closing softly as her lips remained glued to the straw. Cirrus couldn't help but giggle. After wiping off his hands with a damp cloth, however, Russell glanced once more over at Marsha, regretting that he had neglected to take her order earlier, so he walked over to her and cleared his throat.

"H-howdy, Miss Marsha." he said timidly without making eye contact with her. "Is there anything you would like?" She squirmed in her seat and twirled her blonde hair before she managed to say anything.

"Well..." she nervously chuckled as she felt her face warm up. "There is something I would like, yes, but..." Russell flipped a sheet of his notepad around and readied his pencil. "Oh, no. You don't have to write this down." she said as she swallowed hard to keep her heart inside. At that moment, Russell seemed concerned and leaned closer to Marsha; so close that she could almost feel his freckles tickling her.

"What's the tale, nightingale? Was it what I said earlier?" Russell anxiously asked as he looked at her. The awkward tension had suddenly vanished from the both of them once she saw the interest in his eyes. Curtis never looked at her that way, nor did he ever ask how she was feeling. She could see how much he really did care for her just by that single expression.

"I'd like for you to be my date for the Sodapop Bash!" Marsha finally asked and nestled her fingers in Russell's hands, who looked as shocked as could be. "Never mind Curtis. I'd rather it be you!"

♩ ♪ ♫ ♪ ♫ ♩ !!!

Cirrus jumped back in his chair by the sound of loud rock n' roll bouncing off of the walls. Viva had also slapped her chest from the sudden noise. The gear he had retrieved was a success. The jukebox had been fixed and the teens all gathered around Cirrus to praise him, at least before Russell's father had thumped his way over and bear-hugged the living daylights out of him first.

"You did it, boy!" the portly man juggled Cirrus in his arms. "You've saved the party! Let the Sodapop Bash begin!" Russell's father hopped back into the kitchen while everyone else grabbed a partner and began to dance to the beats. Little did Cirrus know, Russell and Marsha were one of the couples in the dancing clique. He watched proudly as they delightfully twisted and shimmied with one another.

"The folk back in the Faerie kingdom sure never danced like this before." Viva spoke out as she finished the rest of her maltshake. Cirrus felt relieved to hear her speak again; perhaps it was a wise decision to bring her along with him to these worlds. At that moment, all seemed fun and free, before the door bells chimed as Curtis entered the diner. He tracked mud after each step he took. Cirrus felt his spine rattle once he had witnessed Curtis noticing Russell and Marsha dancing together.

"Hey, you!" Curtis called out with a huskily, deep voice. Russell gulped and took his hands off of Marsha, whose face was full of fury once she saw Curtis. He stomped over to Russell and grabbed him by the collar of his shirt. Marsha had caught Cirrus fumbling around behind the counter out of the corner of her eye. He had pulled out a can of whipped cream and began pointing to it, diabolically raising his eyebrows. Marsha smiled devilishly.

"Ya got cheese wedged in your ears, Freckles?" Curtis growled. Russell didn't say a word, but continued to fight back with a strong, steady glare. "Marsha's my girl. Understand?"

"Hah, 'fraid not, Curty Boy!" Marsha tauntingly huffed as she popped the lid off of the whipped cream can and sprayed him directly in the face with it. The cream sputtered, decorating Curtis once again with a delightfully speckled topping. The teens gasped and began to laugh among themselves.

"What gives, doll?!" Curtis shouted as the cream from his chin frosted his knitted vest. Marsha miffed at his ignorance and sprayed him once more.

"That's *exactly* how you treat me, like a lil' doll who you can just play around with until you find a better toy!" Marsha shouted. Curtis wiped his face off on his sleeve and tensely stood.

"Y-ya got it all wrong, sweet cheeks!" he bumbled and tried to maintain his false suaveness, but Marsha was having none of that. She sprayed him one last time, filling his mouth and nose with sweet cream, until he finally admitted his disloyalty. "Fine, so it's true. I'm smoochin' with Holly. She's no fake out like you! So go ahead and have your little cream puff. You two were meant for each other!" He revved up his feet and skedaddled out of the diner with a red face. Marsha placed her hands on her hips as her face beamed with pride. Every one began to root and whistle at Marsha as if she had just scored a field goal during a game, but then promptly carried on with their dancing.

"Golly, Marsha. You are the bee's knees!" Russell said in awe. Marsha laughed and wiped the little bit of whipped cream off of his nose.

"Let's boogie!" she smiled.

"Righto!" he agreed joyfully as they picked up where they had left off . Cirrus remained on the padded stool as he clapped his knees together to the beat until Russell's father dumped a large bag of malt balls on his lap.

"100 malt balls. Just as promised!" the stout man's curly mustache shook blissfully. "Oh, and here is the other little extra gift that I had mentioned. Cirrus spun around to see a miniature jukebox sitting atop the counter. It was just as big as his hand.

"Thank you so much, sir!" Cirrus bowed with his head. "How cute!"

"Let me tell ya somethin'." Russell's father whispered closely. "This lil' jukebox's music is so loud, it could wake up a bear in hibernation. So listen to it sparingly! You wouldn't want to wake your parents!" The round man chuckled thunder, but confusion had sparked in Cirrus's mind.

"Um, sir." Cirrus whispered back. "Why didn't you just use this jukebox as a backup in case the other jukebox broke? I mean, if you say this one works fine and loud…you didn't really need me to—"

"Shhh." Daddy-O patted Cirrus's shoulder. "You've helped repair the *one and only* jukebox. That jukebox over there is special, ya hear. It would not have been the same without it. You kept the spirit of the party by repairing that good ol' music box that has been around for years and we are deeply grateful."

The Greatest Cake of the Globes

Cirrus returned a silent smile after the man finished talking and accepted that he had done something great. There was no denying that everyone at the party was happy and having a great time. He looked down and examined the palm sized jukebox, wondering if it was really as loud as it claimed to be. He suddenly had an idea…

The gnome couple in O'Cottage rattled awake in their chairs as Cirrus and Viva held their ears tightly in an attempt to block the rock and roll mayhem. He hit the off switch on the miniature jukebox as soon as he saw the gnomes frantically patting their chests from the sudden startle. It worked! Finally, they were awake! They quickly regained their small stature after catching their breath and stood silently at Cirrus. However, rather than looking confused, they seemed to be worried or disappointed. They repeatedly looked back at one another and began to mutter; however, Cirrus could still hear them.

"Oh, no! Did we ruin the plan?" the woman gnome whispered to her husband.

"We were supposed to stay *asleep* around this lad." he replied quietly. Cirrus crossed his arms and tapped his foot.

"Whadd'ya mean *stay asleep*, huh?" Cirrus cleared his throat trying to sound inquisitive. "You mean to tell me you were awake the entire time I was here before? That you were just pretending to be asleep?

"You be earwigin'? It wasn't easy, laddie." the gnome man said grumpily. "Especially when yeh ate our food and started playin' with us like dolls! Givin' us weird voices n' such. I don't talk like that one bit, all country n' not pronouncin' my G's." A flush of red was painted over Cirrus's face once he had realized that the gnome couple was awake the entire time he was supposedly talking to himself. *How embarrassing...*

"Oh, dear. Come off it, now." the gnome woman smiled as she twiddled with her braided red hair. "He did come to the rescue when me mulligan stew was boilin' about. All we did was sit all plain n' gammy. This young man's as sound as we'll get."

"Aye, I be a mog." the gnome man agreed. "Yeh did prevent our gaff from firin' down, yeh did."

"Uh..." Cirrus felt bewildered after hearing their quick and unfamiliar accents and he didn't quite understand them. Viva had let out a soft chuckle and bent down by Cirrus's ear and whispered.

"They are saying thank you for preventing their house from burning down." Viva said softly. "I've lived around this accent for many years. I'm pretty used to it."

"Oh." Cirrus nodded, but then promptly turned back to the gnome couple for more questioning. "Well, you're welcome, but that still doesn't explain why you were faking your sleep!" The gnome couple sighed and looked at each other.

"In all honesty..." the gnome man began. "Me wife n' I were told to fake a slumber. Only with yeh around, though."

"As soon as yeh would leave the globe, everythin' would go back to normal n' we could carry on wit our lives, or so the magic lad said." his wife explained. "Did yeh even notice how quiet it was here? Didn't even hear the water rushin' or the hay crunchin', ya?" As soon as the woman finished speaking, Cirrus realized that he could hear his foot tapping on the wood floor, he could hear birds chirping outside and the faint sound of water rushing from afar. She was right. Everything was silent when he first showed up, but how?

"How yeh ask?" the gnome man straightened his red, pointed hat. "Wit a little magic from yeh-know-who. We met em in

FaeAway when we used to live there. Wanted a farm, we did. So we came here." Cirrus thought for a moment of all of the magical beings he had encountered over his quest. The Faerie Queen and King was his first guest, but then he remembered the mysterious Nimbus...Luname's brother, perhaps he was the one behind it.

"I know who you mean, I think." Cirrus admitted a bit disappointingly. "But, I still don't understand why he made you two ignore me."

"Nothin' against yeh, lad." the gnome woman spoke. "Just to see what yeh'd do about an ol' boulder in the road; to make things a tad bit harder, a challenge if yeh will. But know this..." She and her husband walked up to Cirrus and took off their pointed red hats, kneeling down to him as if he were a king. "Yeh could have ran away in fear when me fire pit was sparkin' outta control, leaving me husband and I to watch our house catch fire, but yeh came in the house as quick as a rabbit and stopped the flame in a heartbeat, yeh did, and we owe our deepest thanks. Yeh saved our hides. Yeh are brave, ya are."

I saved their lives? Cirrus thought to himself for a moment while he tried to grasp the meaning of those words. He did! He saved their lives. *I. Saved. Lives.* He felt like those words would have never been used to describe the useless globeling he thought he was, but the more he thought about it, the more he realized what an impact he had been for the people he had recently met. The useless globeling saved the gnomes from having their house burned down. The useless globeling was the reason the Sodapop Bash celebration could continue. The useless globeling freed the moth from the spider's web. The useless globeling saved an entire city from an inevitable demise from pollution. The useless globeling brought happiness to a human. The useless globeling was able to free the love of Lorne's life.

"I..." Cirrus could feel his heart beating fast over how happy he felt.

"Aye, yeh did good, laddie." the old gnome man smiled as his cheekbones puffed above his curly, white beard. "But yeh be runnin' outta time if we keep blabberin'. We knew yeh'd pass the magic lad's test so we took the liberty of roundin' up all the materials yeh need." His wife sprung up like a flower in the sun and bounced to the small, wooden cabinet and began shuffling around the interior shelves. She had pulled out a good sized white basket that was decorated with a red and white checkered cloth.

"O-oh!" Cirrus gasped. "Thank you very, very much!" He gratefully accepted the basket and looked inside. There he saw several containers of creamy butter wrapped in ribbons, an array of delicious brown eggs, and nearly six glass jars filled with fresh milk; the milk was such a pure white that it reminded him of...

"S-snow!" Viva cried out as she felt the soft flakes of snow melt down her cheeks. Cirrus helped bundle Viva up with a magenta colored shawl and a knitted, pointy hat that PeppyMint had handed to them.

"It was *I* who picked out that lovely shawl for you madam." SpearMint boasted. "A lovely shawl for a *lovely* lady."

"No, I was the one who said she would look best in magenta!" PeppyMint argued.

"Are you saying that this beautiful woman would only look good in one color?" SpearMint appallingly spoke. "My, any color would highlight her angelic appearance."

"Oh, don't you rearrange my words, you—"

"Ah ah ah!" Cirrus wagged his finger in front of the two nutcracker guardians. "What did I say before? No squabbling during the holidays!"

"But, it's always the holidays here!" PeppyMint whined. Cirrus raised his brow and nodded his head. "D'oh, alright. Well, it's still a pleasant surprise to see you again, for you are always welcome here." Both of the soldiers gestured for them to pass through the entry gate.

"Mind you, the whole town slumbers, so do be quiet. Everyone must be asleep in order for the jolly one to arrive. Ol' Saint Nick should be passing through any moment." SpearMint informed. The mention of Santa made Cirrus's inner child scream internally, but held in his holiday cheer as he and Viva walked through the town quietly. SpearMint was right; not a single globeling was to be seen around town. It was so quiet, as a matter of fact, that the crunching of snow beneath his feet sounded like it would cause an avalanche. Though Viva stood behind him, he could tell that she was experimenting with her breath to see the cloud of steam form from her lips. Her new found winter innocence pleased him, but he continued searching for Silly's home. For some reason, Cirrus had a feeling that Silly would be the only child awake in the town, thus preventing Santa to pass by.

Suddenly, a speck of light flickered on the snow in front of him. He caught a glimpse of a shadow through the dotted curtains of a small, gingerbread cottage and noticed that it was of a small child with a pointed hat. He gestured for Viva to quietly sneak over to the window to get a better look. Once he squinted through the curtains, he could tell that it was Silly who was pacing back and forth next to a wooden table that held a plateful of cookies. Though, the glass next to the tray of cookies lacked milk. Cirrus reached for a jar of milk without taking his eyes off of the empty glass on the table.

"This is what he needs." he whispered happily.

"Shall we knock on the front door and give it to him then?" Viva asked quietly.

"No." he shook his head. "I can't just simply deliver it to him through the front door. I need to do something better. More...*festive*." Viva had become confused, but watched as Cirrus circled the house as if he were looking for another way in. He noticed that the chimney was not releasing any smoke and saw a candy cane ladder that lead up to the roof. That had done it. He unlocked his master plan. He was seconds away from clapping his hands together from pure genius when he remembered to not make any noise. A glass bottle of milk was placed in his satchel as he flung it over his back like a sack of toys.

"I'll be right back." he winked at Viva and scurried up the sugary-sweet ladder. She quickly returned to the window to see the surprise that was about to unfold. Several puffs of soot began to trickle down the chimney and she noticed the little boy stare at the fireplace in awe. She watched as Cirrus had abruptly plopped himself in to the house and was greeted by the ecstatic child. His cotton night gown dragged beneath his feet as he trotted his way over to Cirrus and embraced him. Cirrus handed the boy the bottle of milk and they began to talk. Though Viva could not quite make out what they were both saying, the scene warmed her heart and she could feel tears beginning to form. She watched as Cirrus had knelt down and held the glass as the little boy poured the milk in to it. The only words she managed to hear were of the little boy saying 'thank you' over and over again. Her warm tears started to freeze on her cheeks, so she turned away from the window and began to softly cry. Out of nowhere, she was reminded of Lorne. No matter where she looked, she felt Lorne. Cirrus had brought so much joy to her as of late—joy she had not felt in over twenty years—and it felt sickeningly nostalgic, for she could never feel the joy from Lorne ever again.

The Greatest Cake of the Globes

```
*Side Quests Achieved: Fix Jukebox.
Wake up old gnome couple. Give Silly
milk.

*Obtained 100 malt balls, miniature
jukebox, fresh milk, eggs, butter, and
cinnamon

HP: 30/70
BP: 50/50         *MAX BAKER PTS*
MP: . . . . . . .
```

✮Chapter Twenty-Two✮

Home in the Clouds

      Shortly after parting the world of twinkling lights and glistening snow, Cirrus and Viva—faces thawing from the previous winter chill—stood before the entrance of the Cloudscape globe. Excitement, nervousness, and sadness tickled its way through our hero's mind. He couldn't help but feel anxious to see Luname again, especially since he now knew that she was the mastermind behind The Greatest Cake of the Globes. He could not wait to tell his parents the journey he has had over the past few days, yet he was uncertain how they would react to Viva. To tell the truth, he was curious how Viva was to react to his home once she stepped in the globe. She hadn't said a word since JingleJangle. As soon as Silly had given Cirrus the cinnamon he needed and went to bed feeling at ease about Santa's cookies, Cirrus left and found Viva in an empty daze, isolated on a hill as she stared deeply at the snowy mounds that surrounded her. The loss of Lorne was still troubling her no matter how hard she was trying to cover it up. Cirrus could tell. However, before they reached the top of the spiral staircase, he sat on the top step and took Viva's hand.

    "Are you sure you are going to be okay staying here for a while?" Cirrus asked openly. Viva blinked with sleepy youth and nodded as if her head was to fall off if she moved too quickly. He accepted her bare response as positivity and continued forward, lifting The Bubble entrance above his head. The comfort of home welcomed him with a warm, floral breeze, and he spoke, "Step out, Viva. Come see the flowers of Cloudscape Town—my home in the clouds." He sounded so noble—like a brave man who was just knighted by a queen—and he gracefully lifted Viva out of the hole in the ground.

The Greatest Cake of the Globes

"A-ah!" Viva caught what little breath she had as the flower field lit up her eyes with wonder. She had never seen such a vast gathering of flowers even while living in the world of fae for two decades. Her tattered dress softly grazed over each petal as she leaned down to smell a batch of sun washed primroses. Wishing not to disturb her, Cirrus stood silently behind her and smiled, until he heard her softly weep once more. "I have not seen a primrose this beautiful since the day I left my home, after I placed one in Lorne's hair those many years ago." Viva whispered to herself, but Cirrus didn't say a word. However, before he was able to place his hand on her shoulder to comfort her, something had caught his attention from the corner of his eye. There was something standing on the top of one of the flowery mounds from afar, but he could not tell what it was from where he was standing. It looked like wooden poles were sticking up from the ground. He carefully placed his satchel of ingredients down beside Viva, who was still quietly fiddling with the flowers, and began to squint to see if he could get a better look at what was over on the other hill. He decided to investigate.

"I'll be back in just a minute." Cirrus said nimbly.

"I'll be here." Viva replied, but he did not hear her.

After a minute or so of shimmying through the flowers and making his way to the top of the hill, he noticed that the object standing was indeed made of wood, and it appeared to be an old easel, with many rusty brushes and messy paints placed around it. *Huh? What is this doing here?* He curiously circled the easel and saw a canvas that was half painted on the other side. Thick applications of paint depicted the very same flowers that he stood on, and the sky was the identical brushed blue, but a woman was portrayed in the very middle of the canvas. She had long, burgundy hair and was wearing a beautiful forest colored dress. *Who is she?*

"Cirrus, dear boy! Is that you?"

A familiar voice called from behind and his body bubbled up with goose bumps. It took a moment for him to turn around and see who was behind him, but his hopes had already risen and tugged at him as much as they could. *Please. Please...please be you.*

He finally turned around and saw him...Lorne, standing with a huge smile on his newly brightened face as he cleaned several paint stains off of his hands with a wash cloth. Lorne was different from before, though. His face seemed brighter, though still gray, and his candle hat and long, dusted overcoat were nowhere to be seen. He wore a stained, white, buttoned up shirt—sleeves rolled up—and high-waist overalls. Cirrus remained completely smitten with shock while Lorne spoke.

"I just finished washing up my hands in that beautiful spring below the hill." Lorne said happily. "It's marvelous here, Cirrus! I could not bear to wait, so I left DrearyDrough within minutes after you left. I'm sorry about leaving without warning. I just—" Cirrus interrupted him by throwing his entire weight in to Lorne and hugged him tightly. "Oh!" Lorne chuckled. "Nice to see you again too!" But Cirrus hastily drew back, still entirely speechless, and pointed to the other hillside without taking his eyes off of Lorne's face. "What is it?" he asked, as he followed Cirrus's index finger, which was seemingly pointing to the canvas. "Ah, yes. Viva. I painted her a few moments ago. She would have loved to see this flowery field. If only she—" Again, Cirrus interjected at him by shaking his head frantically as he pulled Lorne to the side of his painting, allowing him to see the hill on the other side—allowing him to truly *see* what stood on the other side. Lorne fell still.

"W-what..." Lorne felt air slide from his lips. "Oh, my stars...is that...Viva? VIVA!" His legs took off before his mind could even comprehend what was happening. Viva shot up like an early firework after hearing her name and saw Lorne jetting down the hill as he tripped with every step he took. Viva thought that she was in a dream. Lorne could not possibly be here. She must be dreaming! Soon enough, after shrugging away her doubts, Viva took flight by running to her long, lost lover and flew in to his arms. Cirrus wordlessly made his way down the hill in disbelief and in tears as he watched them become locked in a strong, tender embrace. *I did it...I did it!*

"What is happening?!" Lorne's voice buckled. "H-how? W-what?!"

"Lorne! My love, is that you?!" Viva held his face in disbelief.

"Darling, I thought you were taken from me!"

"I thought I had lost you!"

"I healed, my sweet, I healed!"

"Oh, Lorne!"

The two of them shared a long, awaited kiss—a kiss that made up for the last twenty years of forlorn sadness and loss—and Cirrus could see their faces glowing; literally glowing. In the midst of the kiss, their skin had abandoned the bland gray and began to blush with a fresh, rosy shade as their hair fell smooth and glistened amongst the sun. Viva's hair painted the wind burgundy as Lorne's dark, hazel hair grazed his beloved's blossoming cheeks. Their worn clothing appeared to have mended itself in front of Cirrus's eyes—a forest bloomed around her dress while a navy, blue sea washed over Lorne's overalls. Their color had come back to them.

"This is remarkable!" Lorne roared with cheer. "How is this possible?" His eyes were layered with questions, but his tears of delight kept them back. Viva nestled her head among his chest and shivered from the tranquil thumps of his heart, but then began to praise Cirrus for her rescue.

"Cirrus is the reason we are together, my Little Primrose." she explained. "I was trapped within another globe—under a spell, if you will— and Cirrus set me free." Mouth still agape, Lorne rushed to Cirrus and mirthfully shook him.

"C-Cirrus, you—you marvelous globeling, you!" he jousted his grateful words to the sky. "I can't even…how can I...the thanks I have are beyond comprehendible."

"I'm just so very glad that I was able to make this happen." Cirrus honorably sighed. "This is everything that I could have hoped for." For a moment, he had felt as if all of his problems had melted away. After all, there was no harm threatening his hometown anymore—no evil sorcery and no kidnapped damsels in distress—but still, he still felt the urge to bake that *legendary* cake—not just for his self-satisfaction, but to prove once and for all that he can bake a decent cake and help give his family's bakery a better name. He closed his eyes and took the most enlivening breath as he grasped the golden Baker's Brooch that sat upon his chest. For the first time, he felt like he could do anything he could ever dream of doing.

In that instant, the brooch began to illuminate like the setting sun around them. Cirrus looked below at his chest and blinked curiously as the brooch oddly quivered while it faded from color to color. Blue, purple, pink, yellow green blue pink red orange pink bluepurplepinkyellowbluepink- *BURST!!* The brooch began to strobe color so fast that Lorne and Viva suddenly drew back from Cirrus, whose cape was violently fluttering as if a tornado's wind was only focused on him. Cirrus's feet became light as a feather as he slowly began to hover above the flowers.

"W-what is happening?" he questioned as he tried to keep his balance while being inches from the ground. Seemingly toxic fumes formed in front of him and the reunited couple. Cirrus knew those venomous cloud puffs; the Poison Prince was about to make his final appearance. However, just as Cirrus had begun to prepare for the phony prince's confrontation, the aura of clouds became a festival of cotton candy and greeted him with a sweet, acquainted face.

"You did it!" Luname congratulated him with an excited wave. "You gathered all of the ingredients for The Greatest Cake of the Globes! Now, you can stop the Poison Prince once and for all!" She bounced over to him as he remained suspended in the air, flopping around as he tried to get down. Luname continued to praise him. "Wow, look at all of these things you've gathered. I am so proud of you, Cirrus!"

"A-ah!" he gasped. Proud....*proud*! That's the word he had been hoping to hear for so long. She was proud of him. "Really? I'm so happy that you think that!" He tumbled in slow circles, but a smile remained on his face. "I'm so sorry that I have caused you so much trouble though..." he said embarrassingly.

"W-what do you mean?" Luname asked as she looked around nervously. Cirrus took hold of her hands, which helped him gain balance in the air, and took a moment to explain.

"I know why you did it." he began. "I must have seemed pretty pathetic back then, huh? Always messing things up." Luname gripped his hands tighter and pulled him closer to her.

"No, that isn't it at all!" Luname protested. "Being a frequent visitor of your bakery, I couldn't help but notice the trouble some of the customers had been giving you, and you always seemed so doubtful of yourself. And, the other day, I had noticed that you were playing The Journey of Super LoLo so I thought—" She caught her tongue before she said anything else, but then realized it was too late. She couldn't help but know that Cirrus had found out about her and the recipe.

"Heh, it's alright." Cirrus gave her a warm smile.

"So..." Luname blushed heavily. "You know?"

"Afraid so." he spoke softly.

"You know that I made up that recipe?" she asked.

"Yeah."

The Greatest Cake of the Globes

"You know I wasn't really kidnapped?" she moved closer.

"Yeah…"

"You know that the Poison Prince was actually just my brother in disguise and he knows magic and is the reason that you are floating right now?" she moved even closer to his face and he closed his eyes.

"Yeah...wait—"

THUD!

Cirrus fell flat on his stomach on to the flowers beneath Luname's feet. *Woah. Were we about to kiss?* He thought.

"Ugh!" she groaned. "Nimbus! You could have waited a bit."

"Oopsy!" a lively voice called from strangely nearby. "My bad~" The figure of the Poison Prince appeared beside Cirrus and Luname. "Darn. Why can't I look like this all of the time? Oh well." he sighed and snapped his fingers, causing him to get a full blown makeover. His hair was a darker blue than Luname's, but

Cirrus could definitely tell that they were siblings. Come to think of it, he could now recall standing by him at the cake competition announcement. *Man, I need to start paying more attention to things.*

"I'm so sorry, Cirrus." Luname apologized and helped him to his feet. "I put you in danger and played you like a fool by having Nimbus portray that villain. I wanted to see if I could help you—to motivate you somehow—but I know that was wrong of me to pry on your personal life. I'm so ashamed."

"No, you've got that all wrong." Cirrus declared. "You have helped me overcome a lot more in a couple days than I have in my entire life. Thanks to you, I've been able to find out my true potential and I've met and helped out a lot of other globelings along the way. Lorne and Viva, for instance." He guided Luname's sight to them and she felt incredibly shocked for she did not even see them standing there that entire time. They greeted her with bright smiles and Cirrus introduced them.

"I actually have much to tell you all, but there is one thing I need to do first." Cirrus stood and dramatically swung the satchel full of ingredients around his shoulder. He gave Luname a striking look of bravery and spoke:

"There's a cake to be baked."

```
*Quest Complete: Find ingredients for
legendary recipe.

*Side Quests Achieved: Reunited Lorne
and Viva!


HP: 70/70
BP: 50/50
MP: . . . . . .    *FULL POWER*
```

☆ Chapter Twenty-Three ☆
Bake it or Break it

Though our hero was happy to return home and see his parents—to finally tell them of his great achievements—he stood in the doorway of the kitchen with sheer horror on his face.

"I completely forgot about our oven being broken!!!" Cirrus screeched and began to pace around the kitchen as the burnt oven taunted him from across the room. His mother tried to calm him down, but Luname had quickly poked her head through the kitchen window and proposed an alternative.

"Come use the kitchen at town hall!" she suggested in a chipper voice. "Really, it's no biggie! My father won't mind at all."

"Oh, thank you so much!" Stara said happily. "You are so kind to help our son."

"Heh, you have no idea, Mom." he replied and rewarded Luname with an appreciative smile. Shortly after that, Atmo came through the kitchen door with Lorne and Viva behind him.

"Well, I've got good news!" he cheered and took Stara's hand. "Looks like we can finally rent out the place next door. Cirrus found us a happily married couple with some creative ambitions of their own."

"Viva and I have decided that we will open our own floral shop!" Lorne said eagerly. "And I'll be giving painting lessons over at the art workshop. I've already met with the owner and he said he'd love to have me around." Seeing the merriment on Lorne and Viva's faces was enough of a reward that Cirrus could have ever wanted, causing him to become completely speechless for a few moments. Literally an hour earlier, Lorne was "dead" and Viva was an empty shell, but they are now alive and well, together and happy—and they were even going to start their own business. Cirrus could not help but think to himself: *None of this could have happened without me. None of this could have happened without Luname. But it did. It happened and it happened because of the two of us!* He could feel himself trying to fight the urge to jump out of his boots to kiss Luname with gratification, but his father loudly cleared his throat, "I hate to burst your bubble, son, but the cake judging starts in nearly an hour or so." Atmo informed. "Think of the pre-heating, boy!"

"Ah, you're right! I have to get started now!" Cirrus gasped and ran around the kitchen yet again like he was on a time limited shopping spree. He grabbed bags and bags of flour, baking powder, sugar, shortening and salt. "I need this and, oh, I got that, oh, uh, this, and, uh, oh yeah, this too."

"Hahaha." Luname chuckled and walked over to him as she picked up his chef hat and placed it on his head, halting him from his frantic striding. This time, however, his hat did not slump in front of his face. "You'll definitely need this." she said softly, and kissed his pointed nose. His cheeks shivered with glee and he bashfully itched at his chin. "Oh, but there is one thing I should mention." she began. "You will be baking in the same kitchen as Nimbus, but the kitchen is a good size, so there will definitely be room for two."

"I see..." Cirrus pondered. "So, I'll be baking alongside the Poison Prince. Never thought I'd see that coming."

"Aw, I bet it does seem a little odd, doesn't it?" Luname embarrassingly raised her shoulders and giggled awkwardly. "I'm sorry, he really *is* a nice guy—a little touchy-feely perhaps—but other than that he is just my older brother."

"It's alright. I'll take your word for it, haha." Cirrus said as he went to lift the bag of ingredients, but then his dirty, ink and blood stained gloves caught his attention and he shrieked once more.

"AGH! I can't bake wearing this!" He gently set down the bag, shot up to his room, and, within seconds, returned wearing a polka dotted apron that wrapped around a white, buttoned up shirt. His parents stood frozen with their eyebrows raised high.

"H-he's wearing the uniform!" Atmo whispered to Stara, who replied with a stunned nod and a gradual smile. A quiver from his father's lips could be seen above his goatee. Cirrus could instantly tell that his parents were pleased with him and it made his motivation beam uncontrollably. They both walked up to their son and aided him with some comforting words of encouragement. "No matter if you win or lose..." his father began. "You have already made us so proud, sweetie." said his mother as they both hugged him. It was a nice hug, a little too tight according to Cirrus—actually, it was a very tight hug—*urgh*, but it was full of love, nevertheless.

"*Th...anks!*" Cirrus gasped for air as they let go. "Gah, but, yes! I am happy I can finally show you both what I am capable of. You have done so much for me over the years and I want to make it up to you. Besides, if I do happen to win, I can buy a new and better oven with the twinkles prize! Yes, I am ready. Let's get to baking!"

"We will be rooting for you all of the way! Our son's going to make the best cake around." Stara boasted. "Ah, but while you are baking, your father and I will be showing Mr. Lorne and Mrs. Viva around their new home."

"Dear boy, we cannot wait to try your cake!" Lorne spoke eagerly. "And knowing that my beloved's blueberries are a needed ingredient makes it all the more special to us." Viva also merrily nodded as she embraced her love.

Everyone wished Cirrus the best of luck before he ventured to the Cloudscape Courthouse alongside Luname, who was lending him a hand by carrying some of the many ingredients. The streets were already decorated with a plume of pastel balloons and curtained with many delicate colored streamers. The courthouse itself was adorned with every birthday party favor imaginable.

"My dad really likes to go all-out with this birthday decorating business." Luname embarrassingly admitted. "But I appreciate every bit of it." Cirrus nodded in agreement because his parents were the same way. As they walked in to the courthouse and made their way through the halls, they finally arrived to the kitchen. "Here we are!" her voice echoed which startled him a bit—especially since it was a long, quiet hallway. "Now, don't let this intimidate you, but Nimbus is one heck of a baker himself. He's always been good at it and the townspeople are usually drawn to his cakes."

"Why's that?" Cirrus asked curiously.

"Well..." she blushed. "He's one for traveling and, usually during his travels he would pick up a few ingredients from other globes. He always told me that gathering one ingredient from each globe would make a cake taste great and be extraordinary at the same time. It would make the cake have a story of its own."

"Gather the pieces of your life and make your story." Cirrus softly spoke aloud. He saw her eyes light up a smile as he grazed his hand across the golden Baker's Brooch. *"Inside the star...beats the heart*! It all makes sense now!"

"I'm happy to hear that you remember that saying." said Luname.

"Still..." Cirrus pondered. "I could have sworn that I've heard that before from somewhere else."

"Ohhhhh." she twirled her hair and lightly chuckled. "I'm sure you'll figure it out soon enough." She placed her hand on the kitchen door and hesitated to push it open. "Are you ready to bake an extraordinary cake, Super Cirrus?"

This is it. The time has come! He couldn't believe what he was about to do. Within two days he had become someone that he hadn't been in twenty years and yet...it seemed so simple. The cake hadn't even been made and he felt like a great baker on the inside, nor did the thought of confronting customers and other globelings strike fear into him like it used to either. *I feel great! I feel so lively. The dreams I have can finally be made true.*

"Yes!" Cirrus answered proudly and stood as straight as a pole "I am ready to bake for you, Princess Luname!" They both laughed as she slowly opened the door, cheeks dusted with pink sugar, and revealed a kitchen with tableware whirling in the air as a lanky man fancifully conducted each fork and spoon to its rightful location. Cirrus's jaw dropped from such a sight.

"Nimbus! Dad said no magic while baking." Luname playfully nagged.

"Wah! I'm not baking, yet!" Nimbus defended. "Just doing some dishes, sistah! Gotta keep this place nice n' tidy, especially if your cute lil' friend is here."

"Cirrus is going to be baking alongside you for today. Is that okay?" she asked concernedly. Nimbus's eyes sparkled when they locked with Cirrus's. He seductively dusted his indigo hair behind his ears as he swayed toward him. "You could bake with me any day, darling." He temptingly grazed his hand down Cirrus's cheek and blew a kiss. *Oh, that's what Luname meant by "touchy-feely".*

"Nimbus..." Luname scowled at her brother and rolled her eyes, but promptly lit up a grin when she looked back at Cirrus. "Best of luck to the both of you!" Before she stepped out of the room, she gave her brother a hug and kissed Cirrus on the cheek. A few moments of silence passed once she had stepped out, leaving Cirrus to finally get the chance to meet the phony Poison Prince face to face. Despite him being the enemy for the last couple of days, Cirrus was strangely able to feel comfortable around him. Nimbus, after all, did play a huge role in helping him along his journey by basically leading him down the correct path.

"Ah ah! Before you say anything," Nimbus abruptly spoke. "Don't think that just because I have super-duper-fantasticle-magical powers I will be helping you out with your baking." His eyes darted from each corner of the room, but then returned to Cirrus once more. "But, I will lend you a couple of tips that every baker must know!"

"Ah! Thank you." Cirrus replied. "I appreciate it. I have tons of room for improvement in this dorky mind of mine." Nimbus held up a few measuring cups in his hand and began to laugh to himself, causing Cirrus to wonder what was so funny.

"Oh, you remind me too much of myself when I was younger." Nimbus laughed. "You see, I always wanted to be a magician, yet I had no talent for it—never being able to cast the right spell nor brew the correct potion—and I was too afraid to go to others for answers. I feared what they would think of me since I felt so different, yet when I ventured to the very last globe on the shelf and spent months training alongside the faerie king and queen, I became who I am today. You should know how it feels, and if you don't, pity, for that had been Luname's intention." The sudden change in Nimbus's tone chilled Cirrus enough to cause tenseness in his arms. It was spoken so seriously; too seriously—like a villain or something. *No! He's not the Poison Prince. Just shake the thought out of your head, Cirrus, and get to baking!*

"You don't have to worry about that." Cirrus justified. "I am so grateful for what Luname has done for me. I know exactly what you are talking about!" He reassured his understanding by giving Nimbus a thumb's up.

"Goody!" Nimbus shouted and excitedly clapped his hands. "Now, let's get started!"

Cirrus had enough of his mental preparation and began retrieving each ingredient that he had obtained from the other globes. He positioned them across one side of the long counter top, examining them thoroughly to make sure he had everything that he needed. He watched as Nimbus did the same thing with his own items and studied the way that he measured out the flour and shortening. Nimbus brushed off the excess powder from the top of the measuring cup before placing each scoop in the mixing bowl—which was something that Cirrus never usually did and made him realize that might have been a reason why his cakes had always turned out so dry. The more he observed Nimbus's routine the more he understood how to properly make a cake.

Thirty cups of cake mix and sugar scooped, eight cups of water and twelve of milk poured, eight eggs cracked, ten cups of butter plopped, honeysuckle nectar drizzled and cinnamon sprinkled; the cake was nearly finished! Cirrus combined the ingredients in a mixing bowl that was nearly the size of a bath tub; all thanks to Nimbus and his magic, that is. The cakes needed to be baked at a big enough size to feed the entire town, and in order to prevent a mountain of dishes, Nimbus used his magic to increase the size of two mixing bowls. Cirrus held up his whisk and gulped at how tiny it was compared to the bowl. It was going to take a lifetime to mix everything together with such a tiny whisk. However, with a wave of his hand, Nimbus had caused the whisk to triple in size in a blink of an eye. Within minutes of feeling like he was rowing a boat in pudding, Cirrus was able to create a smooth and creamy texture of cake batter with the help of the giant whisk. It did not have chunky, dry clumps of cake batter floating in it or a slimy, runny texture like the previous cakes he had made. He was beginning to feel impressed!

Then came the coating of the cake pans and the pouring of the batter. Cirrus had a total of seven round cake pans that he could use, which all varied in size. He chose to fill each cake pan from largest to smallest in order for them to be stacked up nicely when they were cooled. During the baking of the batter, Cirrus was able to get a head start on the frosting. He had washed out the mixing bowl—after sneaking a taste of the batter with his finger, of course—and began adding butter, sugar, water, and the freshly grounded blueberries that Lorne had given to him. The icing became a beautiful shade of violet and mesmerized Cirrus the more he stirred. The sweet, warm scent of the cake that seeped from the oven was so strong it would not surprise him if the human could smell it from her room.

About thirty minutes later, both of the bakers recovered their cakes from the ovens and began to place them on racks to cool. Cirrus watched as Nimbus's cakes easily fell out from the pans once they were turned upside down. That was the part that worried Cirrus the most about baking. It never failed; his cakes always stuck to the pan and end up pulling huge clods out, eventually causing the cake to crumble. *But, here goes nothing.* He flipped over the biggest cake pan—the base—and the cake slid out, but his eyes and teeth were clenched from fear of the disaster that he might see.

"Ah!" Nimbus gasped as he looked over at Cirrus's cake.

"Oh no!" Cirrus exclaimed with his eyes still closed. "I screwed up! I knew I couldn't do it right! Aw, man! I'm so sorry, Luname!"

"No! Look!" Nimbus shouted. Cirrus opened his eyes and saw the most delicious, plump, golden-brown cake that he had ever seen. Not a lump in sight. Cirrus promptly grabbed the next cake pan with oven mitts and flipped it on top of the base. It also slid out of the pan unbelievably easy. He flipped over the next cake and, again, it slid out effortlessly. Each cake easily fell onto one another and stood tall and sturdy.

"I-I can't believe it..." muttered Cirrus, but then he began to jump for joy. "I did it! I actually made a decent looking cake! Wow!"

"Way to go, bro!" Nimbus congratulated him. "But you aren't finished yet. Let's see if you can get this baby decorated with some frosting." Cirrus agreed and did not hesitate to go scoop out some icing from the large mixing bowl.

After a good while of applying thick, swirly gobs of violet icing, Cirrus's cake towered nearly two feet higher than his actual body. He beaded the purple frosting with the many maltballs that

Russell had given to him, but he felt like he was forgetting something. The top of the cake seemed pretty bare. He wanted something to stand out; something bright, something shiny. *Ah-hah!* He scurried to his satchel and fumbled around inside until he pulled out the very last ingredient: the golden apple! As he went to place the apple on the very top of the cake, he realized that he couldn't reach it, nor did he frost the very top of the cake with icing either. He sat the apple on the counter and struggled to reach the top of the cake with a knife covered in icing. Suddenly, Cirrus began to float in the air when he then realized that Nimbus was using his powers on him again.

"Better hurry before I decide to drop you." Nimbus chuckled.

"Ah! Okay!" Cirrus replied as he nodded his head. With a few swoops of the knife, the top of the cake was blanketed with the frosting and topped with the glossy, golden apple. After a quick "OK" hand gesture, Nimbus lowered Cirrus and they both took a step back to appreciate their finished cakes.

☆Chapter Twenty-Four☆

The Last Level

Outside of the Cloudscape Courthouse, beneath the star-lit streets and the twinkling of the descending sun, the whole town was gathered in anticipation for the cake tasting. Cirrus's mother and father were among the crowd as well as Lorne and Viva, and they all were trembling with eagerness to see Cirrus's cake. Atmo tried to avoid the thoughts of Cirrus's cake ending up being a total disaster, but Stara comforted him by wrapping her arm around his, reassuring that their son was going to be great either way. She was right; he knew that and he couldn't help but smile. Suddenly, a parade of horns welcomed Mayor Sphere with his daughter following behind him, mirthfully waving to the townsfolk.

"Welcome, everyone, to the well renowned cake competition!" the mayor announced. "I want to thank you, the globelings of this town, for being here today in order to celebrate my lovely daughter's 22nd birthday and—let's not forget—the wonderful bakers who are competing for the tastiest cake around. Let's see what our contestants have cooked up—or should I say—baked up!"

Atmo and Stara watched the main doors of the courthouse open as each of the five contestants wheeled out their cakes on curtained tables and stood beside them in a single file. Each cake was uniquely colored and constructed. Miss Eva Portation looked as fashionable as ever with her diamond ruff hugging her neck. The wavy hair on her head was as white as her voluptuous lipstick while her large eyeglasses reflected starlight from the sky. Her cake seemed just about as gaudy as her dress did; silver sequin with sugar-made diamonds over the frosting.

Stratus the II was caught ogling Miss Eva several times on stage, but tried covering up his actions by tugging on his high-priced golden tuxedo and tipping his gold, shimmering top hat to all of the young ladies in the crowd. The cake he stood by was even more expensive looking than he was; it was pretty much gilded in gold and looked like it was some sort of rare treasure that he had found hidden in an ancient temple or something. The frosting looked metallic and was sprinkled with edible gold shavings; it figuratively screamed *look at how fancy I am.*

Crystal Droplett rocked back and forth as she stood between the golden cake and her own, which delighted the audience with its soft, pink frosting and rainbow stars made from fondant. The colored confectionary stars complimented her hair decorations that sat upon her pink braid. She stood frowning nervously until she was able to spot her grandparents in the audience; then she finally showed a smile.

The blue shades of Nimbus's cake felt reminiscent of the night sky that encompassed the town of Cloudscape. A sea of blues and indigo gradually faded darker near the top of the cake. It seemed a little too bland to be Nimbus's cake, but then he snapped his fingers and caused an array of small fireworks to sparkle from the rims of each layer. There it was; that was definitely his cake now.

☆ 223 ☆

Ciara Jackson

Atmo and Stara's eyes were both glued to the last cake that was presented.

The Greatest Cake of the Globes

A purple, frosted fortress towered above the table as the radiance of the golden apple glistened like a star atop a Christmas tree. Despite the cake seeming a bit off balance, the cake looked so professional that it couldn't have been Cirrus's cake, yet when they saw the baker standing beside it, it was indeed their son. It was too beautiful to be true! The both of them became astonished as the mayor continued to speak.

"My, my! Aren't they all lovely?" Mayor Sphere proclaimed. "Now, before we begin the judging, let's have each of our contestants stand to the mic and tell us about their favorite part of the competition. Atmo and Stara were both stricken with horror at the thought of Cirrus speaking in front of such a huge crowd, but the more they looked at their son and noticed his surprisingly calm face, they started to feel more at ease.

"Ahem~" Miss Eva cleared her throat and struck a pose in front of the podium. "Hello, darlings. Well, the best part of the cake competition, by far, is the fact that all of you are able to witness the incredible beauty of myself…and my cake here on stage. Thank you all~" She batted her eyes at the audience as they returned a round of applause. Stratus the II shimmied his way passed her as she cat-walked back to her cake.

"Mmm, yes. Hello." he said as he wriggled his goatee. "Ah, well I should say that the best part of this competition was being able to bake a lovely cake for a lovely young lady." He romantically winked at Luname and made slight kissing gestures with his mouth. She turned away and rolled her eyes while she tried to fight the itch in her throat from laughing. Soon after he had sat down and the clapping stopped, Crystal inched her way to the stand.

"U-um. Hello everyone." she hesitated and twisted side to side in her stance. "I am happy to say that, well, the best part of this contest was having my grammy out of the hospital and being here to see me on stage. Hi grammy! Hi grampapa!" The crowed cheered as they saw an older couple close to the stage. Crystal's grandma sat happily in a wheelchair as her grandpa tended to the

The Greatest Cake of the Globes

cast on her broken leg. They both waved eagerly at their granddaughter until she reached her seat, allowing Nimbus to begin.

"It's great to be home again, especially for my sister's birthday." Nimbus sighed happily. "So, I have to say that the best part of this cake competition is the fact that I am home and to have all of you, friends and family, try a piece of my cake. It is all of the magic that I could ever want. Thank you!" As Nimbus walked back to his seat while being serenaded with cheers, he gave Cirrus a quick pat on the shoulder. Cirrus rose from his seat and headed toward the podium. His parents about fainted when he spoke his first few words into the microphone.

"Hello everybody..." Cirrus began as he tried not to stutter. A sudden rush of realization struck him. He had finally reached the last level of his adventure. Before he could continue his speech, he began to feel his hands tremble and it nearly caused him crack up. After all, the entire town stood in front of him—hundreds of strangers—and he could even hear several of them quietly gossiping of what an awful baker he was and questioned why he was in the competition in the first place. Though, despite being in such a nerve wrecking situation, he finally met eyes with his parents and saw Lorne and Viva standing in the middle of the crowd. They all waved at him and instantly made his anxiousness melt away. He felt a hand gently touch his shoulder and noticed that it was Luname. She smiled and gave him the most comforting nod that he had ever seen. Suddenly, his words began to effortlessly flow from him. "The best part of this competition was realizing my true potential. I discovered who I am and what I am capable of. To learn that you can do whatever you dream and that you can make a lot of new friends along the way; that was definitely the best." Atmo let out the most shrill and abrupt noise that anyone could create and caused the globelings around him to flinch. He cleared his throat and let his hands do the cheering while his wife and the others around him did the same. The symphony of clapping drowned out the muffled pounding of Cirrus's heartbeat as he began to make his way back to his seat. His muscles became as frail as wet noodles from the amount of relief that rushed through him. The mayor raised his arms in the air in order to quiet down the townsfolk.

"There you have it, folks! What wonderful contestants we have in our town. Now, let me explain how the judging will work." Mayor Sphere began as he gestured an OK to Nimbus. A melody of *ooooh's* and *ahhhh's* filled the main street as all of the cakes hovered over the crowd and were gently lowered on to long tables prepared with paper plates and other utensils. Nimbus had used some of his magic to transport the cakes easily for the judging. "Each cake has its own table and next to them are baskets of paper. There is a symbol pictured on each slit of paper. Whenever you have tried a piece of each cake, choose your favorite by picking out a slip from the basket and placing it in the box next to said cake. When everyone has voted, we will tally up the scores and announce the winner! Let's eat!"

Within minutes, nearly every globeling was wandering around with a plateful of cake samples in each hand as they chatted amongst themselves. Cirrus's parents, of course, were not hesitant to grab a slice of his cake for sampling. All four of them examined it thoroughly before digging in.

"It seems nice and spongy." Stara pointed out as she poked the inside of the cake with a fork.

"Look! Not a sprinkle out of place." Atmo replied.

"Goodness, let's just try it already!" Viva laughed with her fork in position. They all agreed as Atmo took the first bite. His mouth opened in mid chew, displaying an unpleasant, colorful mush settling on his tongue, but his eyes beamed with surprise.

"Close your mouth when you eat, dear." Stara said as she just finished taking a bite, which caused her mouth to suddenly drop as well.

"Does it taste bad?" Lorne asked cautiously as Stara and Atmo both swallowed. They remained wordless for a few moments, but then smacked their lips together and took another bite.

"It's incredible!!!" Atmo exclaimed. "So rich and full of flavor!"

"So soft and sweet!" Stara marveled. Lorne and Viva could not bear to wait any longer and decided to finally try it themselves.

"Magnificent!" Lorne praised. "Do you taste the frosting, my love? Do you taste the accent of your blueberries?"

"I do!" Viva replied in awe. "This would go great with tea, darling! Oh, Mr. and Mrs. O'Zone, you must be so proud!" They all grabbed a slip of paper with Cirrus's symbol on it, which displayed an image of the Baker's Brooch, and placed it in the box for judging. Meanwhile, as everyone was finishing up with the taste testing, Cirrus remained seated alone on the porch of the courthouse when Luname decided to hop up next to him with a slice of his cake on her plate.

"Well, how are you feeling?" she asked as she pulled up a chair next to him.

"I feel incredible, really." Cirrus took a deep breath and sunk back in to his chair. "I feel like I finally accomplished some great things."

"I am so happy to hear you say that." she replied, but then stuck her fork in to the slice of cake.

"A-ah! Wait!" Cirrus gasped and wriggled his legs. "Is that my cake?"

"Yes, it is!" Luname drew back in shock. "You're not telling me that you are still too nervous to have me taste your cake, are you?"

"Not at all." Cirrus fidgeted in his pocket and retrieved a plastic fork. "I wanted to try it with you." He surprised her with a wink and she blushed immensely, but she held the plate closer to him, allowing him to pick a piece off for himself. *Now's the time for the moment of truth. Is this truly the greatest cake I have made?* They both simultaneously took a bite and their mouths were immediately welcomed with a carnival of pleasant tastes.

"Wow! Cirrus, this tastes amazing!" Luname gasped and licked her lips, but then noticed that Cirrus's face had went blank as soon as he had swallowed and, out of nowhere, tears began to bubble from his eyes. "Ah! Cirrus! What's the matter? Are you—" Her words were halted by a sudden, soft kiss on the lips from Cirrus himself. She could taste the frosting that he had on the side of his lip as her eyes softly closed. Her neck tingled from the touch of his hands cupping her head, and she felt one of his tears trickle against her cheek. He quickly pulled away so he could secretly wipe his nose on his sleeve and bashfully looked down at her hands.

"I'm sorry if that was sudden. I just wanted to thank you for all that you have done for me." Cirrus sniffled and held one of her hands. She sat the paper plate on the ground beside them so she could hold his other hand as well. "Listen, I don't care if I win or lose. The cake that I just tasted was one of the best I have ever had and I made that one all thanks to you. I met others who could have lived the rest of their lives in misery if it weren't for you. I just want you to understand that none of this could have happened without you. You've saved my life, Luname. So, with that said…Happy Birthday."

"You've made me so happy, Cirrus." she replied softly as they both joined lips once more. Little did they know that, as they were sharing a passionate kiss, the whole town had nearly gathered back to the front of the main steps as they patiently waited for the results.

"Oooh la-laaa~" Nimbus jokingly jeered from afar, causing the two love birds to jolt away from each other after realizing they had been putting on a show for the entire town. Atmo could be heard rooting for him somewhere in the audience. Cirrus and Luname both laughed from embarrassment, but they knew that the kiss felt completely worth it.

"I hope you all got enough to eat today, folks, but the time has come!" announced the mayor as he held up an envelope. "Are you all ready to find out who made the greatest cake in town? Let's find out!"

Cirrus kept a steady gaze on his parents as he sat anxiously in his seat, waiting to hear the results. Nothing—not even losing—was going to change the fact that he had come so far and learned so much, but he still could not help but to feel eagerness tickle at his stomach. The mayor excitedly tore at the envelope and pulled out three small sheets of paper.

"Our third place winner, who will be receiving a gorgeous, bronze trophy and ☆*200* twinkles is..." the mayor paused for dramatic effect. "NIMBUS!"

"Woo hoo!" Nimbus sprung from his seat with his arms in the air as the crowd cheered and he walked over to claim the trophy, shaking his father's hand. The crowd became quiet as soon as he sat back down. Cirrus felt a little uneasy after hearing that Nimbus only won third place. There was no way that he could have made a better cake than that talented, magical baker. He took a few deep breaths as he prepared to not hear his name called. He knew he did the best he could and that is all that mattered.

"For runner up, our second place winner, who will receive ☆*500* twinkles and a beautifully crafted, silver trophy goes to..." the mayor stopped for a moment and his eyes widened. "Well I'll be! CIRRUS O'ZONE! Congratulations, son!"

"Huh?!" Cirrus gasped as the sound of the audience roared with praise. He caught a quick glimpse of his parents hopping up and down as they latched on to each other, but the excitement on their faces was priceless. The fact that he had won second place dumbfounded him. On the outside, Cirrus looked like a deer in the headlights, but on the inside he was screeching with joy and disbelief. It was only second place, but—by the stars—that was all that he needed.

"You did it, Cirrus! You did it!" Luname frantically clapped her hands and hugged him tightly. "Go on! Go get your prize!" He felt himself waving at the crowd as he walked to get his check and trophy, but he could not even tell if he was dreaming all of it or not. Everything seemed so surreal, but he was there, awake and proud. He shook the mayor's hand and accepted his trophy. "Oh my goodness..." he panted as he slumped in his chair, beaming a blissful smile. Luname patted him on the back and giggled at his exhilaration. The mayor held up the final piece of paper that contained the name of the first place winner.

"And now for the grand prize winner..." Mayor Sphere cleared his throat and loosened his tie. "The lucky globeling that will take home a whopping ☆*1000* twinkles and an immense, gold trophy goes to..." Right before he had announced the victor, Cirrus quickly took a peek at the final three contestants who could be the winner. They all looked just as nervous as he did: Miss Eva frantically fanning her face, little Crystal's tiny legs trembling, and Stratus the II drooling over the sight of the golden trophy. The mayor stopped dawdling and signaled Nimbus to release the streamers and balloons. "CRYSTAL DROPLETT!!! You are the grand prize winner of this cake competition! Congratulations, youngin!"

Balloons danced in the air as a snow storm of confetti sprinkled on the applauding audience. Crystal Droplett skipped up to the podium in her bouncy, bubblegum dress and sweetly bowed to everyone. Her grandparents were cheering as loud as they could, and even Miss Eva and Stratus the II showed their appreciation by clapping ever so posh. Needless to say, the celebration was a

The Greatest Cake of the Globes

huge success for everyone, especially for our hero, Cirrus, who was finally able to become the baker he had always dreamed.

☆*☆*☆

Days of merriment passed peacefully in Cloudscape Town ever since that day. Everyone carried on with their colorful lives along the twinkling streets. Viva and Lorne's flower shop became a huge success just as the O'Zone Bakery had gained popularity from the high demand of Cirrus's cakes. After all, since he had won some prize money from the contest, he was able to purchase a brand new oven for the bakery and it was even better than the first. It seemed like everyone wanted to get their hands on some of his baked goods so he had to act fast, and—this may even come as a surprise—Cirrus had returned to the shelf in order to share some of his cake with the giant spider that he had roughly encountered before. Let's just say that he and the spider are currently on good terms.

Things were going great for Cirrus, though there was just one thing that had been bothering him for quite some time—he still hadn't beaten the Poison Prince in that video game! One night, after a long day of baking and spending time with Luname, he was about to head to bed. However, just as he was about to snuggle under his celestial blanket, the video game cartridge depicting the Super LoLo logo on the cover beckoned him to pick up the controller and try to finally beat the game, and within seconds, he turned on the GameCloud and began quietly pressing buttons. The game booted up and there stood Super LoLo idling beneath a save point before a large, locked dungeon door that had a poisonous aura seeping through it. On the door was a star-shaped indention. Cirrus knew that he needed to place something star-shaped into the door in order to unlock it, but he looked everywhere in the game and could not figure out where it could be. Obviously, he knew it was the Baker's Brooch that he needed, but where it was, he did not have a clue. As he was controlling Super LoLo to search the room, he came across wall graffiti that was hidden behind a jar that produced poisonous bubbles. He had never noticed that there before. He broke the jar and was able to read what it had said:

> *"Gather the pieces of your life and make your story."*

"No way!" Cirrus loudly whispered to himself, and just like that, he knew exactly what to do. He opened up the menu screen and searched through the list of rare treasures that he had collected over his journey. There, he had come across seven oddly shaped jewels that were each colored differently. He selected each of them and hit the *combine* option. A short cut-scene played that showed the seven jewels circle around Super LoLo and eventually mended together to create the golden Baker's Brooch. The character placed the brooch within the door and it unlocked in almost an instant. Cirrus's heart began pounding once he was able to finally battle the Poison Prince. After about a half hour of studying the Poison Prince's fighting strategy, Super LoLo—or Cirrus—was able to take down that dastardly prince and restore peace among the sugary kingdom once and for all. However, the ending was a total shock to him. Just as Super LoLo was about to strike his final blow to the prince, Princess LuLu ran to the prince as he lay injured on the ground.

"`Don't hurt him, Super LoLo!`" her text bubble cried as she held the prince in her arms. "`You've already done enough. Look. He's coming back to us...my brother...`"

"WHAT?!" Cirrus shouted and flinched back at the thought of waking his parents up, but he continued to intently watch the ending of the game. All of a sudden, the Poison Prince's clothing faded from it's ghastly purple and slimy green to a soft blue and yellow. The prince opened his eyes, revealing an innocent charm.

"`Super LoLo, you've saved me.`" the prince sighed happily. "`One day I was practicing magic and the next thing I knew, I ended up cursing myself and became a disgusting, sour`

```
creature who hated the very sight of all
things sweet and good, including my dear,
dear sister."
```

Cirrus sat the controller down with his mouth agape and lifelessly fell on to his bed, not taking his eyes off of the game's screen. He watched as the kingdom returned to its usual sweet self and sighed as the credits began to roll. After staring at the end screen that featured LoLo and LuLu for a few moments, he rested his head on his pillow and stared deeply at his ceiling as he recollected all of the great things that he has experienced. His eyes made their way to the recipe vial that sat beside his silver trophy.

"And thus, The Journey of Super LoLo has reached an end." he said softly. "But, The Journey of Super Cirrus is only beginning." He closed his eyes and dreamed of the other adventures that await him. "Save and Continue…"

☆*☆*☆

Back outside in our world, the human, Destiny, was busy writing away as her husband quietly stepped in with some more of her favorite tea. He sat down the teacups and pulled up a chair next to her.

"How's your story coming along?" Zachery asked curiously.

"It's picking up! I think this will be a good one." she said as her face lit up brighter than the lamp on her desk.

"Mind if I hear the intro, hun?" he asked.

"Sure thing!" she squealed. "Okay, so, this is what I have written so far:

"We all live in a globe. Everything, living or not, exists inside a globe called Earth. It is our world, our home—where we learn to love and grow. However, little do we know, there are thousands of globes within ours that exist as well. Perhaps you have seen them before—in a souvenir shop, a gift store, or have even received one as a present. These globes which I speak of are none other than snow globes. As they sit on the shelf, not making a sound, another world flourishes within. The creatures that live in these tiny worlds are called "Globelings". Now, globelings look similar to humans, only smaller…a lot smaller."

The Greatest Cake of the Globes

The End

☆ABOUT THE AUTHOR☆

"When I was little, my grandma was given a snow globe as a Christmas gift. It was fascinating and beautifully crafted and even played the most soothing music. One day, I picked it up without realizing how heavy it was and I ended up dropping it—shattering it into pieces and, oh, did I cry! I felt really bad for breaking my grandma's beloved snow globe, but I remember mostly feeling sorry for the people that lived inside it. I was sorry for destroying their home and I still feel bad to this day."

—*Ciara Jackson*

Ciara Jackson sprouted from a little, dirt patch in the small town of Rivesville back in 1991 and currently resides there today. Most of her childhood was spent drawing her own characters, watching cartoons, and playing tons video games, especially on her much-loved Super Nintendo. Her drawing determinations lead to many wonderful opportunities for her to become known in the state of West Virginia. Ranging from t-shirt to poster design, Ciara has won first place in many artistic contests. Her most recent achievements involved winning first place in the West Virginia International Film Festival with her *Dracula* animation short back in 2009, first place animation in the West Virginia Theatre Festival in 2010, and first place winner of the 2011 West Virginia Wine & Jazz Festival's poster/logo contest.

Writing is a passion that she had discovered not too long ago. She had a variety of themes and stories to tell, but could not decide on which one to go along with. She chose to write a story that would describe many different worlds in order to learn what style of writing was best for her. Thus, *The Greatest Cake of the Globes*, with its vast variety of worlds and themes, was written.

☆ SPECIAL THANKS ☆

Ashlyn Larmeu

Stefanie Webb

Kim Jones

Steven Krolikowski

Fredrick Lowe

Sean Lee

Zack Heck

Mary Dunn

....

Jerred Foster

Michelle Proulx

Genny Yosco

Christine Weigandt

Lauren Flinner

Regina Humphrey

Daniel Buckley

Kyrstin Myers

Sam Dunn

Ariane Weathers

Ryan Schell

Cydney Jackson